"Stop it!"

He whirled around, and she backed away, frightened of the anger in his face. "If there's anything between us, it's only because we're forced to be together all the time."

"It's much more than that. You know it is," she insisted.

"More than what? You say I'm strong, but has it occurred to you that I'm smart enough to know it would be one hell of a mistake to make love to you?"

"A mistake?"

"A mistake. You're not my type. Maybe you don't mind slumming, *Lady* Emma, but I'm a little more choosy."

She flinched at the insult. "That is not true," she said, her voice carefully even, "and you know it."

"I don't know anything except that you're not my type, any more than I'm yours." He turned his back on her, staring out at the night. "Go to bed, Emma."

Emma hesitated, opened her mouth to speak, then closed it again, turned in silence and walked to her bedroom.

Dear Reader,

When two people fall in love, the world is suddenly new and exciting, and it's that same excitement we bring to you in Silhouette Intimate Moments. These are stories with scope and grandeur. The characters lead lives we all dream of, and everything they do reflects the wonder of being in love.

Longer and more sensuous than most romances, Silhouette Intimate Moments novels take you away from everyday life and let you share the magic of love. Adventure, glamour, drama, even suspense—these are the passwords that let you into a world where love has a power beyond the ordinary, where the best authors in the field today create stories of love and commitment that will stay with you always.

In coming months look for novels by your favorite authors: Kathleen Creighton, Heather Graham Pozzessere, Nora Roberts and Marilyn Pappano, to name just a few. And whenever you buy books, look for all the Silhouette Intimate Moments, love stories *for* today's woman *by* today's woman.

Leslie J. Wainger
Senior Editor and Editorial Coordinator

Emma's
War

LUCY HAMILTON

Silhouette Intimate Moments

Published by Silhouette Books New York

America's Publisher of Contemporary Romance

SILHOUETTE BOOKS
300 East 42nd St., New York, N.Y. 10017

ISBN: 0-373-07331-3

First Silhouette Books printing April 1990

All the characters in this book are fictitious. Any
resemblance to actual persons, living or dead, is
purely coincidental.

®: Trademark used under license and
registered in the United States Patent and
Trademark Office and in other countries.

Printed in the U.S.A.

Books by Lucy Hamilton

Silhouette Special Edition

A Woman's Place #18
All's Fair #92
Shooting Star #172
The Bitter with the Sweet #206
An Unexpected Pleasure #337

Silhouette Intimate Moments

Agent Provocateur #126
*Under Suspicion #229
*After Midnight #237
*Heartbeats #245
The Real Thing #278
Emma's War #331

*Dodd Memorial Hospital series

LUCY HAMILTON

traces her love of books to her childhood and her love of writing to her college days. Her training and the years she spent as a medical librarian translated readily into a career as a writer. "I didn't realize it until I began to write, but a writer is what I was meant to be." An articulate public speaker, the mother of an active grade-school-age daughter and the wife of a physician, Lucy brings diversity and an extensive knowledge of the medical community to her writing. This native of Indiana lives with her family and three friendly felines.

Chapter 1

The seven o'clock nonstop from Washington, D.C., landed in New York an hour late, much to the disgust of the impatient crowd gathered at the arrival gate.

The waiting quiet was finally shattered when the walkway was rolled out to the plane and the gate agents opened the doors. The river of disembarking passengers was greeted by cries of welcome and relief as irritated business travelers threaded their way through laughing, hugging, family groups, mothers tried to keep track of their children, and an elderly couple argued gently over claim checks for their luggage.

The young woman in the bland beige suit was one of the last to leave the plane, attracting little attention. She was slender and blond, ordinarily an attractive combination, but her limp hair was an undistinguished dishwater shade, there were circles beneath her eyes and no color in her sallow cheeks—even her lips were pale. Her beige suit was a size too big for her slim frame, giving it the forlorn air of a hand-me-down. Her name was Emma.

Emma shifted the strap of her carryon as she walked, easing the weight on her shoulder. Thankful for her sensible, low-heeled shoes, she walked quickly, threading her way through the crowd, dodging hustling businessmen and wailing children. A limousine driver, oblivious to oncoming traffic, walked in front of her, holding a hand-lettered sign above his head. She sidestepped neatly, dodging around a volubly reunited family, and escaped into the concourse.

The crowd was thinner there, so she balanced the heavy bag against her hip and increased her pace. She could feel a cold prickling between her shoulder blades, and though she didn't turn her head to look around as she walked, she slid her gaze from side to side, searching the faces of the people she passed, trying to pretend she wasn't terrified.

She was, however, scared to death, and she didn't like the sensation. She forced herself to take slow breaths, trying to steady her heartbeat. She'd almost managed to do that when she saw the man in the drab trench coat.

Her heartbeat jumped, and her hand tightened convulsively on the bag she was carrying. He was looking for her. He wanted the information she carried, and she knew that he'd spotted her. She would pass him in three more strides, and he would follow her.

He didn't know her real identity, though. She reminded herself of that. He didn't know who she really was, and for her safety, and the safety of her friend, she had to keep it that way.

Emma held her facial muscles still as she passed him, not betraying by even a flick of her eyes that she knew he was there. She didn't turn to look, but she knew the moment he stepped away from the wall to follow her, keeping his distance, but always with her in sight. When she glanced back as she rode down the escalator, pretending to look at a large clock on the wall, she saw that he wasn't alone.

A stocky, rawboned woman of about thirty had joined him. Emma would never have known they were together if she hadn't glanced back at just the moment he bent to murmur something to the woman. Emma quickly faced forward again before they saw her watching them.

She knew what she was to do; she'd been instructed in great detail. Whether she could pull it off with two people following her was anybody's guess. Emma swallowed hard and stepped off the escalator, following a chunky man in a tight suit.

This whole situation was crazy, but as far as Emma was concerned, her life had been upside down since that morning. Half a day. It was difficult to believe so much could change in so short a time.

It had started so simply, with a nine o'clock appointment at her bank's branch office in Washington. The note in her appointment book had said, "Romanian Ag," and she'd flown to Washington early that morning to begin negotiations with the Romanian government.

They were requesting the loan to purchase agricultural equipment and expertise for collective farms. Her family's bank, Strathclyde Bank International, made loans to industries and governments around the world, so the appointment with the Romanian agricultural attaché was standard procedure for Emma.

She hadn't anticipated anything out of the ordinary resulting from her meeting with the Romanians, but all that had changed when the intercom buzzed in her Washington office.

"The Romanian attaché is here, Miss Campbell," her secretary said.

"Thank you, Mrs. Johnson. Have them come right in, please."

Emma stood and came around the desk, and moments later the secretary opened the office door to admit the visitors. For five full seconds Emma stared at the woman standing there, scarcely noticing the man looming behind her. As a wide smile spread across Emma's face, she cried,

"Mina!" and threw her arms out to hug the small dark-haired woman. The stocky heavy-featured man watched, unsmiling.

Emma stepped back, smiling. "Mina, I can't believe this! Why didn't you tell me you were the agricultural attaché?"

"I wished to surprise you. And I did, did I not?" Mina's smile didn't quite reach her eyes, but Emma was too excited at first to notice.

Smiling, she turned to Mina's companion. "How do you do, Mr.—?"

"I am sorry!" Mina apologized. "Emma, this is Stefan Alexandru, attached to the embassy here in Washington. Stefan Alexandru, may I present Lady Emma Campbell, vice director of the Strathclyde Bank."

"And Mina's very old friend," Emma added as she shook hands with Stefan. His hand was damp, his handshake oddly lifeless. "We were at school together when her father was ambassador to Britain."

Stefan nodded briefly. Everyone in Romania knew of the distinguished Ambassador Grigoras. "You knew the ambassador?"

"Yes, indeed," she said, smiling. "He and my father enjoyed playing chess."

Her father had found a friend in the ambassador, and she had found a friend in Mina. Their shared role as outsiders at their exclusive London girls' school had created a strong bond between them. As a child Emma had attended the local village school in Scotland, while Mina was schooled in Bucharest. Neither had fitted in with the tight cliques at the London school. They were too different—Emma, with her thick Scottish accent, and Mina, the foreigner in England.

In self-defense they'd formed a clique of two, finding they'd had considerably more in common than the fact that they were outsiders. They'd become fast friends—lifelong friends.

Though Mina's father had only been posted to London for a year, she and Emma had kept in touch after that with letters, telephone calls and rare, precious visits. The few times they'd seen each other again it was as if they'd never been apart.

The greetings were complete, but when Emma reached out to lead Mina to a chair, she found that Mina's hand was icy and trembling slightly. About to remark on that, Emma looked at her friend's face, and what she saw kept the words unspoken. Instead, she walked around her desk and sat back in her deep leather chair with a bland professional smile.

"Is there anything you'd like to tell me about the proposal before I give you my questions?"

She addressed the question to them both, but it was Mina who replied. In fact, it was Mina who did all the talking during the hour of discussion that followed. Mr. Alexandru remained stolid and silent throughout the meeting, watching their faces, flicking quick, sharp glances at the papers they passed back and forth across the cherrywood desktop. When Emma directed a question at him, he simply passed it over to Mina.

Finally Emma began to understand. Stefan Alexandru wasn't an agricultural expert. He was a policeman—secret police, to be exact—and he was there to watch Mina. And Mina was obviously afraid, not of him, but of what he represented.

"Well," Emma said as she shuffled the papers into a neat stack, "I think that's everything. I'll put this information in decent order and send an offer to you at the embassy, Mina, if that will suit you."

"Thank you. That will do very well." Mina rose and tucked a folder into her briefcase, then set it down again. "Emma?"

"Yes?" Emma glanced up absently, and found Mina watching her with wide, frightened eyes.

"Could you direct me to the loo before we leave?"

"Oh, of course. It's just through—"

Stefan interrupted with a sharp, unintelligible burst of Romanian.

Mina replied in the same language, her voice tart, and a dark flush crept up his neck. He said something short and grudging, permission perhaps, and Mina turned to Emma again. "I apologize, Emma. You said it's through that door in the corner?"

Emma nodded, and Mina walked across the office, leaving her briefcase and purse on the small sofa. As she entered the powder room, she opened the door wide, giving both Emma and Stefan a clear view of floral-patterned wallpaper, a vanity with sink and a brass towel stand. Then the door swung closed behind her.

Emma wasn't sure what was going on, but she didn't see any reason why she shouldn't distract Stefan Alexandru from his intent study of the powder room door. She shuffled through the papers on her desk, then looked up with a puzzled frown. "Mr. Alexandru, I don't seem to have the annual payment breakdown. Could you see if Mina put it in her briefcase by mistake?"

"Eh?" He looked startled for a moment, then lifted Mina's briefcase and opened it. Emma noticed he didn't show any reluctance to search inside someone else's case. He rummaged for a moment, then held the briefcase out to Emma. "I am not certain what paper it is that you need. Do you see it here?"

Emma selected a folder from the case, opened it and nodded. "This is it." While Stefan watched closely, she took a sheet from the folder and photocopied it on her desktop copier. "Thank you," she said. She returned the paper to Mina's case, then put the copy that she didn't really need in her own folder.

"Is something wrong, Emma?" Mina asked from behind them.

Stefan turned, frowning. He apparently hadn't heard her enter the room, and that clearly bothered him.

Watching him, Emma replied to Mina's question. "I forgot to keep a copy of the payment breakdown. I hope you don't mind, but I made a copy of the one in your case."

"Of course I don't mind." Mina picked up her coat and slipped it on, then closed her briefcase. "It's been lovely to see you, Emma. It's been too long."

"Far too long." Emma moved to give Mina another hug, and the other woman leaned close to whisper into her ear, "Look behind the WC."

Emma blinked in surprise, but Mina stepped back, smiling with her lips, pleading with her eyes.

"We must see each other again while you're here, Mina. As you say, it *has* been too long." As Emma smiled, she gave a slight nod. "I have more business in Washington, so perhaps we can have dinner together before I leave."

"I would like that."

Stefan mumbled goodbye and began to shepherd Mina out, but just outside the door she paused and turned back. "Emma?"

"Yes?"

"I saw a chemist's shop in the lobby downstairs. Is it a good one?"

Emma had used the lobby drugstore on occasion. "I think so," she replied. "I've found the pharmacist quite helpful."

For a moment Mina's eyes showed both fear and determination. "Thank you," she said quietly, and walked out of Strathclyde International's offices at a brisk pace.

Emma watched her go, with Stefan hot on her heels. Her first impulse was to run to the powder room and search behind the toilet, but she didn't. She wouldn't put it past Stefan to make some excuse to come back. His suspicion had hung in the air like a thick fog while he was in her office.

Mina was afraid of him, or at least of what he could do. That had been clear, though she'd valiantly tried to hide it. Emma walked back to her desk, dropped into her big chair and swiveled it around so that she could look out the window at the street below. Several minutes passed before she saw her friend leave the building.

Mina carried a small paper bag, and Stefan walked close beside her, close enough to grab her arm if she made a sudden move. Stefan signaled a cab, and when it pulled up, he practically pushed Mina inside. Even from three stories up Emma could see her stumble. The cab pulled away, and Emma watched it out of sight, then reached for the intercom.

"Yes, Miss Campbell?"

"Would you hold calls and visitors for a few minutes, please?"

"Certainly."

"Thank you." Emma cut the intercom off, shoved herself out of her chair and locked the office door before she entered the powder room.

It looked the same as ever, with floral soap bars in a dish, the spicy scent of potpourri from a ceramic jar on a shelf. She locked the powder room door, too, then turned to study the toilet. The functional white ceramic fixture appeared undisturbed, but behind it...? She bent to look underneath, but there was nothing on the floor. Behind the tank, then.

She slid her fingertips along the edge of the cold ceramic lid, then down the sides, gingerly reaching as far behind the fixture as she could. At least it was clean back there, she thought wryly. She would have to congratulate the building's cleaning staff on the next tenants' questionnaire— Suddenly she froze, her heart thumping in her chest. The fingertips of her left hand had brushed something that felt like folded paper...or an envelope. "My God!" So Mina *had* left something there for her.

Emma shifted her position, pushing her hand farther behind the tank, straining to get a grip on whatever was there. She squeezed her hand into the narrow gap, feeling her knuckles scrape against the rough, unglazed porcelain. Ignoring the pain, she pushed again, inching her fingertips against the paper and pressing it against the wall to draw it slowly out.

It was a plain white business envelope, slightly crumpled from being concealed inside Mina's clothing. Ignoring her scraped knuckles, Emma turned the envelope over in her hands. There was nothing written on it, but it was well filled, with what felt like several sheets of paper as well as something small and stiff.

Emma pulled up her vanity stool and sat down to carefully tear the envelope open. It held four sheets of paper, with a small computer disk folded inside them. Three of the sheets were typewritten lists, while the first sheet was a handwritten letter.

My dear Emma, it began, *I am sorry for involving you in this, but I have no one else to turn to and you will know the proper persons to show these papers to.* Emma was to take them to someone who would know what to do with them, but she was, above all, to keep herself safe. *I will contact you when I am able,* Mina concluded.

The lists appeared to be nothing more than names of cities and towns. Though they meant little to Emma, she knew someone who might understand their meaning, as well as whatever information was on the disk. She tucked the handwritten note into her pocket, folded everything else back into the envelope and took it out to her office, where she pushed the envelope deep into her purse.

She locked the purse in a drawer and sat back, swiveling her chair around to prop her Italian snakeskin pumps on the desk, her face thoughtful.

Several minutes passed before she sat up straight and reached for the intercom. "Mrs. Johnson," she said when the secretary answered, "would you place a call to Lord Latham in London please?"

But her godfather wasn't in London. He was, of all things, in New York, Emma's home base. When she finally reached him there, his instructions were brief. Call a certain number, ask for a certain name and she would be instructed. And so she'd been instructed for nearly two hours that afternoon by a colleague of Lord Latham's. Plane reservations were made under an assumed name, and now here she was, playing a deadly serious game of cat and mouse in a situation that was both absurd and insane.

Nevertheless, she had to follow the plan. She walked down the concourse into the main terminal and slowed her pace at a gift shop. She walked in, glanced at the headlines on the newspapers, riffled through a New York tourist guide and picked up a magazine and a pack of chewing gum.

She put her bag down while she searched for her wallet. From the corner of her eye she could see one of her pursuers. He'd followed her into the gift shop and was pretending interest in a gaudy "Souvenir of the Big Apple" mug. Emma paid for her purchases, stuffed the gum and magazine into her briefcase and dropped her change. Coins rolled across the floor, and she watched the man in the trench coat look the other way, sending an exasperated, "This is taking forever" glance to his partner waiting outside.

That was her chance.

She took a deep breath, stooped as if to reach for a coin, then wrapped her fingers firmly around the handle of her bag. Her heartbeat accelerated, pounding in her ears. Her mouth was dry and her hands shook, but she rose in a smooth, rapid movement, the heavy bag in her hand, spun on her heel and walked quickly out of the gift shop, leaving her change spread across the floor.

"Hey, lady! You dropped your money!" a small, sharp-eyed boy yelled as he scrambled for the coins. But she was already gone.

A few yards down the concourse, a side hallway led off to the left, connecting the concourse with the ticket counter area. There would be a ladies' room there with two sets of doors leading in and out.

Emma walked rapidly to the hallway, turned and broke into a run as soon as she was out of sight of the concourse. She sprinted past the first set of rest room doors, then the second, and there—just where she'd been told it would be—was a closed door marked Employees Only.

She grabbed the knob and twisted. For one terrifying moment her sweating hands slipped on the knob. Then it turned, the door swung open and she almost fell into the darkened room. She spun around, pressing her weight against the door to close it quickly. Not until she heard the latch click did she let out the breath she'd been holding.

The room was pitch-dark and silent, but she could feel the presence of someone else.

"Are you there?" In spite of herself her voice quivered.

"Yeah."

The lights flashed on, temporarily blinding her. She blinked into the brightness, gradually focusing on the toughly built, dark-haired, unsmiling man standing in front of her. He looked her up and down. "I've been waiting. It's about time you got here."

Emma blinked in surprise, then stepped away from the door, holding her head very high. "The plane was late."

"But you're here now. Did you have any trouble?"

"Only what I was told to expect. A man and a woman followed me when I got off the plane."

"And you spotted them?" There was a hint of disbelief in his tone, but Emma only nodded.

"The man in D.C. told me what to look for. I dropped my change in the gift shop and ran in here. I'm sure they're still outside, though."

"I'm sure you're right." He walked over to lock the door. "But if you did your job, they think you're in the ladies' room."

"I did what I was told to do." Emma's reply was clipped, her Scottish accent more pronounced than usual.

"And do you always do what you're told?" He turned the phrase around on her and watched her face tighten.

"I do what's right," she said, her tone calm, her eyes angry. "What I'm told may or may not have anything to do with it, Mr.—?"

"Davis. Tyler Davis. And you are—"

"Emma Campbell," she supplied, holding out her hand politely.

He didn't shake her hand, but looked at it, one eyebrow lifted expressively. "A handshake? Shouldn't I bow?"

"Whatever for?"

"Well, aren't you really *Lady* Emma Campbell?"

The sarcasm wasn't subtle; it was an insult, and Emma stiffened. "Actually," she told him in her best boarding school drawl, "it's Lady Emma Margaret St. Clair Campbell, but Miss Campbell will do nicely." She hefted her carryon again and carried it into the small bathroom on the other side of the room, closing the door behind her with a very definite thump.

Safely inside, she braced her hands on the edge of the sink and counted very slowly to ten. It didn't cool her temper in the least. Blast that man! She was coping the best she could with an incredibly trying situation, and all he could do was insult her family name!

She hated to admit it, even to herself, but a moment of appreciation, perhaps even of comfort, would have been nice after the tension and fear of her recent ordeal.

She lifted one hand and watched it shake with a fine tremor. She was still frightened, but she wasn't going to get any comfort from Mr. Tyler Davis. He didn't even see her as a person. To him she was just someone with "Lady" in front of her name.

She'd encountered that attitude before, but it no longer had the power to hurt her. Her father had always told his two children that one might be born to a title, but one must earn the right to be proud of it. Hard work and social responsibility were his touchstones, and his children were never allowed to forget that duty took precedence over privilege. Emma took pride in the accomplishments she'd worked hard for, but as far as she was concerned, her title was nothing more than another part of her name. She doubted her ability to make Mr. Davis understand that, though.

She raised her head to look into the mirror and grimaced at the sight that met her eyes. Between the sallow face and the limp hair, she didn't look fit to lift a spoon, let alone to outwit agents of the secret police.

She bent over, feeling at the nape of her neck for the pins, then pulled the wig off with a sigh of relief. She shook her own hair loose, then twisted it out of her way and quickly stripped out of the ill-fitting suit. As she bent to wash her face, her thoughts were on the man in the other room.

She might not look fit for much, but Mr. Tyler Davis looked fit for just about anything. He must have been a soldier at one time. Though he wasn't overly tall, perhaps an inch short of six feet, he had the lean, tough build of someone for whom exercise and discipline were second nature, and the erect carriage of the longtime military man.

His hair was thick and dark brown, neatly cut and brushed back from his square, strong-featured face. His nose was straight, and his eyes deep-set beneath straight, dark brows. His lips, which might have been sensual, were held in a firm line that paradoxically emphasized their clas-

sically carved shape. His eyes were a color somewhere between gray and blue, surprisingly light against his tanned
face. They'd been cool and hard when he'd looked her over,
concealing his inner thoughts.

Emma felt a little quiver of appreciation in her stomach.
He was an undeniably attractive man. There was an inner
strength to him, the kind of arrogant toughness that drew
women like bees to honey. And that was when he was being
deliberately insulting. She could barely imagine his devas-
tating effect if he chose to be charming.

Chapter 2

Tyler hid his grin as he watched Lady Emma stalk into the bathroom. She did "haughty" very well. Of course, he thought as his grin faded, with her background she'd probably learned about the stiff upper lip in the cradle. She had backbone, though. She hadn't crumpled when he needled her, but had done her best to put him in his place despite her own discomfort.

She acted haughty, but she looked like the wrath of God. He had to admit they'd done a good job on her disguise. The State Department people had faxed him a picture of the pharmacist the Romanian woman had made a point of talking to after she left Lady Emma's office. When he compared the picture to Lady Emma in disguise, he could see they'd done well. She looked as drab and tired as the face he saw in the picture. He couldn't help but wonder how much of that was disguise and how much was her.

He'd been standing in the middle of the room, staring at nothing for long enough. "You're getting senile, Davis," he muttered to himself. He'd wasted enough time. Lady Emma had to get changed and get out of here.

He pushed the bathroom door open about six inches. "You going to be in here much long—?" His voice died away.

A woman was bending over the sink, her hair beneath the faucet, but she was a woman he scarcely recognized as the one who had run in from the corridor. This woman was slim and shapely, wearing nothing but stockings held up by lacy garters, and a one-piece bit of silk, the kind of thing he thought they called a teddy. It was a pale silvery color, with ribbon straps over her shoulders and tantalizing bits of lace at the neckline and legs.

And those legs. They were endless, long and smooth, from slim feet past delicate ankles and shapely calves in sheer stockings, to the gap of smooth, ivory-toned skin between her stockings and the lace.

"What—?"

She twisted her head to look at him while keeping her wet hair in the sink. Tyler caught his breath. Her breasts were small and round and moved gently against the silk as she twisted her body, looking at him from beneath one lifted arm, blinking the water out of her eyes. He could just see the shadowy tip of one breast through the silk, a faint hint of rose against the creamy ivory of her skin.

"What do you think you're doing?" she demanded.

Tyler had to clear his throat. "How soon will you be ready to leave?" His voice sounded odd, even to himself.

"I'll be ready as soon as I color my hair and dress. *If* you don't mind." He didn't take the hint and close the door.

He was staring at her hair. Though it was wet, and darker than it would be when dry, it was a fabulous color—a rich, dark reddish-brown, the color of cinnamon and autumn leaves. It waved into the sink, thick and alive, a single wet strand clinging to her cheek.

"What color will you make it?"

"Cool brown," she replied after a glance at an aerosol can standing beside the sink. "Now, if you don't mind—!"

"Oh." Tyler got the message at last. "Sure." He pulled his head back and closed the door.

Emma heard the latch click, then rested her head on her wet hands. "Oh, my dear heavens!" Of all the embarrassing, mortifying positions to be caught in, standing in her underwear with her sopping hair in a sink! How was she going to walk back out there and face him?

With her head in the air, of course. She almost laughed aloud. She could hear her father say that in his rich, rumbling burr. *You'll do it with pride, girl. With your head in the air.* He felt difficulties should be faced head-on and bravely. She tried to live up to his standards, even in situations like these. But holding her head high in front of a man who'd seen her in her smalls? Emma groaned and began toweling her hair.

In a half hour she was ready. Aerosol hair-coloring mousse had changed her warm auburn hair to a cool walnut-brown, and ten minutes with a brush and blow-dryer had straightened the natural wave. She'd scrubbed off the sallow makeup and the circles beneath her eyes and altered her redhead's ivory-and-rose complexion again, this time to a California tan.

She brushed a hand through her newly colored hair, then shook her head so that it fell into place, reaching a couple of inches below her shoulders. She checked her makeup, then stepped back to survey the rest of her new disguise.

She wore a wide-shouldered tunic in vivid purple over matching knit leggings, with high-topped leather sneakers. Huge silver loops dangled from her ears, swinging and gleaming with every move, her eyes and lips were strikingly made up and a large pair of sunglasses perched on top of her head. With the dark hair, vivid coloring and trendy clothes, she was in nearly every way the diametric opposite of the pale young woman who'd left the plane less than an hour ago. She didn't think they would recognize her. She certainly hoped they wouldn't.

A capacious nylon tote bag had been folded inside her carryon. She packed it with her own clothing and toiletries and left the disguise of suit and wig hanging on the back of the bathroom door. She wiped her palms down her thighs once, then picked up the bags and opened the door.

Tyler Davis, waiting on the small vinyl sofa against the far wall, looked up at the sound of the door opening. For just a moment she thought she saw his eyes widen, but then he blinked and they were shuttered again, concealing his thoughts.

She walked as far as the center of the room, dropped the two bags she was carrying and let her arms fall to her sides. "Well?" she asked after several silent seconds ticked by. "Will they recognize me?"

Tyler stirred his finger in the air, and Emma obediently turned in a circle. "If they do," he said when she was facing him again, "they have better eyes than I do."

He gave her another head-to-toe survey, and Emma felt heat wash into her cheeks. *Don't be a fool,* she told herself. He wasn't looking at her, just at her disguise. Still, she watched his face, and when a rueful smile appeared there, she released the breath she didn't realize she'd been holding.

"If I hadn't seen you go in there and come out again, I wouldn't know you were the same person. You don't even look like you're the same height and build."

Emma had to laugh. "What could one tell about my build in that dreadful suit? It's two sizes too big!"

"Well, this outfit fits . . . nice." There was nothing objective about the look he gave her, and Emma tried to keep from flushing again. All she could think of was the fact that he'd seen what she wore underneath.

"Thank you," she said briefly, and glanced at the door. "When can I leave?"

"Soon. I'll take the information now. There's less risk for you if you don't carry it any longer."

"All right."

Emma unzipped the carryon, then pulled a small penknife from her purse. As Tyler watched, she pushed the clothing aside and carefully snipped a seam in the lining fabric. When she'd opened several stitches, she took both sides and pulled, ripping the lining open for several inches. She pulled an envelope from inside the bag and handed it to Tyler.

He rubbed it between his fingers. "The computer disk?"

"Just a moment." She slid her hand farther into the depths, tugged and produced a small black envelope. "I knew the bag would be X-rayed, so I put the disk in one of these antiradiation envelopes. That should have protected it."

Tyler turned the envelope over in his hand, then opened it and looked inside. "Good idea. Do you know anything about computers, Lady Emma?"

His use of her title fell just short of sarcastic. Emma's chin lifted a fraction. "I work with them every day."

"Uh, yeah. I'm sure you work very hard." His words of agreement were contradicted by the disbelief in his tone. "You have a few minutes before you have to leave. Tell me about the Romanian."

"About Mina, you mean?"

"The Romanian woman, yes. Why did she come to you?"

"Her name is Mina Grigoras," Emma corrected him. "She came to me because she's my friend."

"What!" His head snapped up.

"Didn't they tell you? I've known Mina since we were thirteen years old. She and I were at school together when her father was ambassador in London."

Tyler nodded his head as a few pieces fell into place.

"She knows she can trust me. And since her government has business with the bank, she had the opportunity to see me."

"What did she think you could do?" His tone made it clear that she was the last person *he* would ask for help.

"She knew I would find a way to help her."

"Who else came to your office?"

"Stefan Alexandru. Mina introduced him as an attaché, but it was clear that he doesn't know anything about either banking or agriculture. I got the impression he was there to keep her from doing anything the Party doesn't want her to do."

"What gave you that impression?"

"She was afraid, not of him, but of what he represents."

"Did he know she was afraid?"

"I don't think so. She behaved naturally enough."

"If he was watching her so closely, how did she manage to leave the papers with you?"

"She asked for the loo, and left them behind the WC." When he frowned, confused, Emma gave him the American translation. "She asked for the powder room. She left her briefcase and purse in my office where he could see them, and she put the envelope with those papers and disk in it behind the toilet tank."

"Resourceful."

"I think so." Emma hesitated, fiddling with her tote bag. "Will you be able to help her?"

"It depends." He glanced at the envelopes in his hand. "If this information can be verified, and if she can prove her own value to us, then maybe we can help her."

"Prove? What does she have to prove?"

"Whether she has anything to offer us."

"What she has to offer isn't the point! She came to me because she knew I would help her. I can't let her down!"

"She may have come to you because she knew you would help her," Tyler said, and paused. "Or she may have come to you because she knew you wouldn't question what she told you."

Emma stiffened, then forced herself to take a deep, slow breath before she spoke, her voice ominously quiet. "Are you saying that you think Mina is using me?"

"I don't think anything—yet. Until we've reviewed this information and checked her out, I won't form an opinion. Right now she's just a woman whose only recommendation is that she was a school buddy of yours." He glanced at his watch. "You'd better get going," he said before she could protest his assessment of Mina. "There will be a yellow cab waiting in the arrival area. The driver will have a sign for Miller. That's you."

Emma nodded curtly. Technically he was in charge of getting her away from the airport unobserved. She had a great deal to say to Mr. Tyler Davis about his methods and assumptions . . . but she could wait until the time was right.

She picked up the tote bag. "I'm ready."

He looked her up and down. "Your tails are probably still outside, so I'll go out first and draw them away. If you spotted them, I shouldn't have any trouble, but tell me how they're dressed, anyway."

Emma wanted to bristle at the insult, but considering it was only one of many, she decided to save her anger for another time. She described the man and woman who had followed her, and Tyler nodded.

"Okay. They're still looking for the dishwater blonde, so they shouldn't give you a second glance. Only don't do anything stupid, okay?"

Emma gave him a saccharine smile. "I'll try my very best not to wink at them as I pass by. Now, shall we go?"

"You—" Tyler bit back the words. "By all means, Lady Emma." He inclined his head in a little bow toward the door.

At the door she stiffened in surprise when he reached behind her to turn off the light. He felt her tense, and placed his arm across her shoulders for a moment. "You okay?" His voice was oddly gentle and devoid of hostility.

Emma nodded. "I'm all right."

She felt muscles flex as he bent close to her, felt the warmth of his body, smelled the faint lingering scent of spicy after-shave. Just for an instant she let herself lean into him, taking comfort from his strength.

Then she straightened again, stiffening her spine and pulling slightly away. He dropped his arm from her shoulders and moved her behind the door before he twisted the knob. Emma heard the lock click free. "Good luck," he murmured, and walked out.

She eased the door almost closed and peered out at the corridor as Tyler walked away. He didn't approach the man who'd been following her, but as she watched in astonishment, he let the man approach him. They spoke for a moment, then Tyler walked a few steps away, pointing down the concourse toward the boarding gates.

She waited until Tyler maneuvered the man so that he had his back to her, then slipped out the door and sprinted the few steps to the ladies' room. There were half a dozen women in the large room, washing their hands, combing their hair and reapplying makeup, and one young woman changing a baby's diaper.

Emma slid her gaze past them with the disinterest of the tired traveler as she walked across to the sinks. She washed her hands, flicked a brush through the ends of her hair and freshened her lipstick. Satisfied, she turned away from the mirror and felt herself freeze.

The woman from the secret police was just inside the door, looking around suspiciously. Emma forced herself to keep moving, hoping the momentary hesitation in her step had passed unnoticed. She tucked her brush back into the tote bag as she walked nonchalantly toward the door, then lowered her head to glance at her watch as she brushed past the woman, close enough to touch her, and emerged into the corridor.

Three steps and around the corner to the concourse, and don't look back, don't look over your shoulder, don't give yourself away.

She walked on, neither hurrying nor hesitating, asked directions at an information booth and crossed to the ticket counter area by another of the side corridors. To reach the taxi stand she had to backtrack right past Tyler Davis and the man from the secret police.

They were there at the end of the corridor, Tyler talking, gesturing toward the other end of the vast airport, while the man listened impatiently, frowning and checking his watch. Emma strode past without glancing in their direction, all her attention ostensibly focused on a sign at the end of the concourse, directing her to the taxis.

The cab was there, the cabbie waiting for "Ms. Miller." She gave him her address and sat back on the cigarette-smoky upholstery with a shaky sigh of relief. She barely noticed the drive into Manhattan and downtown to Gramercy Park and, grateful for his lack of conversation, she gave the cabbie a tip that startled him into fervent thanks.

An elegant, older structure that overlooked the private park with its ornate wrought-iron fence, her building boasted high ceilings, Gothic windows and a lobby that welcomed her as she walked inside—all dark, polished wood, Oriental carpets and gilt-framed mirrors. There were two elevators behind polished bronze doors, a large one with a uniformed operator and a smaller one in the corner, operated by a key. It led only to the penthouse, and Emma nodded politely to the doorman as she walked across to it.

Safely inside, Emma lifted a hand and studied it with clinical interest. It was still shaking from the accumulated tension of what had been a very long day, but when she looked at her watch, she saw with surprise that it was only half past nine.

Emma shook her head with a soft laugh. It wasn't even late! She felt as if she'd lived through several lifetimes since she'd left for Washington early that morning. When she felt the laughter returning, she fought it, knowing she was close to hysteria from exhaustion and tension.

What she needed was a hot bath and a cup of tea, and perhaps a piece of real Scottish shortbread—the same as she'd been given when she'd come in cold and wet from school on dark winter afternoons in Scotland. Emma didn't bother to examine her reasons for craving a childhood snack. It was hardly surprising that she felt the need for comfort.

When the elevator discharged her in her twelfth-floor hallway, she walked across to the highly polished mahogany doors and let herself in, leaving her bag in the foyer.

"Emma?"

The voice, coming unexpectedly from her living room, startled her badly. She jumped and gasped, whirling around to confront the intruder. When a tall, distinguished man in an impeccably tailored suit walked into view, she sagged against the wall in relief.

"Uncle Larry!"

"Emma, dear, are you all right?" Frowning in concern, Lord Laurence Latham gave her a quick hug.

She shook her head as she returned the hug. "I'm quite all right, but you gave me a fright."

"I'm sorry, my dear. I didn't want to be seen waiting for you, so Mr. Koback brought me up." He held her at arm's length for a moment and studied her. "I wouldn't have thought one could disguise a red-haired Scot so effectively."

Emma grinned. "You'd be surprised what the cosmetics industry has developed. Will you join me in a cup of tea?"

"I'd love to." He followed her into the kitchen.

In the morning, sunlight flooded the spacious room, but now, blinds were drawn against the darkness, and the electric light reflected off polished copper bowls hanging from the ceiling, next to a string of garlic bulbs and bunches of dried herbs.

Lord Latham watched his goddaughter boil water, set out cups and arrange shortbread wedges on a plate. Her face was calm, her movements easy and automatic, but the tension beneath the surface was obvious. She brought the tray to the scrubbed pine table beside the windows.

"I trust everything went as planned?"

Emma nodded. "I followed instructions, and it appears I got away from them." She handed him his cup before pouring her own. "Actually, I'm a bit surprised I pulled it off."

"I'm not a bit surprised." Lord Latham selected a piece of shortbread. "Emma?"

"Hmm?" Concentrating on her pouring, she didn't look up.

"What was your opinion of Tyler Davis?" He watched with interest as her hand jerked, splashing tea into the saucer.

Very carefully, she set the teapot down and mopped the tea from her saucer with a paper napkin. "Uncle Larry, have you met Mr. Davis?"

"As a matter of fact, I have. I found him quite a resourceful and intelligent young man. I thought you and he would have a great deal in common."

Emma added milk and sipped her tea. "I'm sure he's intelligent and resourceful," she said mildly. "Of course I'd have to add arrogant, obnoxious and closed-minded to the list."

This time it was Lord Latham who appeared startled. "Arrogant, obnoxious—?"

"And closed-minded," Emma supplied helpfully. "I'm afraid the only thing I have in common with Mr. Davis is a mutual antipathy."

"I find that rather surprising."

"Did he call you *Lord* Latham with a sneer in his voice every time he spoke to you?"

"Actually, he called me 'Sir.'"

"I see. So it's me he objects to."

"My dear, I can't imagine that Mr. Davis would have any reason to object to you."

"I don't know his reasons, but he made it very clear he objects to anyone called 'Lady Emma.' Don't worry about it, Uncle Larry. I don't especially like your Mr. Davis, but I'll put up with him . . . for Mina's sake."

"Don't be too harsh with him, dear. He may improve with acquaintance. And all this *is* for Mina's sake." Lord Latham smiled. "I remember her as a girl. A little slip of a thing, with huge, dark eyes."

Emma smiled. "She's not so skinny anymore, but she still has lovely eyes." She leaned toward him, speaking urgently. "I have to help her. She's in danger and she's so frightened. I could see the fear in her, and—"

The telephone rang, interrupting her. She looked at her godfather, and he nodded. She picked it up on the fourth ring, said hello, then handed it to him. He listened without speaking for several moments. "Yes," he said, "That's right. That *is* good news. Thank you."

He replaced the receiver and turned to look at Emma. "The papers and computer disk Mina gave you are now safely out of the airport and in the hands of the proper authorities."

"I see. And what happens next?"

"Tomorrow morning we'll meet with Mr. Davis, and then you and I will fly back to Washington. As far as the Romanian secret police are concerned, you never left the city."

"But what about my appointments tomorrow morning? I have two meetings scheduled."

"That's been taken care of. Your secretary will call the parties and ask if they can be rescheduled, since your breakfast meeting is running late. We'll be in Washington by midmorning. You'll walk into the building as if you've just finished your breakfast meeting and continue with your day."

"And when am I scheduled to collapse with exhaustion from flying up and down the east coast?" Emma grinned, and Lord Latham shook his head at her.

"You can't fool me, my dear. I know you too well to be misled by that air of fragility when I know there's pressed steel underneath."

"I guess I'm feeling rather fragile right now. I'd planned a cup of tea and a hot bath, so now that I've had my tea, I think it's time for the bath, and then bed. Will you be staying the night?"

"I took the liberty of putting my bag in the guest room."

"I'm glad. Actually," she admitted ruefully, "I think I'd rather not be all alone here tonight."

"Don't worry, Emma. It appears we've managed to throw suspicion away from you and onto the pharmacist Mina talked to. She left work early yesterday, and she'll stay home tomorrow."

"How did you manage that?"

His smile was smug. "We sent a gentleman to talk to her and learned that her husband is a commander in the navy. He's an aviator on an aircraft carrier, and she was in Air Force Intelligence until she married and trained to be a pharmacist. She's a patriotic young woman and she was pleased to cooperate."

"That was a bit of luck."

Lord Latham nodded. "More luck than we had any right to expect. She understands perfectly what she's gotten into and she knows what to do."

"Is she in any danger?"

"Probably not. We've assigned protection to her, but I doubt that she'll need it." He started toward the guest room, then turned and looked back.

"I'm not really a superstitious man, Emma, but I'd like you to remember that we've already had one bit of luck. We can't expect any more."

Chapter 3

They met Tyler Davis at seven the next morning.

Emma was back to her real self, having painstakingly shampooed all the coloring out of her hair. Left to dry in its natural deep red waves, it fell loosely over the shoulders of her businesslike emerald silk dress and cream-colored blazer. She wore her usual light makeup and carried a briefcase when she went to face Tyler Davis again, this time with Lord Latham beside her.

She resented the fact that she was edgy about meeting him. After all, it was he, not she, who'd been unforgivably rude. All the same, she could feel the tension in her shoulders as they neared an unused office on the fringes of the airport. She took a deep breath when Lord Latham pushed open the office door, composed her face, then followed him in.

Tyler Davis was there, talking with a tall young man with the same kind of straight-shouldered military bearing. The two men turned quickly when the door opened, the wariness in their eyes easing when they saw who was there.

Emma avoided Tyler's eyes, looking instead at the younger man. Good-looking and blond, he was in his twenties, and his eyes widened in appreciation when he saw her.

"Good morning!" He shook her hand warmly, keeping it in his longer than necessary. "You must be Lady—er—Countess Campbell. I'm Jim Kendall, and I'm really glad to meet you."

"Thank you, Mr. Kendall." She gently retrieved her hand. "I'm Emma."

"Lady Emma," Tyler put in.

Emma ignored him. "Countess Campbell is my mother."

"Sorry about that." He grinned, his bouncy cheerfulness undiminished. "I'm not used to lords and ladies and stuff. They might come to Washington, but they don't get introduced to the likes of me!"

"Please don't worry about it." Emma could feel the anger in Tyler as he stood behind the younger man, could feel him willing her to look at him. She didn't. Instead, she smiled warmly at Jim Kendall. "I seldom use the title in America. It seems to make some people uncomfortable, though I don't know why."

"Maybe they're shy," Jim said, grinning, encouraged by her smile. "But I'm not."

"I can see that." Emma laughed lightly. "Have you met Lord Latham, Mr. Kendall?" She stepped aside, allowing them to shake hands, and found herself finally facing Tyler Davis.

He was scowling, so she smiled. It was what her mother called a tea-party smile—pleasant enough but empty of real warmth. "Good morning, Mr. Davis."

Tyler didn't offer to shake hands, and neither did she. "Lady Emma." He gave her a slight nod, and then turned his back on her, addressing Lord Latham. "Did you tell her what to do?"

"Yes," Emma replied. She didn't like being spoken of in the third person in her own presence. "He told me what to do. It sounds simple enough."

"When you're working with amateurs, you keep it simple."

The insult was clear to them all. Emma heard a quick mutter from Jim Kendall, and her eyelids flickered for a moment as she controlled her temper. "I'm sure we amateurs appreciate your consideration, Mr. Davis." Her tone was deceptively mild.

Lord Latham stepped in before hostilities could escalate. "Do you anticipate any problems for Emma in Washington, Mr. Davis?"

Tyler shook his head. "Not if she does as she's told. As far as anyone watching her office or apartment will know, she's been there all along."

"And Emma will be safe?"

Tyler glanced at her. "If she does as she's told."

"Good." Lord Latham glanced warningly at his goddaughter, bristling with anger, then turned to Jim. "Mr. Kendall, could we check to see if the plane is ready? I'd like to get back to New York as early as is possible."

"Yeah, sure." They walked to the door, where Jim glanced back at Emma and Tyler, standing in opposite corners of the small room like fighters waiting for the bell. He followed Lord Latham out, closing it quietly behind him.

Emma didn't burst from her corner with fists raised, but sauntered out, arms folded, head cocked to the side. She gave Tyler a leisurely survey from head to toe and back again, as if she were examining a new and unusual scientific specimen.

"I'm constantly puzzled by people like you," she said at last.

"What do you mean, people like me?" Tyler turned away, shuffling some papers into a briefcase sitting atop the little office's dusty desk.

"People who are unpleasant to people they've just met, people they know nothing about."

"I know your type."

"My *type*?" she repeated with distaste.

"Yeah. Your type." He turned and gave her the same slow inspection she'd given him. "A rich girl who plays at working for Daddy's bank because she doesn't need a real job. A rich girl who's stumbled into something that's way over her head. You're an amateur, and I know what's going to happen. You'll get in my way every step of this operation, and I can't even order you out of it because the Romanian woman wants to deal with her old school buddy!"

Emma was as startled by the vehemence of the attack as she was by the laundry list of unfounded accusations, but she didn't burst into a furious rebuttal. Instead, after a moment's incredulous silence, she laughed.

"What the hell?" Tyler demanded.

"You—!" she gasped through her laughter. "You're nothing but a prisoner of your own prejudices, aren't you? You don't have to tell me that I'm out of my depth in this international spy business. I know that very well. I'd be lost without the advice and direction of people like you and Uncle Larry, but I'm not stupid, Mr. Davis! I know my limitations and I've no intention of getting in the way. And," she said, smiling at him coldly, "if you're half as good at your business as Uncle Larry seems to think you are, then I have nothing to worry about, do I?"

"You'll—" He took a step toward her, then stopped when Lord Latham strode into the room.

"Emma, dear, come along. The airplane's waiting and it's time for us to be off."

"I think Mr. Davis had something he wanted to say to me, Uncle Larry." She looked at Tyler, but he shook his head.

"You'll be back tomorrow," Tyler told her. "What I have to say can wait until then."

If that sounded more like a threat than a promise, Emma wasn't bothered in the least. She'd had just about enough of Tyler Davis and his superior attitudes, and if he wanted to go another round, she planned to be ready.

"You're looking forward to this, aren't you, Emma?"

Lord Latham sat in a deep leather chair and watched her pace restlessly around her living room. Though they'd flown back to New York that afternoon, she showed no signs of travel fatigue.

"Looking forward to what?" Emma paused by a window and lifted the draperies aside to look out. Her hair glowed dark copper against the midnight-blue velvet, and her skin was porcelain-pale, tinged with rose across her cheekbones. Lord Latham admired the picture his god-daughter made even as he suspected her motives.

"To Tyler's arrival. Since you say you don't like the man, I can only assume you're eager to resume hostilities."

"Resume hostilities?" Emma smiled. "You make this sound like the North African campaign."

"If that's how you're thinking of it, Emma, I'd like to remind you that Tyler Davis isn't Rommel, and you're not Montgomery. You two are on the same side."

Emma's smile faded. She walked across the graciously proportioned room to perch on an ottoman. "I know that, Uncle Larry. I also know that Mina's depending on me, and the danger she's in frightens me. I know quite well that I need help."

"Then why are you so at odds with Tyler?"

"Do you really need to ask? You've heard the man. Every word he says to me is an insult!"

"I know he's a bit abrasive, but give the man a chance, Emma. He's a professional forced to work with amateurs."

"I'm trying to be as professional as I can!"

"I know you are, but look at this from his point of view. You're a banker, Emma, not a spy!"

"I may become a spy before this is finished! I'm afraid our Mr. Davis will force me to!"

"He just may at that." Lord Latham chuckled. "I believe at one time he was a drill instructor for the navy."

"If he tells me to do push-ups, I won't."

"If I tell you to jump out a window, you'll do exactly as I say!"

Emma started, coming to her feet at the sound of a voice from the entry hall. She stood there as Tyler strolled calmly into her living room, shrugging off a battered leather jacket. He tossed it onto a brocade-covered chair and sauntered across the Aubusson carpet to stand facing her.

Emma wondered how much he'd heard. Judging from his expression, he'd heard more than she would have liked. He stood looking at her for several heartbeats before he spoke.

"Remember that, Lady Emma. I'm the boss. If I say jump, your only question should be 'How high?'"

"My memory is excellent," Emma said, giving him a spurious smile. "And good evening to you, Mr. Davis. I assume Mr. Koback opened the elevator for you with no problems."

"Little old man in a red jacket? Very polite while he checked my ID thoroughly?"

"That's him." Emma smiled. "I've lived here for eight years and I still don't know his first name, but I think that's how he wants it. After fifty years in America, his sense of propriety is still very European." She sidestepped around Tyler and went to pick up his jacket. "I'll bring the coffee in, Uncle Larry, and we can begin."

Tyler's jacket was still warm from his body, and as she slipped it on a hanger, Emma caught a faint whiff of a subtly spicy scent. She held the lining to her nose and breathed in the trace of scent that she recognized as Tyler's. Suddenly disturbed, she pushed the jacket into the closet and closed the door.

As she stood in the kitchen, placing cups, coffeepot and accessories on a tray, she mentally dismissed the incident. The fact that she'd recognized Tyler's scent didn't mean anything. She tried to ignore the little voice reminding her that the memories of scents were some of the most powerful, buried deep in the subconscious where important secrets were kept.

She was outwardly calm when she carried the heavy tray into the living room and set it on the low table in front of the sofa. She poured, added a splash of cream to one cup and passed it across the table. "Uncle Larry."

"Thank you, my dear." He accepted the bone china cup and saucer and sat back in his chair.

"Cream or sugar, Mr. Davis?" She kept her gaze on the cup she was pouring.

"Black, thank you."

She nodded and filled the cup. As she started to hand it to him, he reached out and their hands met. Emma jerked, then gasped as hot coffee splashed onto her fingers. It was Tyler who caught her wrist and steadied her hand until he could safely take the cup from her.

"Are you hurt?" He turned her hand over, studying the reddened patches on her fingers. "You should put cold water on that."

Emma shook her head and pulled her hand away. "I'll be fine. It's not burned," she said softly, drying her fingers briskly on a linen napkin.

"Are you certain you're all right, Emma?"

She smiled ruefully at her godfather and nodded. She could feel the heat of a blush in her cheeks and cursed the thin skin that betrayed her embarrassment. "It was clumsy of me. And hadn't we best get on with our meeting? I don't want to waste Mr. Davis's time."

"Very well, if you're sure." Lord Latham studied her face for a moment, then reached into the briefcase beside his chair and brought out a sheaf of papers. "Here's the information I was able to gather on Mina." He gave them each a stapled copy several pages long. "They were telexed to me this afternoon. There's nothing in here that you don't already know, Emma, except perhaps that Mina was attached to the embassy in Washington only six weeks ago. Before that she was in Belgrade, working on an agricultural import program. The rest you know. Tyler—" he turned to address the younger man "—I don't know how much Emma has told you about her friendship with Mina, but it's all in here, including visits by Mina to England and Scotland and Emma's visit to Romania a few years ago."

"Okay." Tyler flipped the closely typed pages, scanning the contents. "Do you know what puzzles me?"

"Hmm?"

"How did someone as young as Mina Grigoras get so far in the Party hierarchy?"

"Didn't you know? Her late father was a Romanian national hero. A war hero, a founder of the Communist government and ambassador to several countries before he went back to work in the government in Bucharest. He died three years ago."

"And his daughter inherited his position?"

"Not his position. That would be too much. But Mina did advance through the ranks faster than usual because of her father's renown. She was born to it, you might say."

"I see." Tyler glanced from one to the other, then closed his copy of the report. "As you said, I can read this later. Right now we need to go over the plan."

"Yes," Emma said, leaning forward, arms folded on her knees, eager to hear. "What *is* the plan? How are we going to get Mina away from them safely?"

"Is that what you think we're planning?" Tyler asked.

"What else?"

Tyler shook his head over her naiveté. "We're not making plans to get anyone away. Not yet."

"Then what?"

"We let Ms. Grigoras prove her worth to us."

"What?" Emma stiffened in surprise.

"We can't just blindly accept the word of everyone who says they want to defect. We have to protect our own interests. We need proof that she is who and what she says she is, proof that she's sincere about her wish to defect and sincere about the potential danger to her if she doesn't."

"How is she supposed to prove those things?" Emma demanded. "She can hardly go to the Party and ask them for a letter certifying that she's in danger if she doesn't defect!"

Tyler shot her an exasperated glance. "Nevertheless, there are ways she can prove herself. She can provide us with information to prove that she's sincere and that she's not a double agent."

"And when will that be? She's already put herself at risk by passing information. Wasn't that enough?"

He shrugged. "It'll be enough when we're satisfied. And don't ask me to put a time frame on the process, because I can't. We'll know when we know."

"And in the meantime?" Emma asked. "Mina waits on a knife edge of fear, not knowing if she'll be allowed to defect, or if she'll be sent back—to prison or worse?"

"In the meantime she waits," he agreed.

"You don't understand, Mr. Davis. Mina is my friend! How do I tell her that I can't help her?"

"You *are* helping her, but this is a process that can't be hurried. Don't worry about your friend, Lady Emma. I'm sure she already knows all this. If she's really sincere about defecting, she'll expect to be checked out, and if she's been planted by the Party, she would be suspicious if we didn't do so."

"She's not a plant!" Emma snapped. "You didn't see her, Mr. Davis. You didn't see her fear, and her desperation."

"No, but you may not have seen it, either. What you were seeing may have been nothing but good acting, taking advantage of your friendship. It's a very clever ploy, really."

"It's not a ploy!" Emma shoved herself to her feet and glared down at Tyler. "It is not a ploy," she repeated, spacing the words evenly for emphasis. She kept her voice deliberately low, as if allowing the volume to rise might also allow her temper to escape the tight rein she was holding on it. "Mina is terribly, desperately frightened and alone, and she came to me for help. I won't allow you to slander and insult her."

"I'm doing neither. I'm merely being objective, something you obviously aren't capable of right now."

"Objective? That's ridiculous. A human being is more important than this idealogical nitpicking! We should get Mina to safety, and then worry about what information she may be able to provide."

Tyler threw up his hands. "Did I say she was naive?" He addressed the question to the ceiling, then lowered his gaze to Emma. "This proves it. And if you can't be realistic about this, Lady Emma, you might as well get out right now. Chances are, we don't need anything the Romanian woman can provide, and we'd save ourselves a lot of time and trouble if we just let her go back to her own country right now."

"No!" Emma spun away from him. Beside the long windows that overlooked the park, she whirled around. "You can't do that. I won't let you!"

Tyler didn't reply right away. He was watching Emma, startled by what he saw. Her cheeks were pink with emotion, her hair glowed like polished copper against the dark foliage, her eyes were bright with outrage. Whatever hostile words Tyler might have spoken were caught on a pang of guilt. Deep inside he was an idealist, not the hard-nosed cynic he was making himself out to be, and he was a little ashamed to realize that he'd spoken more to shock the elegant Lady Emma than because he meant what he'd said literally.

But when she looked at him like that, angry and impossibly, heartbreakingly beautiful, he knew she had only to ask and he would take back the words. He might do anything—if she asked him.

Lord Latham rose and went to her taking her hand and drawing her back to the sofa. "Emma, my dear, I know how concerned you are for Mina. I'm concerned for her, too. And I understand that you believe in her absolutely."

"Don't you?" Emma asked.

Lord Latham hesitated. "I want to believe her," he said at last. "But whatever my personal feelings about the situation, I have to act in the best interests of my government. As Tyler does. Because of that, we can't believe too easily."

"I believe her."

"I know you do. But in this case certainty has to include proof. Something concrete, something tangible to show both our governments, to prove that Mina needs our help. The information she already gave you was the first sign, but she knows we'll need more."

There was a long pause, then Emma sighed. "I see."

"Emma." Lord Latham waited until she looked up at him. "If you want to help Mina, you must help her get the proof for us. That's the best thing you can do for her."

"I will, then. I'll help her get proof, because I know she's telling the truth. And I hope all the doubters—" she shot Tyler a frigid look "—choke on their doubts!"

The apology that he'd been forming died unspoken. He wasn't apologizing to "Her Haughtiness." Let her think what she liked, he told himself bitterly. She'd made it perfectly clear she didn't want anything to do with him, and the feeling was damn well mutual!

Chapter 4

What he wanted, of course, counted for very little.

Only days later, Tyler was sitting beside Lady Emma in a luxurious limousine, riding back into Manhattan after a Sunday afternoon meeting with Lord Latham in Westchester County. Under other circumstances he might have relaxed and enjoyed the comfortable ride, but circumstances made that impossible. He didn't like accepting the perks of her title and wealth, and he didn't like what he'd just been told he had to do. He glanced at her, then looked away.

"Stay at her apartment," Lord Latham had said as calmly as if he'd just offered him tea. Tyler had seen Emma stiffen in wordless rejection of the idea, and she wasn't alone in her dismay. He'd argued the point, but Lord Latham had been adamant. He didn't necessarily believe that Emma was in danger, but he didn't want her alone in her apartment. Neither of them had been able to convince him otherwise.

Neither of them, as they left Westchester and traveled back into the city, had spoken of what weighed so heavily on their minds.

Think of it as medicine, Emma told herself firmly. *Unpleasant, but good for the soul.* If she could negotiate loans with governments around the world, surely she could deal with Tyler Davis for a few nights. Settled in the limousine, she opened a thick envelope filled with papers and began to read.

"I wonder," Tyler said as the traffic grew heavier as they headed into the city, "why you keep hiding behind those papers. Are you afraid of me?"

For a moment nothing moved. Then Emma lowered the thick prospectus to her lap and turned an icy gaze on him. "I am not," she said very distinctly, "afraid, and certainly not of you. I have several meetings scheduled for tomorrow, not just the one with Mina."

"Which is why you're reading those papers so intently?"

She nodded.

"What are they?"

"Confidential, for one thing," she replied. He gave the papers a skeptical look, and she sighed silently. "I can tell you that I'm considering a loan to a South American country, for agricultural development."

"You mean they're buying a couple of tractors?"

"No, I mean agricultural development. Their prospectus concerns development of the agricultural industry in this nation over the next five years."

"And you'll decide to approve or reject? On your own?"

"Yes."

Tyler blinked, then whistled softly. "I had no idea you would be handling something that big."

Emma favored him with a tiny smile. "You've made it clear from the start that you think I'm nothing more than a figurehead."

"So why aren't you trying to change my mind?"

"I never argue with beliefs, Mr. Davis. If your narrow little prejudices make you happy, I won't waste my time arguing with you.'' She opened the prospectus and resumed reading.

Tyler sat back and watched the passing scenery, off balance. Paradoxically her refusal to argue did more to convince him than a listing of her professional credentials would have. So Lady Emma Campbell, despite her age and family connections, really was a working banker. Not even her own father would entrust such important accounts to an incompetent.

Okay, he thought, so he'd been wrong about her professionalism. One new fact wasn't going to change his overall opinion of her. She'd grown up with wealth. It showed in the expensive clothes, in the air of quiet assurance she wore as unconsciously as she wore silk and cashmere, in the limousine. Tyler could neither forget that wealth, nor forgive it.

He did his best to keep his distance that evening, but that wasn't as easy as it should have been. Little things, unexpected things, disarmed him. Like dinner, for instance, at her Manhattan apartment. Tyler expected something like caviar on thin toast. He hated caviar.

They had pizza with everything. Emma phoned in the order to a pizza place around the corner, chatted briefly and warmly with someone called Luca and tipped the delivery boy, whom she also knew by name, more than generously.

Tyler would have enjoyed the pizza more if he hadn't been distracted by the astonishing sight of Lady Emma eating with her fingers from a cardboard carton and drinking a hearty, inexpensive red wine with every evidence of enjoyment. When dinner was finished, she declined his offer to help, put the box in the trash and carried her wineglass into the living room.

She switched on the television and curled up in an armchair with a piece of needlework to watch the evening news. Tyler slouched comfortably on the sofa, his glass cupped in his hand. He meant to watch the news, but kept looking from the screen to Emma.

Her needle moved rhythmically, painting glowing colors on the canvas. A pile of brightly colored wools spilled across her lap, and from time to time she searched through it for the next color she needed.

He found it oddly soothing to watch her, for Tyler had never watched a woman embroidering. His unmarried mother had had no time for fancy needlework.

When he was a child he would wait for her to come home at night from her job in the café. She'd smelled of cigarette smoke, cheap perfume and the French-frying kettle, and she would slump on their sagging sofa, pale from weariness. Ten-year-old Tyler would bring her the supper he'd made—a sandwich and a can of soda. She would thank him and eat the peanut butter or the bologna more out of kindness to him than because she was hungry. Then she would take out her cigarettes and smoke one after another, staring through the haze at the flickering black-and-white television until she went to bed.

Without really understanding why, Tyler had known that her life was hard. Though his mother never hinted that he was to blame, neighbors and schoolmates talked behind his back and called him names, and he knew that he was in some way responsible for her lot. He knew that to ask his mother about the names they called him would hurt her, so he didn't ask. She loved him, though she was usually too tired to show it, and he did his childish best to ease her burden.

He wished he could have done more to take the weight of care from his mother, wished he could have given her the leisure and the energy to make pretty things.

He couldn't despise Lady Emma for her pastime, though, for beauty nourished the soul. And she was very beautiful.

His lips tightening, he took a newsmagazine off the coffee table, opened it and tried to concentrate on an article on the never-ending arms negotiations. He couldn't have said he lost himself in the state of the world, but by determinedly reading one page after another he managed to pass the next hour.

When he glanced at his watch and saw with relief that it was late enough to go to bed, he lowered the magazine and looked across at Emma. His breath caught in his throat.

She'd bent her head toward the light as she worked on an intricate bit of the design, and she was singing under her breath with the Mozart she'd put on the stereo after the news was over.

Tyler knew he'd never seen anyone more beautiful. She worked at the timelessly feminine task, her hair falling around her shoulders in coppery waves. Her skin was as pale as alabaster, so delicate that he could see the faint hint of veins beneath the skin.

Her breasts would look like that, he thought, creamy pale, with a delicate tracery of blue veins beneath the skin, rosy nipples and— He caught himself, cursing his thoughts. Indulging in pornographic fantasies about Lady Emma wasn't only puerile, it was stupid. He threw the magazine onto the low table in front of him with some force, and she looked up, startled.

"Is something wrong?"

"No." He could hear the huskiness in his voice, and cleared his throat. "I just noticed the time."

"Oh." She glanced at a baroque clock on the mantel. "I didn't realize it was so late."

"Yeah, well, we might as well get some sleep. Tomorrow's going to be a long day." It was the most banal of remarks, but she took it at face value.

"You're probably right." She was gathering up her bright wools and tucking her work into a wicker basket as she spoke. "I'll show you the guest room."

She was the perfect hostess as she showed him his room, but there was an unavoidable intimacy to two people spending the night in the apartment. They were both edgy, though they tried to hide it.

Tyler tried to clamp down on his wayward thoughts, but to little avail. As he followed Emma down the hallway, he watched the sweet syncopation of her walk. Then, standing in the doorway beside her, he breathed the lingering scent of her perfume, light and flowery with darker undertones of musk and spice, and knew he wanted her.

Emma stepped into the guest bath to check on towels, then backed out, satisfied, and bumped into Tyler. His body was big and solid and warm, filling the narrow doorway. Though she instinctively flinched, he didn't move back to let her pass.

"Pardon me." She waited for him to move out of the way.

"I don't think so."

She frowned. "Tyler, please let me pass."

Without speaking, he moved closer and she backed up until her spine was against the wall.

"What *are* you doing?" She was trying to sound indignant, but he could hear the huskiness in her voice.

He smiled then, a slow, lazy smile that sent heat to her cheeks. "Research." He put his hands on her shoulders and drew her slowly toward him. "We've both been wondering—"

"What?" It was a silly question. She knew exactly what he meant. "Tyler, no." She'd meant to sound firm, emphatic, outraged, but the words had emerged in a whisper.

"Emma...yes." He bent close, his smile fading as his eyes darkened. "We've both been wondering what it would be like," he murmured, "and now we'll know...."

When he took her mouth with his, the first shiver of delight that slid down Emma's spine was followed by heat. Her accelerating heartbeat sent the heat flushing her skin, beating through her veins, knocking her wildly off balance. She clutched his shoulders, seeking some kind of stability, but when she did, Tyler wrapped his arms around her and slanted his mouth over hers to deepen the kiss with dizzying effect.

It caught like wildfire, a sudden conflagration, destroying pretense and illusion. Emma's lips parted beneath the seductive pressure of his, and as he sought the secrets of her mouth, she melted against his body in surrender. When he wrenched his mouth from hers, she clung to him, and with a stifled oath he practically pushed her out of his arms.

"Now I know." His voice was strained. "And so do you."

Emma stared at him, clutching the wall for support. Her eyes were huge in her pale face, and she pressed a trembling hand to her lips. "You—" Her whisper broke. "You had no right." She looked at him a moment longer, then turned on her heel and stalked into her bedroom. The door closed firmly, then Tyler heard the lock slide home.

"Damn!" Tyler yanked his shirt off with enough force to pop a button. It clicked on the floor before disappearing under the bed. "Damn, damn, damn," he swore, less with heat than with despair, then slumped onto the bed, head in his hands. He had to be completely out of his mind to grab Lady Emma and kiss her like an adolescent, hostage to his hormones.

He'd felt passion rise in her, quick and hot, as he kissed her, but the last thing he'd seen in her eyes had been a cold disgust that chilled him to the core. He didn't blame her. The passion that had surged within him had been damn near uncontrollable.

That was totally out of character for him. Tyler dragged a hand over his face. He'd never lost control like that. He'd never been a victim of his own desires that way. If he'd thought at all, which he would freely admit that he hadn't, he would have thought a kiss would defuse the simmering tension between them, dull the attraction and get her out of his system.

He now knew just how wrong that assumption had been.

Emma stood in the kitchen at six the next morning, fully dressed, carefully made up, watching the coffee drip. If she'd been alone, she would have padded to the kitchen in her robe and read the paper with her first cup of coffee before going to shower and dress. Instead, after an unrestful night, she'd put on all her business armor before she'd left her room and risked facing Tyler. She even had her shoes on, though the jacket that matched her silk dress was draped over a chair.

The coffee maker had almost finished its cycle when she heard footsteps in the hall. Quickly she picked up the butter dish and a plate with sliced bread stacked on it.

"Good morning." She sent a bright, meaningless smile in the direction of the doorway, then set the bread and butter on the table. "I usually have coffee and toast for breakfast, but if you'd like eggs, that won't take a moment." She went back to the counter and picked up two jars of jam.

"Coffee and toast are fine."

"All right. The coffee's nearly ready." Still with her back to him, she was taking out cups and plates.

So, Tyler thought, they weren't going to discuss last night, and the kiss. Well, that was all right with him. If she didn't want an apology, then he would be spared giving her one. He sat at the table and watched as she bustled around making a production of her simple chores.

She was already in her business armor, as he was, but if she considered that dress any form of protection, she was quite mistaken. It was peach-colored silk, and it skimmed lightly over her body, whispering when she moved. The style was prim, with a stand-up collar and a skirt that brushed her calves, but the dress made him think of peach ice cream and warm summer afternoons... and of the lacy things he was certain she was wearing beneath it. It was all too easy for him to remember what she'd worn under the dreary beige suit of her disguise.

His throat was suddenly dry. He took a too-quick swallow of the coffee she set before him and burned his tongue.

He kept the mistake to himself, added milk to the cup and sipped carefully.

"Nanny would be shocked at me, feeding you such a skimpy breakfast." The toast popped up and Emma passed it to him, then dropped more bread into the slots. "She believed in a good Scottish breakfast. Porridge, kippers, bacon, eggs, fried bread, tomatoes, toast and marmalade."

"All that?"

"And she'd watch to see that we ate it, too."

"Coffee and toast are fine," he said.

"Nanny would take you in hand. She said she wouldn't let anyone walk through a Scottish winter without a good breakfast. Even in summer she said the same thing."

"And when did you ever walk through a Scottish winter?" he asked sarcastically.

"To get to school." Ignoring his tone, Emma took her own toast and began spreading it with marmalade.

"I thought you went to that fancy private school in London—with Mina."

"That was when I was thirteen and Father moved his main offices to London. Before that we lived the whole year in Scotland and went to the village school."

"Just like everyone else." It wasn't quite a question.

"Just like everyone else."

He crunched into his toast, considering. "What was it like," he asked after a moment, "having servants?"

"Nanny?" Emma smiled. "She wasn't a servant. She was more like a grandmother or a favorite aunt. My father's mother died when he was born, and Nanny raised him, and then us."

"Us?"

"My brother and I." Emma suddenly realized how much she'd said about herself. She changed the subject before taking a bite of toast. "What about you? Where did you grow up?"

Tyler didn't answer right away, but looked across at her, his eyes oddly wary. "Virginia," he replied tersely, then glanced at his watch. "When do you have to be at your office?"

"Nine o'clock." Emma knew an evasion when she heard one, but she watched his face a moment longer, curious. He obviously didn't want to talk about himself, but was that because he simply didn't like her, or because he was hiding something? Either way she had no time to explore his reasons.

They arrived at her office only minutes before her first appointment. Emma apologized as she plopped her briefcase onto the desk and extracted papers. "I'm afraid you'll have a rather dull day. Mina's meeting isn't scheduled until this afternoon."

"Do you have a phone I can use?" Tyler asked.

"Of course. There's a small office next to this one, it's not used much, but there is a telephone there."

"Great. I'll just—" The intercom's buzz interrupted him. Emma pressed a button. "Yes, Mrs. Johnson?"

"The gentlemen are here, Miss Campbell."

"Thank you. Send them in, please. And would you show Mr. Davis the spare office, Mrs. Johnson? He has work to do."

"Of course."

The "spare" office next to Emma's boasted wood-paneled walls with heavy moldings and cornices, as well as comfortable furnishings, including an antique desk and brocade armchairs. There were current magazines on the lamp table, paper, pens and telephone books on the desk, along with the promised phone.

Pretty nice for a spare room, he thought. With a cup of coffee, he settled comfortably at the desk and made phone calls for more than two hours. He scribbled notes on a pad, trying to sort and analyze the facts that were known about Mina Grigoras, organizing his questions for her.

When he realized he was writing the same things over and over again just to fill time, he locked his notes into his briefcase and carried his empty coffee cup out to Mrs. Johnson's office.

The secretary looked up from entering figures into a computer on her desk. "Can I get you some more coffee, Mr. Davis?"

"No, thank you." He grinned. "I just ran out of things to do. Is Lady Emma free yet?"

Mrs. Johnson, a tall handsome woman in her late forties, smiled and shook her head. "Miss Campbell is still in her meeting."

Tyler glanced at his watch. It was half past eleven. "It's been a long meeting."

"Her sort of business takes time."

"I see. Well, when does she take lunch?"

"She usually has lunch sent in. I've ordered for two, and it will be here at twelve-thirty."

"Okay." He had an hour to wait until then, and Tyler thought he would make the most of it. He pulled a side chair over to the desk. "Can I take up a little of your time?"

"Of course." She pressed buttons on her computer and the columns of figures disappeared. "How can I help you?"

"Tell me about Lady Emma." Tyler watched her friendly smile disappear into wariness. Mrs. Johnson wasn't about to violate Emma's confidence. "How did she get into banking?"

The woman considered, and seemed to find the question innocuous enough. "Her family owns the bank."

"I know, but it seems surprising that someone so young is involved in such high-level business."

"But it's hardly surprising for someone who graduated cum laude from the Harvard Business School with a special award in banking and finance." There was an echo of proprietary pride in her voice.

"Very impressive."

"Don't make the mistake of thinking she's a figurehead because of her family connection, Mr. Davis. She's a working banker and she's earned her position."

"She's accomplished a great deal in a short time."

"Yes, she has. She—" The intercom buzzed, interrupting her. "Excuse me, please." Mrs. Johnson picked up a notebook and pencil and disappeared into Emma's office.

Left alone, Tyler sat back, elbows on the chair arms, his fingertips tented below his chin and his eyes thoughtful.

A Harvard MBA, cum laude, no less, handling loans to foreign governments for sums that had to be well into the millions of dollars. Or pounds. Or yen, pesos, whatever.

He was coming to know a very different woman from the one he'd expected, an exceptionally intelligent, well-educated, hardworking woman, possessed of the protective loyalty of her employees.

The Lady Emma he'd thought he would meet hadn't even been interesting.

This Lady Emma was dangerously disturbing to his peace of mind.

Chapter 5

When lunch arrived half an hour later, Tyler was gratified that it turned out to be salad and veal marsala, with zabaglione for dessert. He ate with enjoyment, while Emma took much smaller portions of everything.

"You don't need to diet," he said without thinking.

"I beg your pardon?"

"You don't need to diet. You look fine the way you are." He looked her up and down.

Emma's chin came up a fraction. "I appreciate the compliment," she said coolly, "but I'm not dieting."

"You're not eating, either."

"I'm . . ." She hesitated and looked away, biting her lip. "I'm not very hungry today."

"Nervous?"

"I'm worried about Mina."

"Yeah." He ate the last bite of his veal. "Why don't you tell me about Mina? What was she like as a kid?"

"What was she like?" Emma looked into her memory, her eyes unfocused. "She was beautiful. Most thirteen-year-old girls are all lanky arms and legs, gangly bodies that haven't quite grown into a coherent whole, but she was different. She was like a Greek icon, a perfectly oval face with huge eyes and delicate, curving eyebrows, black hair, ivory skin. All the English schoolgirls with spotty skin were awestruck, and they didn't cope with that very well.''

"What happened?"

"Jealousy happened. There is no group so cruel to outsiders as English schoolgirls.'' She shook her head. "No, let me amend that. From what I've heard, English schoolboys may actually be worse, but the girls are quite bad enough. Mina and I were the new arrivals, the outsiders. That brought us close.''

"You? How were you an outsider?'' To him, she was the ultimate insider, wealthy, beautiful, titled.

She laughed out loud. "I was from the Scottish wilds and had gone to a simple village school. To add insult to injury, instead of having the upper-class drawl, I spoke with a broad Scottish burr. I didn't know the right slang. I didn't have the right clothes. I didn't fit.''

"And Mina was another outsider—the wrong accent, the wrong clothes?''

"That, plus the fact that she was beautiful and they weren't. And she was sweet, with a kind, generous nature that can't comprehend pettiness. They tormented her in nasty little ways. Tripping her on the hockey field, bumping her so she'd spill her dinner plate, putting salt in her tea and sugar in her soup.'' Emma looked at him, her face sober. "Girls can be very cruel.''

Tyler felt a surprising surge of anger at those faceless teenagers. He knew they'd been cruel, not only to Mina, but to Emma, as well. He, of all people, understood how it felt to be picked on and despised. "Yeah,'' he said after a moment, "kids can be rotten. Did she fight back?''

"She wouldn't have understood how,'' Emma told him.

She said nothing more, but Tyler had the feeling that even if Mina hadn't fought back, Emma had. He would bet that she'd done it pretty effectively, too.

"So you and Mina were forced together by circumstances?"

"Uh-huh. At first, we were like the last two survivors on a life raft, friends because we had to be. Gradually, though, we discovered we had a lot in common and became real friends." She smiled. "You can tell who your true friends are when you've been separated. Even if you've been apart for years, it only takes five minutes to feel at ease again."

"And that's how you and Mina are?"

"Yes. We may be apart for years at a time, but we talk on the telephone and write letters, and when we see each other, it's like no time has passed at all."

"What's she like now?"

"In many ways the same. She's still sweet and generous and brave, though she's not a schoolgirl any longer, but a diplomat."

Tyler listened and made encouraging noises to keep her talking, but with every word Emma told him about Mina, she was reinforcing his conviction that she was hopelessly naive and blindly trusting. Emma believed Mina implicitly, for her friendship blinded her to the current unsavory realities of international politics.

At three-thirty that afternoon Tyler was back in the spare office, pretending to read a magazine, waiting. When he heard a tap on the door, he stood, waiting tensely while Emma entered the room. "Is it time?"

"Yes," she said. "She'll be here promptly at four, but there may be someone else, someone watching for—"

"For someone like me?" Tyler asked, finishing the sentence.

"Exactly." A slight smile touched Emma's lips. She turned and locked the door she'd just come through.

"Are you locking Mrs. Johnson out, or locking us in?"

Emma shook her head mysteriously. "You'll see."

She walked across to the wall that separated her office from the one in which they stood. Tyler watched in amused disbelief as she grasped a section of the molding that ran in vertical lines on the paneling and pressed on it hard. He heard a soft click, and a section of the paneling swung open, revealing itself as a door to her office.

Emma walked through into her office, but Tyler stayed where he was, shaking his head. "Secret doors?" he asked quizzically. "Where are the bats and the skeletons?"

"You watch too many movies." She stepped back. "Come in."

As he stepped through the narrow doorway, he ran his fingers over the latching mechanism with professional interest. "Very neat." He examined the edge of the door. "Did you put this in?"

Emma shook her head. "The door was already here, but I had it concealed. I didn't want clients to have the impression there was someone in the next room eavesdropping on negotiations."

"Does it open from your side?"

"Yes. But it's soundproofed, I'm afraid. You'll have to wait in here until we know if Mina's alone."

"If she isn't alone, the soundproofing will effectively destroy our advantage in my being here."

"It probably will, but the only other place you could hide is the powder room." She shrugged toward an unobtrusive door on the other side of her office.

"If I were in there, I could hear what was going on."

"Yes, you could," she conceded. "But hiding in the loo?"

"I've hidden in worse places." Tyler looked into the little bathroom, with its dainty fixtures and flowered wallpaper. He thought of fetid jungles and foul ditches. Hiding in a powder room scented by perfumed soap and flowery potpourri was luxury indeed. "I'll hide in here."

He left the powder room and went to close the secret door. "How does it lock?"

"You press right here." He placed his hand on the molding, and Emma put hers over it to show him the correct pressure. Deep in the wall the latch clicked, and he turned his hand over, catching hers in a firm, warm grip.

Emma looked up at him, startled and wary.

"Come here." With a steady pressure he drew her around to face him. "Remember," he said, his voice low and his eyes intent, "that if she's not alone, you can't even look at that door. You can't give even the slightest hint that there's anything out of the ordinary about this appointment."

Startled, both by the command in his voice and the hard grip of his hand, Emma looked up at him. "I won't."

"Make sure you don't." Tyler relaxed his grip on her hand, but didn't release her. "You'll do okay," he told her more gently, "as long as you're careful."

"I'll be careful."

"Good." He squeezed her hand, then released it.

Be careful, Emma thought. Yes, she would be careful, not because Tyler Davis told her to, but because she could remember the look on Mina's face. She trusted Emma to help her, and Emma couldn't betray that trust.

If Tyler refused to help, if the overly suspicious agents and red-tape-hobbled bureaucrats turned their backs, then Emma would do it herself. For Mina, she would do everything she could, anything she had to.

Promptly at four the intercom on her desk buzzed. Emma jumped, her heart lurching, but Tyler calmly closed the magazine he'd been reading and stood. "Answer it," he murmured.

Emma pressed a button. "Yes, Mrs. Johnson?" Her level voice didn't betray her nerves.

"Ms. Grigoras is here, Miss Campbell."

"Thank you."

Tyler met her as she left her desk, and caught her hand in his. Though she was shaking, his hand was warm and firm, and it seemed that Emma could feel that warmth flowing into her, steadying and reassuring. "I'll be just on the other side of the door," he said softly, then drew her closer, just a fraction, but close enough for him to kiss her lips. When he lifted his head, he studied her face, noting the flush of rose his kiss had brought to her cheekbones. He gave her a crooked grin. "You'll do fine," he told her before disappearing into the powder room.

Emma took a deep breath and opened the door. "Mina, hello! It's so good to see you again."

She didn't look to see if anyone was accompanying Mina, but held out her hands in welcome. They kissed cheeks in the European manner, then stood back, smiling at each other. If there were signs of strain in Mina's eyes, or Emma's, those signs wouldn't have been visible to the casual observer.

"Come into the office, please." Emma stood back to allow her guest to precede her. "How have you been since our last meeting?"

"I have been well, thank you. And you?"

"Working hard, as usual." Emma glanced behind her. "Did Mr. Alexandru come with you?"

"Not today. He is busy."

"I see." Emma turned to Mrs. Johnson. "If you could hold my calls, please?"

"Of course." The secretary switched the phone to her line and settled again at her computer. The keyboard was clicking busily before the office door closed behind them.

Emma locked the door, then turned to hug Mina tightly. When they parted, their eyes were bright with unshed tears.

"How are you?" Emma asked. "How are you really?"

"I am well." Mina sniffed, then smiled a slightly watery smile. "Really."

"Good." Emma led her to the sofa. "Come and sit down. Would you like coffee?"

"Thank you, yes." Mina looked around her. "Is he here?"

"Yes, he is," Emma replied.

"Yes, I am," Tyler said. The two answers came simultaneously.

Mina swung around to see Tyler emerging from the powder room.

"Tyler Davis," he said.

"Mina Grigoras," she replied, and they shook hands.

"Have a seat, Miss Grigoras." He pulled an armchair around and seated himself at an angle to Mina, so that his face was in shadow while hers was lit by the sunshine from the window.

To Emma, at her desk, it looked like a police interrogation, but Mina didn't seem disturbed. She blinked a little in the bright light but faced Tyler, straight-backed, her face calm, her hands folded in her lap. Tyler studied her for several minutes before he spoke.

"Miss Grigoras." Emma jumped when he broke the silence, but Mina never moved.

"Yes?"

"How did you manage to come here alone today?"

"Stefan Alexandru is busy this afternoon."

"That's convenient," he said dryly.

"That's lucky!" Emma corrected in protest.

"Convenient," he repeated, watching Mina. "How did it happen?"

"He was called to meet with the ambassador this afternoon. There was an emergency, just as we were to leave."

"What kind of emergency?"

Mina's lips curved into a tiny smile. "The ambassador's safe was found to be improperly locked. There may have been some papers missing. It was probably nothing more than carelessness on someone's part, but it required Stefan Alexandru's immediate attention."

"How do you suppose it happened?" Tyler wondered.

Mina regarded him with limpid eyes and shrugged.

Reluctantly Tyler smiled. "How did you manage it?"

"I have been in a position of trust all my life. I know where the safe is and I learned how to open it."

"Did you take anything out?"

"I considered that, but no." She shook her head. "I would have to dispose of anything I took, or hide it. Instead I made a mess with the files in the safe and closed it improperly. It will take them some time to make certain everything is there."

"How did you manage to have access to the safe? Why were you there just at the right time?"

Mina's smile faded. "It was difficult to find a time when no one was watching me, but I was fortunate. This morning I was called to the ambassador's office to discuss this loan. He received a telephone call and left me alone in his office. I opened the safe."

"I see." Tyler considered that for a moment. "Did you know how long he would be gone?"

"No. I only knew I could not let such a chance go by."

"You took a terrible risk."

Mina shrugged again. "I needed to create a distraction that would keep Stefan Alexandru occupied."

"Why didn't they send someone else with you?"

"There was no time. Stefan Alexandru is of a high rank in the secret police. He did not appoint anyone else to come with me, and there was no one who could, or would, take the responsibility to make that decision."

"Will they suspect you, now that you have come alone?"

"There will be suspicion, yes." Mina seemed resigned to the prospect. "But already I am suspected. If I return with the papers and information, and tell them what we discussed, they will have no proof of subversion."

"The papers are here." Emma tapped the thick file folder in front of her. "They will account for quite a long meeting."

Mina smiled with pure gratitude. "You are truly a friend."

"And love is blind," Tyler added dryly. Emma scowled, but before she could speak he was addressing Mina. "Your friend has complete faith in you, Miss Grigoras. I don't. Before I can help you—"

"You mean, before you *will* help her," Emma put in.

"Before I *can* I must have proof, for my government and Lady Emma's government, of your intentions, and of your value. Until then I will make no move to help you defect."

They both ignored Emma's gasp of outrage.

"What proof do you require?" Mina asked.

"More information. What you gave Lady Emma last time was interesting, but we must have more. It must be verifiable by intelligence or satellite. Can you do that?"

"I will try," Mina replied.

"Mina, you can't do that!" Emma pushed herself out of her chair, palms planted on the desktop, and looked from Mina to Tyler. "Tyler, you can't ask that of her! She's already under suspicion. If she does this, she'll be risking prison at the very least! You can't ask something like this!"

"I have to," Tyler retorted. "If she is as she seems, then both our governments will do all they can to help her. But only after they're sure. She must prove her sincerity."

"But what if she can't? What then? Suppose she can't get her hands on the kind of information you want? Suppose she brings you information, but you decide it's not good enough? How is she to know what will satisfy you?"

"I think she knows what we want," Tyler replied, unruffled by her vehement attack. "Don't you?" he asked Mina.

"I understand."

"Mina, you mustn't do this! Your safety is the most important thing."

Mina shook her head. "Emma, I know that I must prove that I am as I say."

"But it's dangerous!"

"Emma, I know what I must do and why I must do it."

"Why *are* you doing this?" Tyler interrupted, directing the question to Mina. "Your position in the Party was secure. You could have spent your life safely inside the bureaucracy."

"Yes," Mina agreed. "I could have." She rose and walked toward the window, stopping a yard short of it, far enough away that she couldn't be seen by anyone watching from the street below.

"My father was a war hero, a hero of the Communist Party. He sincerely believed that the Party would bring a good life to everyone in the country, that all citizens would be equal, that there would be no more poverty or hunger. In theory I suppose that could have happened, but in fact it did not. Toward the end of his life he saw the corruption in the government, the failure of his dreams, and it saddened and angered him. He tried to work within the government to change things, but he died too soon." She was silent for a moment.

"And you?" Tyler prompted gently.

"Me? I am the only child of the hero. It was expected that I follow in his footsteps, and I did. I joined the Party, studied agriculture so that I could help to feed our people and I went to work in the government."

Mina studied the design on the chintz curtains intently. "And then I began to see the truth. At first I didn't wish to see the corruption, or the cumbersome bureaucracy that makes efficiency impossible. I tried to deny the problems, and perhaps if I'd never lived in England, or Australia, or France, I might never have known better. If I'd never known things could be different, I might have been able to deny the truth, but I *had* lived in those places. I knew things could be better. At first, I thought I could help to change things, but whenever I tried, whatever I tried, I met a stone wall. 'This is the way things are done,' I was told. 'You cannot change it, and trying will only make you crazy, so why try?'"

"So why did you try?" Tyler asked. "Why are you here now, talking to us?"

Mina turned to face him. "Because people in my country are hungry. They are cold in the winter. They may have money to pay, but they cannot buy the things that are sold in France or England, or even in Hungary. Perhaps it is communism itself, perhaps it is what our government has become, but people are hungry. They have no hope." She paused for several moments. In the silence Emma could hear the soft ticking of her desktop clock.

"I love my country, Mr. Davis," Mina said at last, "but I do not love the government and what it has become. If I cannot change the government from within it, then I will try to change it from the outside."

Her voice was quiet, the soft words carrying more conviction than a shout. Emma walked over and folded Mina in a hug.

"It's nearly five," Tyler said, standing well out of sight of the window. "You shouldn't be here much longer."

"You are right, of course." Mina swiped at her eyes, and Emma passed her a tissue. "Thank you."

Emma nodded, near tears herself. She pushed the loan papers into an envelope, and Mina slipped it into her briefcase.

"We've discussed all the information in there," Emma told her. "I made a few changes in figures so that it looks as if we negotiated hard."

"I will read this in the taxi," Mina assured her. "I will be able to answer any questions they have." She glanced at the window. "Do you see the man waiting in the street? He has seen nothing unusual. He will tell this to Stefan Alexandru."

"What man in the street?" Emma started for the window, only to be abruptly halted when Tyler caught her arm and swung her roughly around.

"Don't be a fool! If he sees you gawking at him, he'll know something's fishy."

"But Mina—"

"She stayed three feet from the window and screened herself with the curtains. At least *she* knows what she's doing."

"He's right, Emma." Mina had pulled on her coat and was ready to leave. "Watch for me to leave the building, then wave to me. You will see him. He is across the street, standing in the doorway of the apartment building."

Tyler stood at an angle to the window and carefully looked outside. "Your classic spy," he said, shaking his head in amusement. "He's even wearing a trench coat."

"He is listed as a chauffeur, but he is secret police." Mina chuckled. "He reads James Bond novels in translation."

Emma looked at them both, disbelieving. "How can you laugh? Mina is walking back into danger and you two are laughing!"

"I must laugh," Mina said, "or I will cry instead."

"All right." Emma forced a smile. "Then I will, too. And when this is all over we'll sit down together and laugh until we hurt."

"As we did when we put the toad in Mlle. Quincy's desk?" Mina's grin was as wicked as when she was thirteen.

"Exactly." Emma found herself grinning back. Though they'd been punished, it had been worth it to see the grim-faced French teacher scream and jump up on her chair.

"I hate to break this up—" Tyler began, and Mina nodded.

"It is time for me to go."

They said a formal goodbye for Mrs. Johnson's benefit, and Mina left with every appearance of normality.

Emma watched from the window as Mina had suggested, waving cheerfully when Mina glanced up before stepping into a cab. The man in the doorway across the street checked his watch, then flagged down a cab of his own. When Mina's car had disappeared around the corner, Emma left the window, her face grave.

"What will happen to her?"

Tyler shrugged. "It depends."

"On what?"

"On what she does."

"Don't you mean it depends on whether she can manage to locate the kind of information you want? Whether she can bargain for her life and win?"

"I mean it depends on whether she's telling the truth, on what she does next and on how careful, or reckless, she is."

His dispassionate tone struck an already raw nerve. Suddenly incensed, Emma whirled around to stand toe-to-toe with him, her eyes bright with fury.

"You just don't give a bloody damn, do you? All you care about is your precious proof! I don't even think you're human. You're just some kind of government-programmed robot!"

She swung her hand up and slapped him as hard as she could.

Chapter 6

The sound of her open palm striking his cheek cracked through the room, followed by an instant of utter silence.

Emma stood stock-still, staring at the imprint of her hand on Tyler's face. He, too, was very still for a moment, then he reached up and touched his cheek with his fingertips. "I wish," he said, his voice low and rough, "you hadn't done that...."

He moved so quickly that she had no chance to evade him, catching her upper arms and yanking her close as he brought his lips down on hers. It was an angry kiss, intended to punish. He clamped one arm around her waist and caught her hair in his hand, tipping her head back as he forced her lips apart to plunder her mouth.

Emma struggled, pushing against his chest, wriggling in his arms, kicking out until she connected, landing a hard kick on his shin. He grunted in pain and lifted his head. "I wish," he repeated, "that you hadn't done that either."

"You deserved it," Emma ground out between gritted teeth.

He looked at her flushed cheeks and her furious eyes. "Maybe, but I don't lose my temper all that often and you're really pushing it."

"Let me go!" She arched her back, fighting his imprisoning arms, then realized, too late, just what that movement was doing.

She froze, suddenly aware of the way she was pressed against Tyler's body, breast to knees, of his strength and of his heartbeat pounding rapidly against hers. His pupils widened as he looked down into her face, and she could feel her own heart lurch into a hurried rhythm, could feel her limbs softening, feel the warmth running along her veins. He started to lower his head again, and she stiffened in sudden panic. "No! Let me *go!*"

"If I do, will you kick me again?"

"Let . . . me . . . go!"

He did, abruptly. He released her and stepped quickly out of range, holding his arms out in mock surrender.

"There. You're loose. Truce, okay?"

Emma wiped a hand over her mouth. Her hair was falling out of its neat knot, and as she angrily shoved it back, a hairpin fell to the floor. "If I were a man," she whispered furiously, "I'd kill you for that."

"If you were a man, it wouldn't have happened," he shot back, swinging away, raking a hand roughly through his hair. He glanced over his shoulder at her. "What time do you usually leave?"

Emma was pulling pins from her hair with angry jerks. "Whenever my appointments are finished for the day." She dropped the pins on her desk and began shuffling papers into a folder.

"Are your appointments finished?"

"They are."

"Can you go, then?"

Emma looked at his back, tense and stiff. "Yes," she said. "I'll just put some things away." She locked away her files and collected her coat and briefcase while Tyler stood at the window.

Emma locked her desk, then straightened and looked around at Tyler. His head was bent, his hands jammed into his pockets, emphasizing his broad shoulders and muscular arms. There was something about his posture, though. He looked vulnerable, and alone.

She looked at him, and her anger drained away. He was so utterly alone, with a weariness in his posture that went deeper than muscle and bone. Yes, she'd been angry, but she could hardly wrap herself in righteous indignation when she'd provoked him as much as he'd provoked her.

"I'm ready," she said gently. His head came up and his shoulders straightened, and when he turned to her, all expression had been wiped from his face.

"I have other business to attend to in town," he said. "I'll meet you back at your apartment later this evening."

Emma opened her mouth to speak, then changed her mind. She nodded silently and went downstairs to meet the limousine. If she'd looked up, she might have seen him at the window, silently watching her departure, but she didn't.

Back at the apartment she changed clothes and went to the kitchen. She studied the contents of the cupboards, frowning, then glanced out the window. The cool, bright, fall afternoon had degenerated into a chilly gray evening, heavy with the promise of rain. As Emma watched, the first drops tapped against the windowpanes, and a gust of wind sent fallen leaves swirling down the street.

"Tea," she said to herself, and began briskly opening cupboard doors.

Tyler paid off the cab and flipped up his coat collar against the rain as he crossed the street. He wasn't sure where the sunny day had gone, but evening was bringing the first breath of winter, with fine misty rain on a sharp wind.

He glanced up at Emma's building and scowled. He didn't want another tense evening with Lady Emma; he wanted a steak and a Scotch, and a ball game on TV. He stalked into the lobby and jammed his key into the penthouse elevator call slot, then used a key to let himself into the apartment.

He could hear Vivaldi playing quietly from the living room and sounds of activity in the kitchen. Shrugging out of his raincoat and suit jacket, he pulled off his tie and approached the kitchen in vest and shirtsleeves.

In the doorway he stopped short, staring at a Lady Emma he scarcely recognized. She was wearing tight jeans and a fuzzy pink sweater with a wide neckline that threatened to slip off one shoulder. Flour and sugar and other ingredients stood out on the countertop, there was a warm smell of frying in the air, and she was mixing something in a large brown bowl.

He must have made a sound, for Emma suddenly looked up, her eyes wide and startled until she saw who it was. Her cheeks were flushed from her efforts, she had a streak of flour on her cheek where she'd brushed her tousled hair off her face, and Tyler knew he'd never seen anyone so beautiful.

"Oh! Hello." Her voice was high and just a bit breathy. "Tea will be ready in a bit if you'd like to have a wash."

"Tea?"

"High tea, to be specific." She smiled. "What you'd call supper."

"Okay. I'll go and wash. When will it be ready?"

"Ten minutes or so. When the scones and the fish are done." She picked up the bowl and tipped a mound of dough out onto a board dusted with flour. It landed with a plop, and a white cloud puffed around her. She sneezed.

"Bless you."

"Thank you." She rubbed her nose and began patting the ball of dough into a circle. "Go ahead." She waved a floury hand at him. "These will be ready soon."

Bemused, Tyler watching her patting the dough with floury hands, her face flushed from the heat of the oven, wisps of auburn hair escaping from the ribbon that tied it at her nape.

"Okay," he said finally. "I won't be long." Lady Emma? he thought as he changed. Lady Emma working in the kitchen, with flour on her face? He'd seen it with his own eyes, but he didn't think he believed it.

When he returned to the kitchen, wearing jeans as old as hers and a deep blue sweater, she wasn't there. There were bowls in the sink and a steaming kettle on the stove, but no Emma.

"In here," she called from the living room, where Tyler found her carrying a heavily laden tray toward a small dining table.

He hurried across, but she'd already set the tray down and begun placing the plates and teacups on the table. "Sit down."

He did as she bid, and she handed him a plate, passed a bowl of salad and lifted the lid to peer into the teapot. "It's almost ready. How do you like yours?"

"The tea? By itself, I guess."

She offered a plate of little sandwiches, cut in triangles, with the crusts removed, and he took one. "There's ham," she said, pointing, "watercress, crab and bread and butter."

"There's also fish," she added, pointing to the herring. "Help yourself."

"Thank you." He tasted the crisply browned fillet and looked at the tray of sandwiches and scones and teacups. "This is good. Is there anything we're supposed to do?"

Emma gave him a quizzical look. "Just eat," she said with a smile, pouring their tea.

Tyler bit into a sandwich and found Smithfield ham, mellow and rich, spread with pungent mustard. It was delicious, as was the fish and the salad with a tangy homemade dressing. It all went perfectly with strong, hot tea.

"It's all good," he said after a moment, "but I don't know what everything is."

"Well, tea sandwiches, salad, herring in oatmeal—"

"Oatmeal?"

She nodded. "The fish is breaded with it. We Scots use oats in everything. Tonight, with the rain and all, I was feeling a little homesick."

"I see." Tyler chuckled. "Well, it sounds weird, but it's good." When he'd finished what Emma referred to as the savories, she filled another plate with the sweeter dishes.

"What are all these things?"

"Scones," she said as she gave him something that looked like a biscuit with currants in it and sugar on top, "and shortbread and black bun. I brought it back from Edinburgh."

He looked at his plate. "I'm almost afraid to ask what a black bun is."

"Would you rather it be a mystery?"

"Do I want to know?"

"It's just fruitcake," she assured him, "baked in a crust. And it's perfect with tea."

When Tyler finally leaned back, finishing a shortbread finger so buttery-rich that it threatened to crumble in his fingers, he realized that not only was his hunger sated, but he'd been warmed from the inside out, his body refreshed, his earlier tension eased. He licked the crumbs from his fingers and smiled.

"That was good."

There was faint surprise in his voice, and Emma laughed softly. "I know how strange it seems, but most Americans like these things after they've tried them."

"I did. Even the fish coated in oatmeal."

"Southern cooks bread fish with cornmeal."

"Somehow I have trouble imagining oatmeal hush puppies."

"They're purely an American invention." Smiling, she stacked used dishes back on the tray. Before she could lift it, Tyler picked it up and strode into the kitchen.

"I can carry it myself," Emma said, following.

"It's too heavy."

"Don't be ridiculous. It's lighter now than it was before we ate, and I did just fine then."

He set the tray on the counter and dusted his hands. "It's a moot issue now, isn't it?" He began unloading dishes into the sink. "You want to wash or dry?"

"I do have a dishwasher, you know."

"Okay, do you want to rinse or load." He rolled up his sleeves.

"You're not letting me be a good hostess, Tyler."

He threw her a glance. "That's because I'm not a guest. You didn't invite me here. I'm here on a job."

"But there's no need—"

"Tell me what you want to do, or I'll rinse."

Emma blew her breath out between her teeth. "I'll load."

"Good." He ran hot water into the sink and lifted the first plate. Emma stepped up beside him, and was suddenly conscious of how small the kitchen really was. Standing at the sink, Tyler seemed to fill the scant space.

He rinsed the china and passed it to Emma, and their hands met on the edge of the wet plate. Emma jerked back and the plate slipped. It would have shattered on the countertop if he hadn't caught it.

"Too hot?" he asked. "I'm sorry."

"No, it was my fault." Emma took the plate, without touching his hand, and placed it carefully in the dishwasher. She watched his hands as she took the next plate— strong, square hands, holding delicate porcelain. His forearms were tanned and corded with muscle, his hands warm and wet, slick with soap.

He handled the fragile dishes with exquisite gentleness. He would be gentle with a woman, too, holding his obvious strength in check, caressing her— Emma gasped at her wayward thoughts.

"Is something wrong?"

She looked up to find Tyler watching her curiously.

"No! Nothing's wrong." She could feel a betraying blush scorching her cheeks. "It was just a hiccup."

"Oh." He handed her a cup. "Do you want a glass of water or something?"

"No, thank you." She bent her head, concentrating on the cup. She knew that Tyler watched her for a few moments, before resuming his chore.

Emma tried to keep a little distance between them, but she couldn't move around Tyler in the narrow confines of the kitchen without brushing against his shoulder or his arm as she passed.

"Excuse me," she said for the sixth time as her hip brushed his. Tyler turned from the sink to catch her wrist with a dripping hand. "What—?" Emma looked at his hand, then up at his face.

"Do not," he said with carefully exaggerated patience, "say 'Excuse me' again. You're excused in advance."

"It's just that this room is—"

"Small," he said softly.

Emma could see the flecks of blue and gray in his eyes, and she could see his pupils widen as he looked at her. She knew he was going to kiss her again, and she knew this kiss wouldn't be punishing, but tender. His lips parted just a fraction, and her heart lurched... just before she twisted away.

Her elbow struck the freshly washed teapot, and Tyler caught it as she spun out of the kitchen. He didn't follow, but put the teapot carefully on its shelf and finished the dishes.

When he returned to the living room, she was seated on the sofa, her needlework on her lap, peering at the pattern.

She looked up, her face carefully blank. "I didn't know washing up could go so quickly."

"In the navy they don't let you stand around and daydream."

"Oh, that's right. Uncle Larry said you were in the navy. Did you pull KP often?"

"Too often." He sank onto the other end of the sofa.

So they'd declared a truce, she thought. She was glad. She and Tyler Davis had to work together, and they couldn't if they were always at loggerheads. She didn't know if they could work together if they were kissing.

He slid lower on the sofa and stretched lazily. "I know you don't drink much, but a brandy would go down real well right now. I don't suppose you'd have any around, would you?"

"Actually, I don't." He grunted understanding, but she wasn't finished. "I have something better, though."

"Better than brandy?"

"Much better." She set her canvas and wools aside and crossed to a cupboard on the far side of the room. Tyler admired the grace of her walk, even as he wondered what she was doing.

She opened a lower door, rummaged inside and brought out an unlabeled bottle filled with a golden brown liquid. She took two heavy cut-crystal glasses from a shelf and carried everything back to the coffee table. With ceremonial care she poured an inch into each glass and presented one to Tyler.

"What is this?" Tyler asked, wondering at the unlabeled bottle

"Uisge beatha," she replied. "Scottish Gaelic for the water of life." She raised her glass to him and smiled. "Single-malt whisky from Scotland."

"Scotch?" He frowned at her quizzically. "I thought you didn't like alcohol much?"

"I don't as a rule. But I'm from Scotland, and this is Scotch whisky. I think I first tasted it before I was five. I had a toothache," she explained when she saw his horrified expression, "and until I could visit the dentist, Nanny put whisky on her fingertip and rubbed it on the ache."

"Did it work?"

"As I remember, it did. This is useful stuff, you know. Good for fevers, chills, aches and pains." She grinned. "I've even heard that some people use it as liniment for lame horses."

Tyler looked at his glass suspiciously. "You're giving me horse liniment to drink?"

"What's the matter? Are you afraid to drink it?"

His head came up in instinctive arrogance. "I'm not afraid!"

"Then...?" She raised her glass in what he recognized as a challenge and took a healthy mouthful of straight whisky. She rolled it around her mouth for a moment, then swallowed. Drawing a deep breath, she closed her eyes as a shudder quivered through her, and then relaxed, slowly opening her eyes. Finally she let her breath out in a long sigh. "Mmm, that's good."

Enjoying her expression, Tyler took a mouthful of his own.

It was smoky with peat, mellow and smooth and strong. It didn't quite take his breath away, but the smoothness camouflaged a fairly powerful kick.

"What do you think?"

"I think it's strong." Tyler was surprised to find that his voice was breathless.

"It keeps you warm on a Scottish winter night."

"I can imagine." Tyler sipped again. "It grows on you."

"Gin drinkers often don't like it," Emma said.

"That's because their taste buds are pickled. Gin tastes like bug spray, anyway."

Emma giggled and sipped her whisky. Getting comfortable, she half turned toward Tyler, curling her feet beneath her. Though two feet of sofa cushion still separated them, it somehow brought them closer, and Emma wanted to talk.

"Mr. Davis?"

"Call me Tyler."

"Tyler." He waited for the question while Emma rolled her glass between her palms, watching the golden swirl of whisky. "You've met Mina now, face-to-face. Why don't you believe her?"

"Because I can't allow myself to," Tyler said. He lounged on the sofa, one arm draped along its back, watching her through half-closed eyes. He reminded her of a big cat, deceptively lazy, watching and waiting for the time to strike. "I can't allow myself to believe without proof, because there still is the possibility that she's simply a very talented actress and spy, seeking to damage the governments of our two countries."

"Very well." Emma acknowledged that with a nod. "But what if she's neither a spy nor an actress? What if she's exactly what I believe she is?"

"Then she's in a great deal of danger and will be in danger until she defects." He sipped his whisky and gave an appreciative murmur as it slid smoothly down.

Emma looked at hers, then banged the cut-crystal tumbler onto the tabletop with such force that the whisky sloshed out.

Tyler looked at the little pool on the polished cherrywood and raised a lazy eyebrow. "Are you upset?"

"Of course I'm upset! Why aren't you? Are you made of ice? Don't you have a heart?"

Chapter 7

"Don't you care," Emma demanded, "that there is at least a fifty-fifty chance, whatever you personally believe, that Mina has told us nothing but the truth? Do you worry that she's in danger? Would you feel guilty if she were returned to Romania and imprisoned?"

Tyler placed his glass on the table with more care than she'd used. "I'm not made of ice," he replied quietly, "but I know what I have to do. I can't let emotions distract me."

"But this is her life!" Emma leaned toward him, pleading Mina's case. "You can't risk a woman's life for the sake of *information*!"

"Lives have been lost for information, Emma. Wars have been fought over it. And it's proof I'm looking for."

"This isn't a war, Tyler."

"Isn't it? Maybe we're not using guns and bombs, but there's always a war of sorts going on, sort of an international chess game, move and countermove. There are little wars being fought all the time, Lady Emma, private wars, and this war belongs to the three of us." He held her eyes with his, cool and hard and determined. "And until we know that all three of us are on the same side, we'll do this my way."

The implacability had been hidden by the lazy manner and casual tone, but it showed now. Emma could argue, but this would indeed, be done his way.

She picked up her glass and took another swallow, savoring the complex taste that carried so many memories of home. She didn't shudder as the spirit went down this time, but studied her glass for a long moment before she raised her head and looked at Tyler.

"You're wrong, you know," she told him. "Mina is telling the truth. Don't ask me how I know. It may be instinct, or woman's intuition, or a fey, Scottish impulse, but I know that she's telling the truth."

"For the sake of your fey impulses, I hope you're right," he said. "And for Mina's sake, I hope she's careful."

"I hope she's safe," Emma said flatly.

"I hope you know that I'm not doing this to be cruel," Tyler said urgently. He leaned forward, his intent gaze on her face. "We have to be cautious, have to be suspicious. We've been burned badly, and we don't want to be burned again."

"How have you been burned?"

"Oh, God." Tyler ran a hand through his hair, shaking his head ruefully. "I don't know where to start. There was a Pole who defected, just to give one example. He was desperate to get away, committed to helping the West. For three years he gave information to the U.S. and NATO. Information about military installations, troop counts and movements, personnel in the Polish government and the Russians working in Poland. In the meantime, because he was trusted, he had access to some of our fairly sensitive military information." Tyler paused and frowned at the carpet beneath his feet.

"And then?" Emma prompted softly.

"And then he vanished. There was much consternation here," Tyler said bitterly. "Fear that he'd been kidnapped or assassinated. After a week he surfaced in Russia, the darling of the Party, having completed his mission of disinformation so admirably. He's now working his way up the ranks in the KGB."

"And you think Mina's the same? Someone who's been planted to give us false information?"

"I don't know if she is or not. That's the problem. Until I *do* know, I can't take a chance on believing her, no matter what I personally might want."

"Do you want to believe her?" Emma demanded, pouncing on his words.

"I'm not a monster," Tyler said, "whatever you think. If she is what she says, I'll move heaven and earth to help her."

Emma looked into his eyes for a long time, then nodded slowly. "I suppose I can't ask for more than that."

"That's all I can give." He spoke the words gently, but the quiet, sure tone told its own tale.

"I wish it weren't," she said quietly. "I fear for Mina because I know she's telling the truth."

"You believe," Tyler corrected her. "You can't know. You haven't seen proof, any more than I have." He shook his head. "I was naive and idealistic once, too. I believed in people, a very long time ago."

Emma looked into his eyes and saw the bone-deep world-weariness of a man twice his age, a man who had seen far too much of the world's ugly side. "There's both good and bad in everyone," she pointed out softly.

He shook his head. "In my experience the good impulses are brief and weak, the bad ones by far the stronger."

"That's a cynical attitude."

"Cynics are made, not born." He glanced at her. "The cynics see clearly, while the naive look at the world with blinders on."

"I can't believe that, so we'll have to agree to disagree," Emma said mildly.

She couldn't say what was really in her mind. Someone who felt as he did must be terribly alone, trusting no one, denying even the basic need for human contact. He was a strong man, but the need for others was fundamental. No man was an island, to borrow from John Donne, but Tyler Davis didn't realize that.

He'd convinced himself that he was better off alone. He believed that to need others was a weakness rather than a strength. She didn't think he had any idea how lonely he was.

She bent over her needlework again, and they sat with their private thoughts until a look at the clock showed that it was time for bed.

Emma finished the last few stitches, remembering the night before, and feeling all the tension she'd managed to keep at bay come rushing back. She didn't want Tyler to think she expected him to kiss her again, but she didn't want him to think she was afraid of him, either. And she didn't know how to get through the next five minutes gracefully.

Her movements jerky, she put her embroidery wools away and began rolling her work to store it, too agitated to be careful. "Ouch!" Punished by her carelessness, she pricked her finger deeply on the sharp embroidery needle.

"What's wrong?" Tyler asked.

"Nothing." Emma put her bleeding fingertip in her mouth to soothe it.

"You hurt yourself." He slid over beside her and pulled her hand from her mouth, studying the pricked finger. "That must hurt." He lifted her hand and kissed the injured fingertip.

Emma swallowed a gasp. His grip on her wrist was strong but gentle; it would leave no mark that it had been there. His lips were warm on her fingertip, and seductive; the kind of touch that would leave an all too painful bruise on her heart.

She pulled away again, and this time he let her go.

"It's...it's late. I'm tired." She was babbling, but she couldn't seem to help it. "I'll just wash these glasses and check the locks...." She started across the room, then paused. "If there's anything you need..."

"I'm fine." Tyler's voice was warm with amusement. "And I'll check the locks for you. Go to bed, Emma."

He'd used her given name so naturally, without the title. It sounded different that way, more intimate. She felt her face flush, and Tyler chuckled softly.

She fled down the hall to the sanctuary of her bedroom. Sleep was elusive, and she was wide awake an hour later when the phone rang. "Hello?"

"Is that any way to greet your beloved brother?" boomed a deep voice with a rich burr. Despite his years at Oxford and in London, Drew still sounded like a boy from the lochs.

"How are you, Drew?" She glanced at the clock. "And why are you calling at this ungodly hour?"

"The sun's just risen. You should be up and about."

"For someone who can figure compound interest in his head, you show the most appalling lack of understanding about time zones. It's after midnight here."

"The shank of the evening, and I need some information."

"At six in the morning? There's no one in London awake and doing business at that hour."

"London should get on its toes. Do you have the Macauley prospectus?"

"Yes, I do. I've been working on it for my next meeting with Angus Macauley."

"Good. Can you give me the annual figures they want? I'm meeting with their comptroller later today and I need to know what Angus is asking for."

"It's in the study. Hold on while I go in there, okay?"

"Aye, I will," he said.

Emma pulled on the thin silk robe that matched her nightgown, and hurried to her study. "Hi, Drew. I'm back." She pulled out a drawer and searched through the files there. "It'll take me a minute to find it, okay?"

"Have I told you how very American you sound?" her brother asked with laughter in his voice. "'Okay,' indeed."

"Don't be a stuffy Scot, Andrew." She pulled a file from the drawer and opened it. "Here it is." She tilted her chair back, lifting her legs and resting her slender feet on the desktop. "Now, for the first year, they want an interest-only schedule. Two payments, if we'll allow it, but they'll go to four."

"That's generous of them."

"Yes, well, here are the figures." She began reading the numbers, slowly enough for Drew to write them down.

In the darkness of the hallway outside the study door, Tyler stood watching, wearing only the slacks he'd dragged on when he heard Emma leave her room. He was holding a gun in his hand.

He listened to her recital of principal and interest figures, and gradually the tension in him eased. He tucked the gun into his waistband, folded his arms over his bare chest and watched Emma.

Lady Emma, he thought. She looked like Lady Emma now, wearing silk and lace, her hair tumbled from the pillow, her long legs crossed at the ankle and propped on the desktop. She'd lit one dim lamp, and it cast a soft golden glow over her skin and hair. Then she moved, reaching forward to pluck another sheet of paper off the desktop.

The fragile silk slid up her legs, baring them nearly to midthigh. She relaxed back into the chair again, and the robe fell off her shoulder, taking one ribbon strap of the nightgown with it.

Tyler's mouth went dry. Her legs were impossibly long, as smooth as the silk that slipped up another tantalizing inch when she shifted position, crossing her ankles again. Her bare shoulder was creamy-pale, the bones fragile under the skin. The lace that trimmed the gown's bodice clung tenuously to the curve of her breast. It covered, but didn't completely conceal, hinting at the rosy crest, taut and erect in the cool room.

He tried to swallow, and found it difficult.

"Drew!" She chuckled and leaned forward again to replace the papers on the desk. "You never stop, do you?" Her voice was low and amused, indulgent and affectionate.

Who the hell, Tyler wondered, was this Drew, and why was she on such familiar terms with him? Tyler clenched his fist as he listened. "I'll take care of myself, Drew. Don't I always?" She laughed again. "I have a long memory, too. Yes. I'll tell Angus you said so." There was a pause then she added softly, "I love you, Drew," before she hung up.

Tyler stepped into the study. "Who is Drew?"

Emma gasped and spun around, coming to her feet in a defensive crouch. She saw him, and then recognized him.

"Dear...sweet...heavens!" She sagged against the desk, a hand pressed to the pulse that hammered in her throat, her eyes huge with fright. "You scared me to death! What on earth are you doing prowling about?"

"Who is Drew?"

She frowned in confusion. "Drew was on the phone. What *are* you doing?" He moved slowly, advancing on her a step at a time.

"I heard you, so I got up to check on you. Who is Drew?"

"Drew's my brother. What did you imagine was wrong?"

"I—" He stopped, his expression arrested. "Your brother? You didn't say you had a brother."

"Of course I did. You weren't paying attention. And what did you think was wrong?"

The tension in him slowly eased. "Nothing specific. I heard the phone, and you got up, so I had to check."

Emma glanced at the gun in his waistband, and her eyes widened. "Do you think they might come here?"

No need to ask who "they" were. Tyler shrugged. "Who knows? We can't take chances. They know you're Mina's friend. It's logical to assume she might go to you for help."

"But we've only met on perfectly legitimate business."

"But that's *not* the only reason you've met. If they suspect you, they're absolutely right. We expect them to be watching you, at least part of the time. Why do you think I'm staying with you, Emma?"

"I didn't know you had a gun." Emma shivered and caught the lace-trimmed edges of her robe, holding them closed across her breasts. Tyler followed the movement with his eyes, and felt tension of another sort begin to build in him.

Though she held the robe's edges together, she seemed unaware that one smooth shoulder was still bare. She'd drawn the bodice taut, and through the fine lace inserts he could see the pale gleam of her breasts and the darker shadows at their crests. The thin silk had little body, so the skirts of gown and robe clung rather than draped, veiling her waist and hips and legs, while suggesting the curves beneath.

Emma shifted uneasily under his scrutiny, then straightened. "I'm tired," she said. "I'm going to sleep."

"Not yet."

Tyler caught her arm as she slipped past him, then swung her around, using her own momentum to bring her into his arms. She braced both hands against the solid wall of his chest, but it was a futile attempt to push away. Instead, with her palms firmly planted on his bare chest, she felt the heat of his skin, the rhythm of his breathing, the strength of his muscles. His heartbeat under her palm was quick and heavy.

She pushed again, and as her hands slid over his skin, she felt his heartbeat accelerate. He released his grip and slipped his arms around her waist, pulling her fully against him. She felt his heat through the silk, and felt an answering heat and a dangerous weakness within herself.

She was no longer pushing him away, but clinging to him for support, melting into the curve of his body as he slid one hand up to cradle her head, turning her face up for his kiss.

He didn't kiss her tentatively, but plundered her mouth, searching its sweetness. He demanded pleasure as he demanded a response, but Emma was already parting her lips, answering his demand with a demand of her own. She felt as if she were melting from the inside out, boneless and lax, pressing into his caresses.

He ran his hands over her back, sliding the silk across her skin, and it seemed that trails of heat followed the path of his touch. He brought a hand up to caress her throat, then let his hand drift down again over her naked shoulder and lower, to her breast, sliding the robe and gown away.

The silk slipped off the upper curve of her breast, catching for an instant on the tight bud of her nipple. Tyler slipped a fingertip beneath the silk and freed it, then covered her breast with his hand. Emma swallowed a gasp at the shock of pleasure that flashed through her like lightning, quick and sharp, leaving a burning heat in its wake. Her head fell back, her fingers digging into his shoulders as her body arched up when he followed the caress of his hand with the caress of his mouth.

She was burning and shivering and aching with need, for a man she scarcely knew. A few days ago she would have said that she didn't even like him. She was on fire for him now, but when he pushed the strap off her other shoulder, she froze.

''No!'' The whisper was barely audible, but she stiffened, pushing instead of clinging, her body straining away from his. He didn't immediately comply, and she knew a moment of stark panic, knowing that if he didn't release her, she wouldn't have the will to resist. She felt his arms tighten around her for a moment, but then, with an incoherent mutter under his breath, he let them fall away.

Emma didn't try to speak. There was nothing she could say that would improve this situation. Clutching her night-clothes to her breast, she fled.

"Damn." Tyler ran a shaking hand over his face, not surprised to find that he was sweating. He dropped into Emma's desk chair and tipped it back, resting his head on the soft leather upholstery.

He tried to relax, but his heart hammered against his ribs, and his body reminded him insistently of what he'd given up. He could have made love to her. He knew that he could have overwhelmed her resistance and made her want him until nothing else mattered but their aching need. That ache would subside, though. And in the part of his mind that remained unclouded by passion, he knew that however badly he might want it now, making love with her would be a disastrous mistake.

He turned off her desk lamp and made his way back to the guest room, where he lay awake well into the night, wondering grimly how long he could maintain his resolve to keep away from Lady Emma.

Emma sat stiffly in the taxi, elbows pulled in, feet directly in front of her to eliminate any chance of accidentally touching Tyler. Beside her, he sat as stiffly as she.

She studied his stiff posture from the corner of her eye, then silently sighed and returned her gaze to the financial statement on her lap. It wasn't holding her interest, and that worried her. She'd never had trouble concentrating on her work, until now.

Then Tyler Davis had shoved his way into her life, and suddenly she couldn't seem to focus on anything more complicated than the weather report in the morning paper.

In the week that had passed since she'd run from the study, running from him, she'd done her best to avoid Tyler.

That had been made simpler by the fact that he'd spent several days in Washington, meeting with American and British diplomats. Emma had flown down only yesterday to receive her instructions.

She had met Mina, and now she was embroiled in this seemingly endless yo-yo of meetings to get information, meetings to ask for information and more meetings for more information. How long, she wondered, would it go on? Between meetings with Mina and meetings *about* Mina, Emma wondered why she didn't just move to D.C.

Uncle Larry had been in Washington, along with several other agents and functionaries of various sorts. They all shared Tyler's unrelenting suspicions of Mina. Emma had steadfastly argued Mina's case, controlling her temper when they accused Mina of all sorts of devious and unsavory actions. She understood their need to play devil's advocate, but she wondered if concern for a human life had gotten lost along the way.

She understood that national security was important, of course, but for Emma, nothing could overshadow the value of a human life. And Tyler? What did he think?

She glanced at him through the thick screen of her lashes but could read nothing in his face. What were his priorities? What was important to him? Emma was usually good at reading people, but Tyler continued to remain a mystery to her.

Was it only the issue of security that motivated him? He kept saying it was, and on one level she believed him. Yet there was another side to him; there had to be. She'd had plenty of time to think, and she kept recalling little things, small events that didn't fit the picture of a callous, single-minded agent.

He'd asked difficult questions of Mina, testing her, yet Mina had said she understood the need for the tests. Emma had been angry, but Mina had seemed to understand Tyler's demands. And even Emma had to admit that Tyler hadn't actually been cruel to her.

She remembered other things, too, and saw them more clearly than she had in the heat of the moment. Specifically she remembered his kisses.

Emma bit her lip. He'd kissed her with passion, but also with tenderness, and when she pushed him away he'd let her go. Even knowing how little it would take for him to change her mind, he'd let her go.

She glanced from her hands to his, tanned and strong, turning the pages of his book. He'd touched her, with strength and gentleness, caressed her skin...

"What's the matter?" He was looking at her with a mixture of impatience and irritation.

"Nothing," Emma replied. "I was just thinking."

"About what?"

"Nothing important." She bent over her papers again, knowing the lie for what it was.

Chapter 8

W ill you stop that damn pacing?"

Emma paused in the middle of another trip across the Oriental carpet to give Tyler a look ripe with dislike.

"If I feel like pacing, I shall pace."

She paced over to the window, and for the twentieth time looked down at the street below. Rain drizzled on the traffic streaming past, a cruising cab pulled into the curb to pick up a fare, and three teenagers who should have been in school jaywalked blithely in front of a delivery van. The van driver honked and shook his fist at the girls, who waved back as they bounced off down the sidewalk. Emma could almost hear them giggling.

"There's no one there," Tyler said from the sofa, where he was comfortably settled, reading the morning paper.

"How do you know?"

"Mina's punctual." He checked his watch. "She's due at three. It's now two-thirty, so I consider it unlikely that she's standing on the sidewalk in the rain half an hour early, just waiting until three o'clock so she can come upstairs."

"Ho, ho. Very droll. The comedians of the world can rest easy tonight."

"Ha, ha." Tyler disappeared behind his newspaper again. "Will you please sit down? You're making me nervous."

"You'll survive." Emma resumed pacing, this time across to the door.

"I wouldn't go out there," Tyler said. "You already asked Mrs. Johnson to buzz you when they get here. You know she will." Emma hesitated, and he added, "And if you bother her again, she'll probably throw her typewriter at you."

"She uses a computer."

"The keyboard, then." Abruptly Tyler shoved himself to his feet and strode across to her. He grabbed her shoulders and marched her back to the sofa.

"What are you *doing*?"

"Saving your carpet." He pushed her down onto the cushions with a thump. "Not to mention your feet and my nerves. Now stay put!" He tossed a magazine into her lap. "Read something."

"I don't want to read." Anger made her Scottish accent more pronounced.

"I don't want to watch a caged tiger. Just sit there, and remember that discipline is good for the soul."

After a moment of silence, Emma laughed out loud.

"What's the matter with you now?" he demanded.

"You sound more like a Scot than me!" With difficulty she mastered her laughter. "We Scots are a puritanical lot, fond of things that benefit the soul. It comes of living in such a dreadful climate."

"The climate can't be that bad if people live there."

"People live above the Arctic Circle," she pointed out, then sighed. "What time is it, now?" The intercom's buzz interrupted her, and she jumped up to answer it. "Yes?" Her voice was breathless.

"The doorman downstairs just called up, Miss Campbell. Ms. Grigoras and a gentleman are on their way up."

"A gentleman?"

"That's right."

"Very well. Thank you." Emma switched off the intercom and stared across at Tyler. "Go through the secret door." She pushed him toward it, but he resisted.

"You know I won't be able to hear what's going on."

"Hold a water glass against the wall. Just get in there!"

"I can hide in the powder room."

"No! I have a feeling...."

"Intuition?"

Emma heard voices in the outer office and gave the door a wild glance. "Go!" she whispered desperately. "Just go!"

She started toward the outer office as he slipped through the secret door and pulled it quietly closed. Emma glanced back, saw that the door was invisible once again and pinned on a smile before she stepped out to greet Mina.

"Mina! It's lovely to see you." They kissed cheeks, and then Emma extended her hand to the bulky, heavy-faced man behind Mina. "Good afternoon, Mr. Alexandru."

"Good afternoon."

His handshake was damp, and Emma resisted the urge to wipe her palm on her skirt. "Please, make yourselves comfortable." Two chairs were drawn up in front of her desk and a coffee service stood ready. "Will you have coffee?"

As Emma poured, she covertly studied Mina's face, pale beneath the brave facade of cosmetics. She could see the signs of strain, and while Mr. Alexandru was adding sugar to his cup, she winked at Mina.

Mina blinked in surprise, then her eyes lit with laughter. For an instant time rolled away and they were schoolgirls again, pulling a prank on the teacher.

"Sugar, Mina?" Emma asked with commendable calm.

"Yes, thank you." Mina wasn't actually laughing, but her voice was less strained than it had been.

"Now, then." Emma sat back in her chair when the coffee was served. "Do we have an agreement?"

"Our government wishes to make some minor changes in the terminology," Mina replied easily, extracting a sheaf of papers from her briefcase.

Pressed against the hidden door, Tyler listened to them negotiate the minutiae of wording, and the fine points of repayment schedules. The door's soundproofing was frustratingly effective. Mina's and Emma's voices were high-pitched and clear, and he could understand most of what they said, but Alexandru's words were little more than an indistinguishable rumble.

The better part of an hour passed before the banking business was concluded to the apparent satisfaction of all. Tyler waited in mounting frustration. He'd known the odds were against Mina getting away from Alexandru for a few minutes, but the appointment was nearly over, and Alexandru was still welded to Mina's side.

"I believe that's everything," Emma said. Tyler could imagine her gathering papers together, preparing to say goodbye. "Would you like to freshen up before you go, Mina?"

Mina and Alexandru spoke at the same time, and Tyler couldn't distinguish much beyond the fact that Mina was declining the offer. There were muffled sounds of movement, then the closing of a door. In the few minutes that followed, Tyler could hear Emma and Mina, talking about the weather and the difficulty of getting a cab in New York.

Then he heard plumbing noises and a door opening, and Alexandru's voice rejoined the women's. Tyler waited behind the secret door while they said polite goodbyes, then he crossed to the other door to listen to what was said in Mrs. Johnson's office. It was nothing but some more goodbyes and a promise from Mina to call the office and check on when the papers would be ready for signing. Emma would check on the agricultural equipment, she said. Mina appreciated that. More goodbyes, and then, at last, the outer door closed.

He stayed in the spare office, waiting and listening.

"Insert the percentage table," Tyler heard Emma saying, "right here, after the narrative, if you can."

"I'm not sure how that will page out. If it doesn't fit here, shall I pull the narrative down?"

"Hmm. Yes, I think so. It will make it clearer, and I—" Emma broke off. "Mr. Alexandru? Can I help you with something?"

"I have misplaced my gloves. May I see if they are in your office?"

"Of course." Emma's heels tapped across the floor, but Tyler didn't hear her accompany Alexandru into her office. "There they are."

Alexandru's voice rumbled.

"I'm sorry you had to come all the way back up."

Another rumble, moving across the outer office.

"Goodbye, Mr. Alexandru," Emma said. The door closed again. "Now are there any other problems with the format?" Tyler nodded approval of the easy tone of Emma's voice as she picked up her conversation with Mrs. Johnson as if nothing unusual had happened.

"I don't believe so."

"Good. I'll be in my office if you have any questions."

Mrs. Johnson agreed in a murmur, then Tyler heard the outer door of Emma's office close. Moments later the latch inside the hidden door clicked and she pulled it open.

"Are you sure he's gone this time?" he asked.

Her eyes widened. "Do you suppose he'll come back?"

"Maybe, maybe not." Tyler walked across and peered through the draperies, watching the sidewalk below. "Yeah, there he is. Mina's holding the cab for him. No, stay back!" He thrust an arm in front of her when she started toward the window. "He wouldn't expect you to watch him leave." He watched for a few seconds more, then stepped back.

"They're gone." He turned to Emma. "How did you know he might come back?"

She looked surprised. "I didn't."

"But you waited out there, talking to Mrs. Johnson, instead of coming to get me."

"I suppose I should have—"

"Don't get me wrong," he interrupted. "It was the smart thing to do, and it's a damn good thing you did it. Alexandru came back, but he didn't find you letting an American agent out of a hidden room. He found you innocently conferring with your secretary. I'm awfully glad you did that."

"Are you saying I did the right thing?" She sounded as if she didn't believe he would actually compliment her.

Tyler's lips curved in a small smile. "That's right. If he'd seen me and guessed what I was doing here, you would never see Mina again."

Emma looked at him for several seconds, then walked slowly across the office with her head bent and her arms folded. She rubbed her upper arms with her hands, as if feeling a chill.

"I'm so afraid for her," she said softly, almost talking to herself. "I want you to help her. I want to say the words that will make you help her, because I can't do it alone."

"You *are* helping her."

"Not quickly enough. I'm terrified each time she goes back to the embassy, back to people like Stefan Alexandru."

"I've never seen him face-to-face. What's he like?"

Emma shuddered. "Frightening."

"In what way? Besides the fact that any member of the secret police is bound to be frightening."

"His eyes," Emma said after a moment's thought. "They're empty, with no life behind them, no soul. It's as if he's dead on the inside."

Tyler nodded. "I've seen people like that. They're both frightening and sad." He cleared his throat. "Well, anyway, was she able to give you any information?"

"Yes." Emma's voice was tight. "Yes, she did. Apparently she had a couple of plans in mind when she couldn't keep Mr. Alexandru away." She walked briskly to her desk and bent over the piles of papers, dashing a hand across her cheek to swipe the tears away. "She has information concealed in the loan papers in microdots or something. I presume you have people who can find that easily enough."

"It shouldn't be a problem." He looked through the papers carefully, one page at a time. "We'll make copies of these for you, so you can go ahead with your loan."

Emma bent to unlock a lower drawer. "There's something else."

Tyler's head snapped up. "She gave you more than this?"

Emma nodded, bent over the drawer. "This." She held up a small envelope. It was sealed and slightly crumpled.

Tyler took it, turning it over in his hands. "When did she give this to you?"

"When Stefan went into the loo, she pulled it out of her blouse. I stuffed it in that drawer and locked it before he came out again. We kept talking while he was in there, so he wouldn't get suspicious."

"I know." Tyler's tone was dry. "I heard you. Is the weather really that fascinating?"

"It comes of having lived in Britain. When in doubt, talk about the weather."

"I guess it works." Tyler held the envelope up to the light, but couldn't distinguish anything inside.

"Why don't you open it?"

He shook his head. "I'll let the boys at the lab do that." He tucked the envelope and the loan papers into his portfolio. "Did she say anything?"

"Just to give the envelope to you. She thinks it's what you want." Emma looked into his eyes. "I hope she's right."

"Time will tell," he said cryptically. "Time will tell."

The flight back to New York was as tedious as ever and it was late when they reached the apartment. Emma had brought work home, but couldn't keep her mind off of Mina. Finally she sighed and closed the file on her lap. "I can't concentrate."

"It's been a long day."

"To say nothing of stressful." Emma let her head fall back against the sofa. "I hope Mina's all right."

"She should be. Because of her family connections they can't act against her without solid proof."

"Which they would have if they'd searched her this morning." Emma spoke softly, but there was no disguising the bitterness.

"But they didn't. She's not without resources, Emma. She's the daughter of a national hero. She seems to know what she's doing. Did she ever have training in espionage?"

"Espionage?" Emma looked over at him. "I have no idea."

"Would she have told you?"

"I think so." After a brief pause, she asked, "If the information you need is in the things she brought today, will you help her?"

Tyler didn't immediately reply, but studied the ceiling for a few seconds, then turned so he could look into her eyes. "I can't say for sure. What she brings us is only part of the package. The rest is herself—her history, her motivations. I have to explore it all."

"Explore it," Emma repeated thoughtfully. "Sometimes I want to explore your mind. I wonder why you're doing this?"

"It's my job."

She disagreed. "There's more to it than that. At first I believed that you were cold and calculating, a robot doing your job. I could have lived with that conclusion, but you gave yourself away.''

''What did I do?''

''You didn't behave like a robot. You weren't callous to Mina. You treated her almost as a colleague. And I saw a side of you that surprised me.'' He raised his eyebrows in disbelief and she nodded.

''There's gentleness inside you. You don't like to show it, but it's there.''

He made a little movement of disagreement.

''Oh, yes, it's there, and that's left me more confused than ever. If you're not a robot, then what are you?''

''Just a man.''

''That's not what I mean.'' She sat forward, seeking to explain herself. ''What are you inside? What do you believe in? What goals do you work for? How do you see the world?''

''Not through rose-colored glasses, that's for sure.''

She blew out an exasperated sigh. ''Are you going to keep hiding behind clichés? Or are you going to talk to me?''

''I don't know.''

''You *are*—''

''A robot?'' he suggested.

''Aggravating,'' she retorted. Then she added thoughtfully, ''And I think a little frightened.''

''Frightened? Of what?''

Buying time, thinking how to phrase her answer, Emma sipped the tea she'd poured. ''I think you're frightened of letting anyone see you. Not the face you show to the world but the real you, that you keep hidden.''

There was a moment of silence. ''That's a crock!''

Emma knew she'd struck a nerve. ''I don't think so. Everyone guards their emotions, but you . . . you've buried them so deeply and guard them so closely that I can't help but wonder why.''

"Maybe because I don't see any point in spilling my guts all over the place."

"I don't think so. I think it's because you've been hurt. And perhaps because you learned over time that letting your feelings show opens you to more."

He snorted. "Is that something you read in one of those women's magazines?"

"No, it's life. And whatever happened in your life to make you this way, I know there is a different man behind that tough-guy facade."

"Oh, yeah? You think you're so smart, Lady Emma? How do you know that?"

"I know that," Emma said, so softly that he barely heard her, "because you kissed me."

There was a moment of silence. "You kissed me back," Tyler pointed out.

You kissed me back. Emma could feel a flush heating her cheeks, but she lifted her chin and faced Tyler bravely. "Yes, I did. But it was you who put an end to it."

Tyler frowned. "What does that have to do with anything?"

Her cheeks were pink with embarrassment, but she managed a small smile. "It has everything to do with it, Mr. Davis. You gave yourself away." She rose and picked up their empty cups. "It's late and I'm tired." Without waiting for an answer, she walked out of the room.

"You're going to explain that."

He'd followed, and stood in the kitchen doorway, watching her stack dishes in the dishwasher. Emma didn't want arguments tonight. She wanted a hot bath and a deep, dreamless sleep. She closed the dishwasher, started it and walked over to the doorway he was blocking.

"Tyler, it's late and I'm tired. All I really want to do is take a hot bath and go to bed."

"Sounds good to me." He folded his arms and gave her a smile that was more of a leer.

Emma just shook her head. "It won't work, Tyler. You can't fool me anymore."

"Who's fooling?"

"You are, and we both know it." Suddenly annoyed, she pushed past him. She'd taken all of three steps along the hallway before he caught her wrist and swung her around.

"I'm not fooling. We're going to talk." He shifted his grip to her arms, pulling her close so that she had to tip her head back to look into his face.

There were small lines of fatigue around his eyes, and beneath the macho blustering she could see his weariness. Her irritation faded into compassion. She reached up, touching his face with her fingertips—tracing the lines, skimming over his features, the curve of his eyebrow, the lean plane of his cheek, the elegant line of his upper lip.

Her caress neared the corner of his mouth, and he turned his head, only a fraction, but enough to capture her fingertip between his lips. Emma gasped, and when she didn't pull away, Tyler wrapped his arms around her waist and she went pliantly into his embrace.

Chapter 9

He kissed her fingertip, her palm and then her lips. It was deep and sweet and gentle, though Emma could feel the passion in him. His muscles were tight, his body tense as she melted against him, parting her lips for his kiss, tangling her fingers in his hair.

He shifted his feet, pulling her between his thighs, slanting his mouth over hers to deepen the kiss. He ran his hands down her back, pressing her hips into his, and a sudden uprush of passion scorched through Emma, unexpected in its force. She had no defense against feelings like this; they were as overwhelming as an ocean wave, pulling her under into the swirling depths.

Clinging to Tyler as her only security, Emma was deaf and blind to anything else. She was on fire for him, her skin flushed and hot with a heavy, empty ache centered low in her belly. Only he could fill that ache, no one else, and she pressed close, her movements inflaming her further. For a moment he responded, the tiny, subtle movements of his body complementing hers in a dance older than time, fanning the flame until it threatened to burn out of control.

And then he went still. Emma moved again, a wordless plea, but he tore his lips from hers, pressing her face into his shoulder, swearing into her hair. She reached up for him, but he caught her wrists in a strong grip, forcing her hands down, stepping back to create some space.

Emma raised her eyes to his, wide and dark with need. "Tyler?" It was barely a whisper, a breath of sound.

"No," he said, his voice harsh with strain. He spun away from her and stalked into the living room to stand at one of the tall French windows, gripping the sides of the frame with his hands, shoulders hunched, head bent. Emma stopped two steps away, her hands clenched together to keep from reaching for him.

"Tyler?"

She could see his muscles bunch and tighten, as if he were bracing himself for an assault. "What do you want?"

"This is what I meant," she whispered. "You have the strength when I don't. You can say no, when I can't…when all I want is to make love with—"

"Stop it!" He whirled around, and she backed away, frightened of the anger in his face. "And stop painting white hats for me, will you? There's nothing between us but proximity."

"It's much more than that. You know it is."

"More than what? You say I'm strong, but has it occurred to you that I'm just smart enough to know that it would be one hell of a mistake to make love with you?"

"A mistake?"

"A mistake. You're not my type. Maybe you don't mind slumming, Lady Emma, but I'm a little more choosy."

She physically flinched at the insult. "That isn't true," she said, her voice carefully even, "and you know it."

"I don't know anything except that you're not my type, any more than I'm yours." He turned his back on her, staring out at the night. "Go to bed, Emma."

Emma hesitated, opened her mouth to speak, then closed it again, turned in silence and walked to her bedroom.

Emma had a great deal to think about during the days that followed. Whatever he said, however he behaved, she knew that behind the rough-edged facade Tyler Davis presented to the world, there was a good man.

It was clear he'd been hurt in the past, and hurt badly, if the thickness of the shell he'd grown was anything to judge by. It was the man underneath whom she was drawn to, and proximity had little to do with it. Proximity alone couldn't create the tension that seemed to crackle in the air whenever they were together.

And yet...they were very different people. She knew very little about him, for he refused to talk about himself. He'd made it clear that he didn't approve of her background, though she wasn't certain if it was the money or the title he objected to. Whichever it was, he'd made it clear that he considered himself and Emma, as her father would put it, as incompatible as chalk and cheese.

Perhaps they were—on the surface. However, beneath those surface differences of money and background and career, Emma had begun to think they had more in common than not. There was an honorable man under the macho posturing, a man capable of compassion and gentleness, a man she admired. And because she admired him, cared about him, this situation was rapidly becoming far too complicated.

The secret police had apparently lost interest in Emma for the moment, so they didn't have to spend their nights in the same apartment, though Lord Latham insisted Tyler escort her home each evening. Emma should have slept better knowing he wasn't in the next room, but instead she seemed to spend too many of her nights wakeful and thinking.

It wasn't yet seven on a cold Friday morning, and the sun wasn't ready to put in an appearance, when the phone rang. Emma was curled in her living room window seat, wearing a length of Campbell plaid like a generous shawl over her silk nightgown.

She picked up the phone. "Hello?"

"Emma?" She knew his voice.

"Yes, Tyler?"

"Are you awake?"

"I am now."

"Oh, hey, I'm sorry if—"

"That was a joke. I was already up."

"Oh. Good. We need to talk. Do you have some time now?"

"Well, yes, I do. What do we need to talk about?"

"Not over the phone. Can I come to your place?"

She hesitated only a moment. "Yes, if you want to."

"Okay. I'll be right there," he said, and hung up.

Emma hung up, and rose from the window seat. She had to get dressed before Tyler arrived. She was halfway across the room when the doorbell rang.

She walked warily into the entry hall, frowning. The bell rang again. "Who is it?" she called through the closed door.

"It's me."

"Tyler?"

"Who else? Are you going to let me in or not?"

"Oh, yes! Of course."

She quickly unlocked the door and stood aside as he walked in past her.

"Do you get a lot of people up here at six-thirty in the morning?" he asked.

"No one but you." Emma watched as, with his back to her, he peeled off his gloves and shrugged out of his coat.

"Then what took you so long? You knew I was coming."

"I didn't know you'd arrive in fifteen seconds."

"I was just across the street." He leaned into the closet to hang up his coat. "I called on the car phone."

"I see." She started for the kitchen. "Well, I didn't know that. Would you like coffee or tea?"

"Whatever you're having is—" he left the closet, turned and saw her "—fine," he said weakly.

Emma felt her cheeks warm. She nodded and pulled the plaid more closely around her as she walked into the kitchen.

Tyler followed slowly, his mind filled with the image of her fresh from bed, her hair streaming over her shoulders, wearing some kind of shawl thing over a silk nightgown. It covered her decently enough, but it had slipped off one shoulder, taking the silk strap of her gown with it. She held it closed with one hand, just at her breasts, and beneath the green and blue and black of the wool was the first shadowy hint of cleavage.

It was far too easy to imagine her in his arms, her slim, soft form swaddled in silk and wool. And he could imagine pulling the wool away and finding her body warm and soft and sweet.... He swore under his breath, almost a groan.

"Tyler?" Emma called from the kitchen. "Did you say something?"

"No." He rubbed a hand over his face. "I didn't say anything. I'm going to wash my hands, okay?"

"All right."

Her voice was low and quiet and husky from sleep, and Tyler wanted nothing more than to carry her back to the bed in the cream-and-rose bedroom at the end of the hall. He turned away from the kitchen door and walked with jerky strides to the bathroom.

Emma was pouring tea when he entered the kitchen. She glanced around at him. "There's toast and marmalade if you like."

"Okay. Thank you."

She set things on the table, then added milk to her tea. She stirred, sipped and decided not to wait for him to speak. "Tyler, why are you here?"

He looked up from his toast. "What?"

Emma shook her head. "You're not here at six-thirty in the morning just for tea and toast."

"You're right. I came about Mina."

"Why?" Emma's cup clattered into the saucer. "Has something happened to her? Is she all right?"

"Nothing's happened, and as far as we know, she's fine."

"As far as you know? Do you suspect something's wrong?"

"No, really." Tyler reached out to take her hand, and she gripped his fingers tightly. "That's not what I meant. We have no indication that anything's wrong."

"Thank heavens!" The tension went out of Emma on a sigh. "What is it, then?"

"It's just that I've assembled all the information we could find on her. I want to run it past you to see if there's anything you can add, and if there are discrepancies between what we've dug up and what you already know."

"Oh. all right, then. What have you learned?"

"I'll show you," he said, hesitating, "If you'll let me have my hand back." Tyler looked at their hands, tightly clasped.

"Oh!" Emma released his hand as if burned, an embarrassed flush rushing into her cheeks. She lowered her head and tugged the plaid more closely around her shoulders. "Well, then." She cleared her throat. "What have you learned about Mina?"

Tyler opened the portfolio he'd brought and withdrew a sheaf of papers. He laid the closely typed sheets on the table and began. "First, about her father. Don't you think it's a paradox that the daughter of one of the highest-ranking Party officials in the country would want to defect?''

''Why is that?''

''We'd expect such a person to be loyal to the Party, and that would increase the chances of her being a plant. But if she *were* a plant, we'd expect her father's history to be concealed.''

''What does that mean, when you add both sides up?''

He shrugged. ''Neither yes or no. They balance each other out. We know a great deal about her father's career, but not much about his personal life.''

He paged through the extensive report, condensing the contents for Emma. Sometimes he'd ask her to clarify a point, and other times she was able to supply information the intelligence agencies hadn't learned, such as why there appeared to have been no women in Nicolae Grigoras's life.

''He loved Mina's mother very much. They met during the war and survived by the skin of their teeth, but they nearly starved, and she was never strong after that. She was over forty when Mina was born and died when Mina was five.''

''What did she die of?''

''I don't know. I don't think Mina knows. Possibly just the weakness she never overcame.''

''Okay.'' He made a note in the margin. ''Mina was born in the town of Cimpina, north of Bucharest, while her father was overseeing collective farms in the area. Shortly after you say his wife died, he became a diplomat and began traveling, taking his daughter with him.''

Emma was astonished at the amount of information that had been assembled. Tyler knew all the places where Mina had lived, both in Romania and throughout the world, during Nicolae's diplomatic career. He knew where she'd been educated, that she had no siblings, that her only living relatives were distant cousins she scarcely knew and that she'd been a manager on a collective farm before becoming a diplomat.

But all his facts couldn't verify her thoughts, her feelings or why she'd decided to defect. Emma had more insight into those aspects of Mina's personality.

"She's afraid."

"That's obvious, but if she weren't attempting to defect, she'd have nothing to fear. Her plans to defect so she can do something for her country by working from the outside sound very idealistic," Tyler said dryly. "But when you get right down to it, isn't she a traitor?"

"To what?" Emma asked. "To communism or to her country? To effect change in the Party that has betrayed her country doesn't sound like treason to me. I'd call it patriotism."

"Apparently she's convinced you."

"Yes," Emma said firmly.

"Why? What proof do you have?"

"You can't prove emotions, but that doesn't make them any less powerful, does it? I know Mina is telling the truth, not because of any tangible proof, but because I simply know."

"Woman's intuition?" he asked, clearly amused.

Emma nodded, annoyed by his patronizing tone. "You can scoff," she said crisply, "but intuition exists, and it's not limited to women. I believe what it tells me about people."

"What it tells you? Come on, you sound like one of those flaky psychics on morning talk shows."

"I've had some intuitive feelings about you."

"Me?" He looked startled.

"You. I don't believe you're as cynical as you try to be."

"Take it from me—I'm cynical."

"You're an idealist. That's why you're so insistent on this proof of Mina's sincerity."

He bristled. "How do you figure that?"

"You feel that national security is at stake when you make a decision. You wouldn't want to make a mistake, because the consequences would be so grave. You take your responsibilities seriously, and that's why you're good at what you do."

"And now that you've figured out that I'm some kind of knight on a white horse, you don't hate me anymore for being so hard on your childhood buddy?" he asked sarcastically.

"I still wish you could believe Mina, because the longer this goes on, the more danger she's in. I get angry with you when you refuse to see things that are perfectly clear to me. That doesn't alter the fact that I can understand your reasons. If you weren't an idealist, you'd be making bags of money on Wall Street instead of working for the government."

"I would, huh?" He leaned back in his chair, but Emma could see the anger under the indolent pose. "Well, you can think what you like, but it's all nonsense. And I don't appreciate amateur psychoanalysis."

"Why not?" she shot back. "You did a pretty thorough analysis of me before you'd even met me—and you weren't a bit interested in the truth.

"I knew—"

"You didn't know anything! You didn't want to risk knowing *me*, because you'd already come to a whole set of conclusions based on your prejudices. The truth might have upset all your preconceived notions, and you still don't want to face it!"

She shoved her chair back and stalked toward the door.

"Emma." She stopped, her back to him. "Why don't you tell me what the truth is? Who are you, Lady Emma?" She turned and found him standing there, toe-to-toe. "What do you want from me?" he demanded, goaded. "This?" He caught her in his arms and took her mouth in a swift, hard kiss.

At first there was anger in the kiss, but he lifted his lips for an instant and looked into her eyes. "Damn you." The curse was a tortured whisper in the instant before he kissed her again, deep and sweet, a kiss of possession, not punishment.

He drew her against the length of his body, bending her head back as the kiss deepened. She was slim and soft and sweet through the folds of wool, close, but he wanted her closer. He pulled at the loosening plaid until it slid free and fell to the floor. He read her with his hands, stroking down her back to waist and hips, then up again, from the sweet curves of her derriere to her shoulders, her throat and then to the curve of her breast.

He trailed kisses down her throat, pushed the satin ribbon strap off her shoulder and followed the path of the drooping silk onto her breast. She gasped when he covered her nipple with his lips, and whispered his name as her head fell back and her eyes closed in delight.

Tyler kissed and caressed one breast, then turned his attention to the other, sliding the remaining strap off her shoulder so that the gown fell to her waist. A shiver ran through Emma as the cool air struck her skin, then she shivered again, in delight this time, as he lifted his hands to her breasts again.

She pulled at his shirt buttons, fumbling to undo them, so dizzy with delight that she scarcely noticed when Tyler lowered himself into a chair, pulling her down on his lap, cradled in the curve of his arm.

The doorbell's ring was like cold water thrown in her face. Emma froze in his arms, startled out of her passionate daze. Tyler held her close for a moment, his lips warm against the soft curve where her neck and shoulder met, then muttered a curse against her skin.

"Are you expecting anyone?"

Emma shook her head.

"Then I'll answer it."

When he got up, releasing Emma, she was painfully aware of her near-nakedness, her gown pooled at her waist and her plaid on the floor near the window. She held an arm across her breasts as she fumbled to cover herself, but Tyler brushed her trembling hands out of his way and gently pulled her gown up. He replaced the straps on her shoulders and scooped her plaid up off the tile. "Turn around."

Emma didn't look at him as he folded it around her but gripped the fabric with icy fingers, clutching it to her breasts and hunching her shoulders defensively inside the warm wool.

The doorbell rang again, and she started toward it, but Tyler spoke quietly, stopping her. "Emma, look at me."

She'd never been a coward. Slowly she raised her head and met his eyes.

"This—" He spread his hands helplessly. "It won't happen again."

Emma studied his face for a moment. "Who are you trying to convince?" she finally asked. "Me or yourself?"

The bell pealed again, and she walked quickly out of the kitchen into the hall. Tyler followed and caught her hand before she could turn the lock. "Who is it?" he called softly.

"Uncle Larry," came the reply. "And who are you?"

"What the hell?" Tyler quickly opened the locks and swung the door open. "Lord Latham? What are you doing here, sir?"

"I might ask you the same thing, my boy." Tall, silver-haired, and resplendent in a vicuna overcoat and cashmere scarf, Lord Latham stepped in. "I came to see Emma, but since you're here, Tyler, I'll be spared repeating myself."

"About what?" Emma helped him out of his coat.

"About our plans, my dear."

Lord Latham stepped back to look at her, then frowned. He glanced at Tyler, saw the ruffled hair and unbuttoned shirt, and his frown deepened. He looked searchingly at Emma, seeing mussed hair and swollen lips.

"I say, Emma, are you well?"

"Of course." She went to hang up his coat, tossing one end of the plaid over her shoulder to secure it. While her back was turned, she composed her face. "I'm a bit tired, that's all."

With a bright smile on her face, she tucked a hand through his arm. "Would you like a cup of tea while you tell us about these new plans? I have Dundee marmalade for the toast."

"You can always tempt me with marmalade, my dear."

When they were settled at the table again, Emma kept her gaze lowered. Tyler still had his top three buttons undone, and though Emma had her expression under control, she couldn't conceal the well-kissed fullness of her lips or the blush of embarrassment that stained her cheeks.

"Uncle Larry," she asked, "can you tell us why you've come here so early?"

"To make plans, as I said, and they must be made quickly. You and Tyler are being watched again."

Chapter 10

What?" Emma nearly dropped her cup.

Across the table Tyler reacted with disgust rather than surprise. "Hell!" he muttered. "When did it start?"

Lord Latham smiled ruefully. "We've suspected it for about a week, and for the past three days we've had our people watching their people, who are now watching you. And don't ask me to repeat that, please. Actually, it's a bit of luck that you're here at Emma's flat so early in the morning, Tyler. It contributes to the impression we'd like to create." He waited for the obvious question.

"Which is?" Tyler asked.

"That you and Emma are...er...romantically involved."

There was a long moment of silence while Emma looked from one man to the other, too astonished to speak.

"I see," Tyler finally said. "So what's the plan?"

"You've been seen coming and going from this apartment, and from Emma's office. They can make what they wish of that, but we want to take appearances a step farther. We'd like the two of you to go away together for the weekend."

"Go *away*?" Emma found her tongue at last. "Uncle Larry, what are you talking about?"

"I'm talking about diverting suspicion from you. What could be less suspicious than a tryst in the country?"

"A tryst?" She tasted the word and didn't like it. "Couldn't we just go to dinner?"

He shook his head. "That isn't enough. Tyler has been spending a great deal of time with you. We'll give them an obvious reason, so they won't go searching for a hidden one."

"Do we have to publicly act as though we're in love just for the benefit of a lot of spies?"

"Semipublicly," he replied. "You won't be performing for an audience, Emma. We simply want to create an illusion."

She folded her arms. "By sending us off to a motel?"

"Not exactly."

"Then what?" Tyler's voice and eyes were hard. "Exactly."

"Sending the two of you to a secluded cabin."

"Where?" Tyler asked before Emma could.

"There's a place upstate where you'll be safe. It's in the mountains. Once you lose anyone who might be following you, you won't have to put on any kind of act."

After a moment Tyler nodded. "All right."

"Good. You can leave this evening." Lord Latham drained his tea and stood. "I'll be on my way, then. Tyler, I'll get the rest of the information to you this afternoon."

"Uncle Larry, wait a minute." Emma rose, too, and put a hand on his arm to restrain him. "Must you go?"

"I'm afraid so."

"I'll walk down with you, then."

He shook his head. "Thank you, but that's not necessary. I'd prefer not to be seen this morning, so I'll use the service entrance."

When she'd seen him out the door, Emma returned slowly to the kitchen. Tyler was still sitting at the table, but he looked up when she stopped in the doorway.

"Tyler, I have to get ready for work."

"We still have to talk."

"What is there to talk about? This situation is embarrassing enough as it is. And I really do have to get ready." She glanced at the kitchen clock, emphasizing her point.

"You can't deny what's happened," he said as he rose from his chair.

She shook her head in a quick, sharp negative. "I don't love you. And you've made it clear you don't love me!"

"Oh, hell!" He raked a hand through his hair. "I don't even *like* you half the time, but...there's something between us. We can't ignore it."

"I'd like to try," Emma muttered, and left.

Later that day she hadn't made much progress.

"Emma? Are you all right?"

"What?" Emma came out of her reverie to find her secretary studying her quizzically.

"You haven't heard a word I said."

"I know and I'm sorry. I've been a little preoccupied."

"I see." The secretary smiled. "What—or should I say who?—has your thoughts all tied up?"

Emma clucked in reproof. "I was thinking about the Romanian agricultural loan."

"Of course," the other woman said dryly. "Well, since your mind's on it, anyway, I'll leave the latest information with you, and you can go over it at your leisure."

"Thank you. I'm sorry I'm not concentrating."

"I understand." There was a world of knowledge in her voice. "I'm going to lunch now. Do you want me to get something for you?"

"If you would, thanks. Just a sandwich, okay?"

"Okay." With a wave, she vanished.

Emma waited until the door closed, then lowered her head into her hands. She hated to admit it, but her secretary was right. Tyler Davis was to blame for her preoccupation. To be fair, she should blame both Tyler and Uncle Larry, since it was Uncle Larry who was sending her off on this pseudo-romantic weekend.

Romantically involved, indeed! She'd seen Uncle Larry's face this morning, and she knew exactly what conclusions he'd drawn. She and Tyler had been kissing, and Uncle Larry probably thought they were falling in love. Well, he'd thought wrong.

She opened the folder she held and determinedly started to read. Absolutely wrong.

Late that afternoon she was still trying to convince herself of that. She wanted to dislike him. Dislike was a simple emotion, easily dealt with. What she was feeling was much more complicated.

She liked his strength, and the fact that he felt no need to flaunt it. She liked his flashes of dry humor, too, even when they were at her expense. She liked his intensity and his commitment to his work. She liked his integrity, and she admired the sense of honor that had prompted him to draw back from making love to her.

It hurt to admit it, but she would have let him. At that moment, in his arms, she'd wanted him more than she wanted air to breathe, with a desperation she'd never imagined. And she was convinced it would have been wrong.

She was grateful for his restraint, but she had to wonder what would happen this weekend. She was almost frightened to be alone with him, almost frightened by the intensity of her feelings.

Those feelings were an aberration, she told herself, rather like a twenty-four-hour virus. She would recover from it. The problem was that this virus was getting worse instead of better. She could only hope that since absence made the heart grow fonder, proximity, in an isolated cabin, would make the passion die.

"Tyler?"

"Yeah?" he answered without looking up from the detailed map of Romania he was studying.

"A packet just came for you. By messenger." Jim stood in the door of Tyler's office, a manila envelope in his hand.

Tyler glanced up. "Oh, yeah, thanks. Just dump it over here, would you?" He tapped the end of his desk, then bent over the map again.

"You . . . uh . . . know what it is?"

"Yeah." Tyler glanced up again. "I know. And you don't need to." He waited a moment. "Thanks, Jim."

"Okay, I can take a hint." Jim put the envelope down and backed toward the door. "By the way, how's Lady Emma?"

Tyler looked up again. His eyes were cold and hard. "She's fine," he said. "Is there anything else?"

"Nope." Jim backed away. "Nothing else. Nothing at all." The door closed behind him, and Tyler tried to relax.

It didn't work. He reached up to massage the back of his neck, where the muscles ached with the daylong effort of forcing himself to concentrate. And instead of a relaxing weekend to look forward to, he had to take Lady Emma off to Lord Latham's cabin.

Tyler smiled wryly. Jim wouldn't complain about taking Emma away. Tyler didn't know what to think about a weekend alone with Emma, wanting her, and hating himself for wanting her. He knew she was wrong for him, but that didn't stop him from wanting her when she was near, and dreaming about her when she wasn't.

He'd found it easy to dislike the idea of a "Lady Emma," with too much money and too much breeding, hoity-toity and conceited. That had worked out fine until he'd met her, and found her beautiful and brainy and hardworking. There were things he admired about her, reluctantly, such as her quick intelligence and her drive. She worked hard, and the people who worked for her both liked and respected her. They trusted her judgment, and he knew they wouldn't if she hadn't earned it.

He never should have kissed her in the first place. He knew that, but second thoughts were a waste of time. It had happened, and he had to deal with it.

Deal with it. His quiet laugh was bitter. His only problem was deciding *how* he was going to follow his own instructions.

"Is this it?" Emma peered into the early autumn darkness, straining to see ahead of the car.

They were over three hours from Manhattan, somewhere in the Catskills. A half mile back they had turned off a narrow country road onto a private lane.

It was even narrower than the blacktop road, and in a woeful state of disrepair. Branches scraped the car as they bumped and lurched over the rutted surface, and Emma braced her hand against the dashboard as she squinted ahead. A small house appeared as they rounded the last corner.

It was unprepossessing, to say the least. A small stone house, it sat in the middle of a clearing that had once been larger. Bushes and young trees were encroaching on the lawn as the woods tried to take back the land. The uncut grass had gone to seed, and the shrubs around the house were overgrown, shooting raggedly up in front of the darkened windows.

Tyler brought the car to a halt and killed the engine. They sat looking at the cabin, uncertainly illuminated by the headlights.

"Are we where the map said we ought to be?" Tyler asked.

Emma checked. "We followed Uncle Larry's directions."

"Then this must be it." Tyler switched off the headlights, and darkness fell on the clearing like a thick cloak. He reached for the door handle, but Emma caught his sleeve. "What is it?"

"Are you sure we shouldn't just go to a nice hotel somewhere?" She tried to make it a joke.

"Nah." She could feel him shake his head. "Just because we're out in the woods, miles from anywhere, it's pitch-dark and creepy, and this place looks like the Bates Motel in miniature—"

"Stop that!" She smacked his arm.

"There are probably spiderwebs hanging in the doorways, and bats in the bathroom, and—"

Emma couldn't help it. Laughter bubbled up and spilled over. "All right! You've made your point!" She opened her door and looked at Tyler as the dome light came on. "But if there are bats in the bathroom, you have the job of evicting them!"

"That's hardly a liberated attitude."

"I decline to be liberated about bats."

Tyler switched on a flashlight, illuminating an uneven flagstone path to the cabin. Emma followed closely, but still she tripped over a stone heaved up by tree roots and winter freezes. She stumbled against Tyler's back, but found herself caught and held by a strong arm.

"You okay?" he asked.

"I just tripped."

"So watch where you're walking." He sounded faintly annoyed, and Emma pulled free of his arms with more force than was really necessary.

"I would if you'd aim that torch so I can see the path."

"Aim what?"

"The torch. You know, the flashlight." She translated the British into American for him. "I can't see the path."

"Come here, then." He pulled her up beside him, shining the beam of light down the stones. With one arm around her waist, he marched her briskly to the weathered stone stoop.

He kept an arm around her as he fished in his pocket for the keys. Emma would have liked to be annoyed, but she was secretly grateful. With Tyler's arm around her, she felt less nervous of bats, spiders and other potential inhabitants of the darkness. On the other hand, his body was warm and solid and strong, resurrecting all the apprehensions she'd spent the day trying to banish. It was an uneasy dichotomy.

"Here it is." With a grunt of satisfaction he produced a ring bearing a long brass skeleton key and a brand-new dead-bolt key. The dead bolt opened with a well-oiled click. "For all that this place looks like a dump, at least Lord Latham has a decent lock on the door." He applied the skeleton key to the larger keyhole and spent several seconds jiggling it before that one opened. "I take back what I just said. That lock would frustrate burglars more than the new one."

"That mightn't be such a bad thing," Emma told him. "Assuming a burglar would come all the way out to the edge of civilization to burgle."

"You never know." Tyler pushed the door open, revealing an even more stygian darkness. He reached in and felt around for a few seconds. "Is there a switch on that side?"

"Let me see." Emma gingerly patted the wall on the other side of the doorway until she found a button and pressed it. A light flashed on, momentarily blinding them.

Blinking against the glare, Tyler drew her inside, and they saw that they were standing in a small entry hall. The overhead fixture cast enough light to show them a living room through one doorway and a hallway leading toward the back of the house.

Tyler turned on a lamp in the living room, revealing a smallish room, furnished comfortably in the English country house tradition. The ceiling was low and dark-beamed, the walls papered in a soft floral and the sofa drawn up before a large stone fireplace with a basket of logs beside it.

"Well," Emma said, looking around, "this is quite nice."

"Not too bad, is it? Want to see the rest?"

"The rest" was equally nice—a large country kitchen, two small bedrooms, each dominated by an antique bed, and a bath with a deep clawfoot tub.

Emma stood in the center of the hallway when they'd finished their tour. "This is really lovely. Why do you suppose it looks so unkempt outside?"

"Unkempt? I'd call it spooky." Tyler returned to the entry hall. "Maybe to keep from calling attention to the place. I didn't see too many immaculate lawns on the way up here."

"You may be right." Emma shivered and hugged herself. "Do you suppose there's central heat?"

"Bound to be. Why don't you look for a thermostat while I get the bags?"

The thermostat was in the hall, and when Emma turned the setting up, she was rewarded with a blast of dusty-smelling air from the furnace vents. It warmed quickly, and by the time Tyler finished with the suitcases, she was in the kitchen, poking through the cupboards.

"Will we starve?"

"Not likely." She closed a pantry door. "As Uncle Larry said, there's everything here but milk and eggs."

"And since we brought those—" Tyler held up a grocery bag "—we're all set." He put the perishables away while

Emma emptied the bag of the other items she'd bought. "Were you going to fix anything to eat?"

"Why?" Emma glanced over her shoulder with a grin. "Are you hungry?"

"Starved."

"It'll only take a minute to fix something."

"I'll see if that garage in the back is still standing."

Toasted cheese sandwiches and tomato soup didn't take much longer than it took Tyler to park the car, and they ate hungrily. After their light meal, they returned to the living room— Emma perched on one end of the sofa, curling her legs beneath her, while Tyler slouched in a chintz armchair.

Emma sat until the silence began to stretch out a little too long. "Well," she said, getting to her feet, "I'm a bit tired. I suppose I'll go—"

"Go to bed?" Tyler checked his watch. "It's barely nine-thirty."

"But it has been a long day, and I'm..." She faltered in the face of his openly skeptical regard. "And I'm tired."

"You just don't want to be in here with me, thinking what you're thinking." He rose and walked lazily toward her.

"You don't know what I'm thinking!"

"Sure I do." His voice was as lazy as his walk. "You're thinking about this morning just like I am."

He took a step toward her, and when Emma backed quickly away, he caught her arm. She flinched at his touch, and he frowned. "For God's sake, you're not afraid of me, are you?"

"Certainly not!" she retorted, but Tyler read a different answer in her eyes. His mouth twisted as he released her.

"You don't need to be." He turned away, pulling his jacket off a chair. "Come on, let's go for a walk."

"In the dark?"

"Sure." He shrugged into his jacket, then held hers out for her. "The moon's out. You'll be able to see just fine. Come *on*," he urged when she still hesitated.

"All right." With no reason to refuse, Emma slid into her jacket and followed Tyler outside.

It was like walking into a fairyland.

The moon had risen, full and fat and silver in the clear, cold night. The bright moonlight bleached the color from everything, painting trees and rocks and grass starkly in black and silver.

Behind the cabin the lawn fell away from a flagstone patio in a long grassy slope. Bushes and trees dotted the hill, and through them Emma could see the gleam of water. She gazed out in wonder. "It's beautiful," she breathed.

"Yeah." Tyler had spoken as softly as she, reluctant to shatter the silence. "Come on." He took her hand. "It looks like there's a stream down there."

Emma followed him down the slope and through the frosty grass to where the land leveled at the edge of a stream that widened into a good-size pond. The water was glassy and still in the windless night, with moonlight in a trail of silver across it.

"Come this way." Tyler picked his way over tumbled rocks on the shore until he reached one that was perhaps five feet high and large enough to sit on. He climbed up and pulled Emma onto the flattish top after him. She hesitated when she saw that there was barely space for her to kneel beside Tyler.

"There's no room."

"Sure there is. It's as good as an armchair. Turn around." Taking her shoulders, he turned her to face the pond with her back to him. "Now sit down."

She sat, gingerly, with her feet dangling several feet above the water. Tyler shifted his position behind her, then extended his legs, one on each side of hers, and pulled her back to lean against his chest. He released her shoulders and dropped his hands to his thighs.

"How's that?" His breath ruffled her hair, and she could feel his voice vibrating in his chest.

"It's ... it's quite nice," she said huskily.

"You warm enough?"

Warm? Leaning into the solid comfort of his body, his unhurried breathing stirring the hair just behind her ear, his legs pressed to the length of hers and his hands resting just beside her thighs ... "Yes, I'm all right."

"Like it here?"

"Oh, yes. It reminds me of sitting by the loch at home."

"Do you do that much? Sit by the loch?"

"When I'm in Scotland. We watch the salmon jump."

"That's about as exciting as watching the grass grow."

"It's peaceful," Emma murmured. "You can feel the tension and worries draining away."

She sat back, watching the moonlight, enjoying the peace of the night. A fish touched the water's surface, sending ripples in widening circles. Time flowed past unnoticed, the moon wheeled slowly higher into the sky, and an owl called somewhere in the distance. Closer to them, something rustled the leaves as it moved through the woods.

Emma started to whisper a question to Tyler, but he gripped her arm, silencing her. The rustling came closer, and then, on the far side of the pond, a masked face peered from beneath a bush, studying the area for several minutes before the fat raccoon lumbered out of the undergrowth. He waddled down to the pond, drank and then spent several minutes hunting and finally catching something small at the edge of the water.

Emma had no idea what it was, perhaps an insect or fish, but she watched, amused, as the raccoon busily washed his meal before eating it. He was hunting again when rustling sounded in the woods, louder this time. The raccoon looked up in alarm, then vanished into the undergrowth as the sounds of something moving through the woods grew near.

Emma tensed, all her concentration focused on the far side of the pond. She didn't know what was coming, but it had to be big. When she shivered, from nerves more than cold, Tyler slid his arms around her, linking his hands in front of her waist just as a deer walked out of the trees.

The doe paused to look around her, then walked calmly down to the water and drank. Emma leaned forward, straining to see, and her shoe scraped the rock.

At the tiny sound the doe threw her head up, droplets of water scattering from her muzzle like diamonds in the moonlight. She looked directly at the two humans and nothing moved for a full thirty seconds. Then the doe, apparently deciding they were harmless, lowered her head to drink again. When she finished, she looked across the pond once more, then melted back into the woods.

Emma listened until the sounds of the deer's passage faded into the night sounds. Then she let her breath out in a long sigh. "Wasn't she beautiful?" she whispered.

"Yeah," Tyler whispered back. "Beautiful." Silence surrounded them for a moment. "Emma?"

"Hmm?" She turned her head to look at him and met, not his gaze, but his lips.

He tipped her face up with one hand and kissed her gently, seeking and sharing a new beauty as they'd shared the sight of the deer. When he lifted his lips, it was only to murmur her name before he kissed her again.

Chapter 11

Emma felt the hunger of his kiss take hold like a flame in dry grass, growing until it threatened to burn out of control. She leaned back, clinging to his sleeve as she braced precariously on the rock. The kiss was enough, for perhaps a heartbeat of time, and then they wanted, needed more.

Emma twisted on the rock, shifting her position to turn toward Tyler... and felt herself overbalance.

"Oh, no!"

Her lips were torn from his as she felt herself slide toward the still, cold water. She grabbed for Tyler, clutching desperately at his sleeve.

Tyler swore as she slid away, and shot out his hand to grab a fistful of her padded jacket. "Hang on!" With one hand twisted in the slippery nylon fabric, he locked his legs against the sides of the rock and pulled. He grunted as she tried to help, gripping the cold, smooth stone. "Just hang on."

Emma clawed at the rock, straining to find footholds until he gave a final heave and pulled her back up. Heart pounding, Emma clutched at Tyler, burying her face in his chest while he wrapped his arms tightly around her. They stayed that way, clinging together as their heartbeats gradually slowed and their breathing steadied.

Tyler lifted his face from her hair. "You okay?"

"Y-yes."

"Well, since we've undoubtedly scared off all the wildlife for miles around, we might as well get down now."

Emma shivered. "We almost did get down—the hard way!"

"Let's try it the easy way this time. Turn around, like this." He helped her turn around and ease off the rock on her stomach, gripping her hands tightly until she could feel the stony shore beneath her toes. Only when she was standing securely on the ground did he release her.

Tyler slid off the boulder to land lightly beside her and dropped an arm around her shoulders. "You all right?"

"Yes, I'm fine."

He pulled her closer. "So why are you still shaking?"

"That's not shaking, that's shivering. It's freezing out here."

"Let's get you inside." He caught her hand to lead her back up the hill. "Your hand's like an ice cube."

"The rest of me is nearly as cold." Emma broke into a half trot to keep up as he pulled her up the hill. The grass was slippery with frost, their breath puffed in clouds in the still air, and by the time they reached the house, Emma's nose and cheeks were red, her teeth chattering.

"G-g-good h-heavens, it's cold!" She stood in the kitchen, hugging herself, shivering hard.

"Come on." Tyler pulled her toward the living room. "I'll make a fire."

It sounded wonderful to her—perhaps too wonderful, to sit in front of a warm fire, alone with Tyler. "No." Emma stopped short. "It's late, and a fire would take too long."

"There's plenty of wood and kindling here." He was crouched by the hearth with a stick of kindling in his hand, but when he glanced over his shoulder at her, Emma shook her head.

"We can't leave a fire burning." She knew her voice sounded thin and strained. "Someone would have to sit up until it died down. I'll just go on to bed." She walked away quickly, avoiding his eyes.

"Emma."

She stopped with her hand on the door to her bedroom and looked back at Tyler in the living room doorway, a tall, broad-shouldered male form silhouetted against the lamplight. "Yes?" she asked softly.

"You can't keep running away from it forever."

Her chuckle caught on a sob. "Maybe not. But for tonight I'm going to keep trying." She dropped her head and slipped into her bedroom, closing the door softly behind her.

She'd thought that a hot bath would warm her, but long after she was tucked in bed under an exquisitely made log cabin quilt, she was still cold.

It was well past midnight when, thoroughly fed up, she slid out of bed, pulled on her robe and padded to the kitchen. A cup of tea should warm her up, and she knew she'd seen some of Uncle Larry's special blend in a kitchen cupboard.

She put the kettle on to boil, located the tea, the pot and a cup, then carried her steaming pot of tea to the table. While it steeped, she sat looking out at the night.

The moon still poured its silver light across the frosty grass, bleaching the colors where it fell and deepening the shadows in the woods to indigo. The raccoon and the deer were in there somewhere, inhabitants of a magical kingdom.

It *had* been magic out there—sharing a glimpse of the secret world of the night...sharing moonlit kisses. Emma touched her fingertips to her lips, as if she could still feel Tyler's lips.

She snatched her hand away, annoyed with herself for acting like an overimaginative adolescent, sitting alone in the dark, mooning over a kiss. She hastily poured a cup of tea, gulped it and burned her mouth. It served her right. She should remember the way she'd let herself be carried away and how she'd nearly fallen into the frigid pond as a result. That was quite a good object lesson about the dangers of passion and Tyler Davis.

She refilled her cup, checked that the stove was turned off and began to pick her way carefully across the darkened living room, taking her tea to bed.

"Going somewhere?"

The disembodied voice from the darkness of the hallway frightened Emma half out of her wits. She jumped and narrowly missed dropping her teacup, catching it in time to do no more damage than spill half the tea into the saucer.

"Dear heavens!" Emma sagged against the sofa, heart pounding in her throat. "Don't *ever* sneak up on me that way!"

"I didn't sneak." Tyler emerged from the hall, gaining form and substance as he walked into the moonlit living room. "I heard noises. And what were you doing poking around in the middle of the night, anyway?"

"I was making a cup of tea!" Emma held it tightly with hands that shook only slightly. "And it's no thanks to you I didn't spill it all over Uncle Larry's Shou rug."

"Is that what that is?" Tyler darted a glance at the Oriental carpet beneath their feet. "Why were you making tea at this time of night? Couldn't you sleep?"

"I was still cold."

"Are you warm now?"

"A bit." She pulled her robe closer around her. "I got more of a chill than I thought while we were outside."

"I'll build that fire."

"You don't need to—" she began, but he was already stacking wood in the fireplace.

"You're cold. We're both awake." He glanced over his shoulder. "Can you honestly tell me that if you go to bed now, you'd be able to fall asleep?"

She hesitated just long enough to make the truth undeniable.

"Okay, then. I'll bank it before we go to sleep and put the screen in front. It'll be safe." He touched a match to the tinder and fanned the first tiny flames with his hand. "If there's any of that tea left, would you pour me a cup?"

By the time she returned with his tea, the fire was crackling, and Tyler was sitting on the hearth rug, facing the long windows. He patted the rug beside him. "Have a seat."

Emma hesitated for a moment. If sitting on a rock in the freezing moonlight was dangerous, then sitting with him in a warm, fire-lit living room was infinitely more perilous. She knew that, but she sat down beside him, tucking her robe around her legs. Tyler sipped his tea and leaned back against the hearth with a sigh of contentment.

"That's good." He tasted it again. "Different, but good. Is it some special kind?"

"Earl Grey. Uncle Larry's favorite."

Tyler nodded and rested his arm on one bent knee, looking out at the night. Behind them the fire popped and the flames jumped briefly. The firelight glinted off Tyler's hair and gilded his face with glowing warmth. Strength, Emma thought, and integrity. Tyler was that rare man, a man of honor. Honor was an old-fashioned concept, unfashionable in this cynical day and age, but she knew that honor, both as a concept and as a way of life, was an integral part of him.

As was strength. His physical strength was obvious as she studied him covertly through the screen of her lashes. He wore an unbelted terry-cloth robe over pajama trousers. The firelight slanted over his muscular chest, gleaming on smooth skin beneath a dusting of crisp, dark hair. Emma helplessly watched the play of muscle beneath the fabric as he lifted his cup, watched the line of his throat as he drank, watched him lick a droplet of tea from his lip when he lowered the cup.

Oh, yes, he was physically strong. He'd pulled her onto the rock and held her in strong arms, then he'd kissed her, tasting and taking and giving.

But he was strong inside, as well. He'd had the strength to resist making love with her when she was there for the taking. He could have seduced her, yet he hadn't, and he wouldn't. She knew him well enough to know that he wouldn't use passion to push her into something he thought she wasn't ready for.

Emma sipped her tea to moisten her suddenly dry mouth. She knew how his code of honor required him to act, but what if he was wrong? She'd thought of Tyler far too much recently to pretend that her feelings were casual. She knew how she felt about Tyler, but she didn't know how he felt about her. He wanted her, but was there more?

As if he felt her thoughts, Tyler turned. "Emma?"

"Yes?" Suddenly shy, she looked down at her tea.

"I wish I could tell what you're thinking."

Emma laughed softly. "I'm as transparent as glass."

"Not to me. You're a mystery, Lady Emma."

"I doubt that."

"Then tell me what you're thinking right now."

She frowned. "Why?"

"Because just then something made your eyes look sad. What was it?"

For several moments the only sound in the room was the quiet crackle of the flames.

"I was remembering something you said." It was surprisingly easy to be truthful, alone in that dimly lit room.

"What did I say?"

"You said that you don't even like me most of the time," she replied without looking at him.

"I said that?"

"You did. And if I'm brutally honest about it, I have to admit that it hurt." She looked up, meeting his eyes. "It was easy enough to dislike you when we met at the airport. You were rude and arrogant and overbearing, and I was quite happy disliking you."

"You made *that* pretty clear."

She grimaced. "As I recall, I was attempting to dislike you politely. Disliking you was easier than this."

"What's 'this'?"

"Liking you," she admitted slowly, "more than I want to."

"Liking me?" He was skeptical. "You don't let on much."

Emma laughed under her breath at his good-humored teasing. "I don't know how you can say that," she said with wry self-mockery, "after what happened out on that rock. I wasn't exactly hiding my feelings."

A smile tugged at Tyler's lips. "Neither was I."

Emma leaned against the hearth, half turning toward him, resting one elbow on the warm, smooth stone. She pulled her robe over her knees and smiled to herself. "I can't decide whether kissing on that boulder was high romance or low comedy."

"A little of each?" Tyler suggested, and leaned back beside her. "What could be more romantic than sitting in the moonlight watching the woodland creatures?"

"Sitting in a nice warm cinema watching *Bambi*?"

He considered that. "It has plenty of cute animals, and we could sit in the balcony and neck."

"And no risk of falling into a freezing pond." Emma giggled. "Though dying of pneumonia in the name of love is supposed to be romantic, isn't it?"

"Coughing and wheezing your way into the great beyond? No way!" Tyler shook his head firmly. "No, romantic is me rescuing you from the icy depths and holding you in my brawny arms."

Emma gave a snort of laughter. "Brawny?"

"Yeah, brawny." He flexed a bicep. "Check it out."

Hiding a grin, she tested his muscle. It was a solid bulge, tensed rock-hard. She lowered her hand primly to her lap.

"So, is it brawny?"

"Oh, for pity's sake!" Emma blew out a gusty sigh. "Very well, I'd say muscular."

"Not brawny?"

She shook her head. "Brawny sounds like those muscle-bound bodybuilder types. Overblown and a bit grotesque."

"But muscular is good?" he asked, and she nodded.

"That's okay, then." He sat back. "I never expected the proper Lady Emma to lecture me on the difference between brawny arms and muscular arms," he commented.

Emma sighed. "I wish you wouldn't keep harping on that."

"On what?" Tyler traced a fingertip down her cheek.

"My title. Calling me a 'proper English lady.'"

"But you are. Why shouldn't I say so?"

"It's not the saying of it. It's what you mean by it." She shook her head in something between a shrug and a shake. "In the first place, I'm not English. I'm Scottish. And I'm perfectly aware that I've never been a proper lady—Nanny and my mother told me so often enough." She hesitated. "And you keep going on about my title."

"It's part of your name, isn't it?"

"But that's *all* it is. The title's not me. It's something I was born with, like red hair. I don't wake up every morning and congratulate myself on it."

"You're not proud of it?"

"I'm proud of what I've *accomplished*, Tyler. The things I was born with are just there." She half smiled. "I'm proud my family has a long history, even though parts of the Campbell history are nothing to be proud of.'' Her smile turned a little sad. ''I rebelled against the title when I was a teenager, then, when I was older, I accepted it. I just wish—'' She broke off.

After a moment Tyler prompted, ''You wish what?''

''I wish that you could see me, really see me.'' She sat up, her face turned away from him. ''You look at me and you see somebody called 'Lady Emma.' You don't see who I really am. Perhaps if you could see the woman apart from the title you could stop applying your prejudices to me.''

Tyler stiffened, taken aback. ''Do I do that?''

''You do. At first I just dismissed you as narrow-minded and governed by prejudice. If you chose not to look beyond the obvious, I told myself, it was your problem.''

''And now?'' he asked softly.

''Now.'' She sighed. ''Now, since I've come to... to not dislike you, I find I wish you saw more.''

Emma saw a flicker of what might have been regret in his eyes. ''I've been very cruel to you, haven't I?'' She started to protest, but he wouldn't let her. ''I have been. I've hurt you, and it's time I corrected that.''

He took her hand and drew her slowly into his arms, her face against his shoulder. He could feel the stiffness in her, the instinctive way she held herself back. ''It was beautiful out there, wasn't it?''

He could feel her smile against his shoulder. ''Yes, it was beautiful.''

''I didn't have an ulterior motive, you know,'' he said. ''I just wanted to show you something nice. It wasn't some stupid planned seduction or anything.''

''You wanted to show me something beautiful?''

''And then I nearly dropped you in the pond,'' he said dryly.

''But you didn't. I didn't get so much as a toe wet.''

''If you had, it would have been my fault.''

"But I didn't, so you've no reason to feel guilty."

Several minutes ticked past in a silence broken only by the soft sounds of their breathing and the crackle of the fire. He held her close and smoothed a strand of hair off her face.

"I'm not so sure there's nothing for me to feel guilty about." He rolled onto one elbow and gazed down at her.

"A kiss?" Emma tried to laugh it off. "That's nothing to feel guilty—"

"It wasn't just a kiss." He combed his fingers through her hair, spreading it around her shoulders. "It was a lot more than that, and you know it."

Emma's gaze fell, her lashes sweeping down to veil her eyes.

"You know how much more it was," he said, stroking her cheek in a gesture that was almost reverent, then slid his fingers down to her throat to rest on the pulse that was racing there.

"I wanted more." He covered her mouth with his for a slow, leisurely kiss. When he lifted his lips, Emma let out a ragged breath. "So much more . . ."

For an instant she moved as if to push him away, but then he lowered his head, and instead of pushing, she slid her palms up to his shoulders, clinging as his mouth settled gently on hers.

Her eyes fluttered closed, and she gave herself up to the kiss. There was no moonlight now, but there was firelight and the slow, languorous kisses melting the last of the resistance in her body. When at length he lifted his lips, Emma's eyes fluttered open reluctantly. She met his eyes, and a small smile dented the corner of his mouth.

He stroked her throat with his fingertips, sensing the pulse that beat rapidly just beneath the skin. "I wanted to unzip your jacket and touch your breasts." Emma caught her breath as he slipped his fingertips down the lapel of her robe. "Your sweater would be soft, but I'd feel the warmth of your skin through the wool." He stroked the upper curve of her breast, the warmth of his hand reaching her through her robe and gown.

"I'd want still more, though, so I'd put my hand underneath your sweater." He slipped his hand inside her lapel. "You might be wearing a lacy little bra, or one of those sexy one-piece things, but it would definitely be silk."

Emma held her breath as she felt his fingers slip down to the swell of her breast.

"I'd slide the silk across your skin." His hand covered her breast, moving the gown as he spoke. "Your breast would be heavy in my hand," he whispered, testing its weight in his palm, "and when I touched you I'd feel your nipple pucker."

Emma clutched his shoulders at the quick shock of delight, her back arching involuntarily, pressing her breast into his hand. She whispered something soft and plaintive, and he buried his face in her hair.

"I'd touch you," he murmured close to her ear, "through the silk, but pretty soon that wouldn't be enough, either. I'd have to touch your skin and see how beautiful you are."

He levered himself slightly away so that he could push her robe open. The firelight flickered over her bare shoulders and hinted at the darker crests of her breasts through the semisheer gown. Her nipples were taut and hard, pressing against the fabric. Emma watched his eyes widen and darken as he gazed at her body.

He drew one thin strap slowly off her shoulder, then the other, peeling the silk away. "I'd see your breasts, so perfect, and then I'd touch them." Emma's eyes fell closed, shutting out everything but his touch on her breasts.

"Your skin would be smoother than the silk, and so warm." He caressed her with his palms, then drew his thumbs across her nipples, making her shiver again. "It would excite me to know that your body responds to my touch...."

His voice trailed raggedly away, and he bent his head to her breasts. She shuddered as he took her nipple with his lips, then tightened her arms to hold him close, moving her body against his, sweetly seductive.

Tyler groaned. He was accustomed to keeping a tight rein on his emotions, but with Emma's arms around him, with his lips on her breast, he let that rein slip just a little.

He dragged her close, tangling his legs with hers as his robe fell open and he felt her hands slip inside, her touch making him shudder with pleasure. Her hands were cool and soft, and her touch left scorching trails on his skin, like brands of tenderness.

How deeply would she brand him if he made love with her?

Self-preservation would dictate that he run from her, run far and fast before it was too late. Emma slid her hands around his waist, caressing the sensitive skin above the waistband of his pajama trousers.

Tyler growled low in his throat. He ignored common sense, abandoned self-preservation and gave himself up to the wonder that was Emma.

Chapter 12

He meant only to kiss and caress her, his need for her as powerful as the need to breathe, though he meant to stop short of lovemaking. He could kiss her, he told himself, and draw back; he could caress her, then pull away. But if he made love with her, he knew that he could never, entirely, go back inside his shell.

He'd meant to maintain his control, to keep a wall around his emotions, but Emma shattered his defenses. Her skin was like velvet, her perfume filled his senses, heady with roses and spice, making his head swim, as if he'd drunk old brandy or young wine.

He tasted her skin, delicately sampling and seeking, brushed his lips over the upper curve of her breast, drifting toward the rosy crest. Her nipple was drawn into a tight bud, and when he closed his mouth over it, her fingers tightened convulsively on his shoulders and her lips parted on a soft moan of pleasure.

Tyler growled low in his throat, and Emma clung desperately to him, rocked by sensations, dizzy from a pleasure she hadn't known existed. When he kissed her breast, pleasure shot through her like heat lightning on a summer night, so overwhelming that she was half afraid of it, even as she wanted more.

Tyler answered her unspoken plea. He traced a path with his mouth to her other breast, repeating his inflaming caresses until she twisted beneath him, scarcely knowing what she wanted but desperate for more.

He suddenly lifted his lips from her breast, levering his body up and away from her. The cool air was chilly on her heated skin, and she whispered a protest, reaching for him.

"It's okay," he murmured. "Just a minute..."

He rocked onto his heels and rose, pulling her up with him. Her gown and robe slipped to her waist as she stood, leaving her shoulders and breasts bare. Emma tried to cover herself.

Tyler caught her hands. "You don't need to hide." He looked down at the silk pooled around her feet, at her bare shoulders and breasts, gilded by the firelight. "Come here." His voice was little more than a whisper.

Before she knew what he was about to do, he bent to hook one arm behind her knees and lift her into his arms. He strode down the hall to the room that was his for the weekend, with its massive cannonball bed in dark old oak. Slowly he lowered her feet to the rag rug.

He took her face in his hands and kissed her, then ran his hands down her throat, across her shoulders and down her arms. A small candle sat on the nightstand, the flickering light behind Emma silhouetting her legs through her sheer gown and gilding her arms and shoulders.

Tyler gently turned her toward the light, watching as the glow slid over her skin, his gaze almost a tangible thing. A wave of shyness swept through Emma, and she turned her face away, bringing her arms up to shield her breasts.

Tyler took her hands in his and lowered them. "You're so beautiful," he murmured reverently. "You should never be shy."

His words sent a thrill of feminine pride through Emma, pride that he found her beautiful, that she could excite him, yet still she was shy. She was unaccustomed to a man looking at her body with hunger and reverence, and unsettled by the storm of emotion he roused in her.

"Emma," he said softly, "look at me." She hesitated. "Look at me, please."

She turned her head and slowly lifted her eyes to his, alight with passion, with hunger, and with something very near to awe. He held her gaze with his, his eyes burning into her as he touched her face with gentle fingertips.

As she stood before him nude, her shyness faded, replaced by something stronger, a heat that started in her center and radiated through her body, flushing her skin and pounding along her veins. She lifted her hands, reaching for him, and he shrugged quickly out of his robe. Emma was sliding her hands up to his shoulders as he peeled off his pajama trousers.

She linked her hands behind his neck as he kicked the trousers aside and swept her into his arms, pivoting to lower her to the bed. He came down with her, rolling her onto her back and covering her body with his.

Emma was all sensation as he kissed and caressed her, stroking the graceful line of her back, from neck to waist, then lower, shaping the soft curves of her derriere before stroking back up toward her breasts, kissing her where his hands didn't touch.

The caresses of hand, mouth and body overlapped one another, running together into a tide of sensation that washed over Emma, threatening to overwhelm her. She wanted to return as much as he was giving her, but lost in the haze of pleasure, she could do little more than cling.

With strong hands, tender lips and a body that was lean and hard and taut with leashed power, Tyler drove her beyond reason. He was far stronger than she, yet she felt no fear, for he wouldn't use his strength against her. He would be tender with her, care for her and protect her from harm.

He drove her, taking her far and fast, until she was twisting beneath him, mindless with need. He pushed her to the edge of sanity, but she could feel the restraint in him, the leash he kept on his own passion. She whispered incoherent pleas as she kissed his throat and shoulders, and when he eased away from her, she clutched at him in panic, lest he leave her.

He soothed her with a murmur and a touch, and after a moment Emma opened her eyes to find him studying her face, searching for something. "You know what I want," he whispered.

"Yes." Her reply was a breath of sound.

"You have to want the same thing."

She nodded, wordless.

"What do you want, Emma? Tell me what you want."

"She swallowed. I . . . I want . . ."

"Emma—"

"I want you to make love with me," she breathed softly. "Tyler, make love with me—"

He smothered her words with a kiss, and the leash on his passion finally snapped. He kissed and caressed her with a kind of desperation, driving them on until neither could wait any longer. His breathing was ragged, his heart thundered against hers, yet he took her gently, fitting their bodies together with a care that was both endearing and frustrating to Emma.

She was touched by the gentleness he showed her, but at that moment she didn't want gentleness as much as his passion. She moved her body, wrapped him in her arms, kissed his face, his shoulders, his chest and drove him past the point of gentleness.

They moved together, knowing by instinct the ways to please, each driving the other. Emma could feel the spiral within her winding tighter and tighter, driving her farther and higher into the storm building on the horizon. She was dizzy, her mind whirling from the thunder and wind, higher and wilder until it could build no more, and she tumbled over the edge into space. She fell through heat and light and sensation for an eternity before coming to earth in Tyler's arms, still gasping from the trip.

For a long time she lay there, her face on his chest, while her heartbeat and breathing slowed, while beneath her cheek she felt Tyler's heartbeat slow, felt his skin cool, felt his arms periodically tighten around her, as if he couldn't bear to let her go.

When Emma shivered, Tyler reached down and pulled the bedcovers over them, then settled back into the pillows, tucking her against his side, his face in her hair, and took a deep breath.

Tyler wished the moment, the night, would never have to end. He could feel her body relaxing, her breathing slowing as she slid toward sleep, but before she slept there was something he had to ask. He had to ask despite the risk. He drew a deep breath. "Emma?"

"Mmm?"

"Was this—" he forced himself to say it "—was it your first time?"

"What?" She tensed in his arms.

He drew a deep breath. "Were you a virgin?"

She bent her head down so that he couldn't see her face. "What kind of question is that?" Her accent was stronger than usual, more Scottish.

"An honest one." He stroked a hand over her hair, trying to reassure her. "And I hope you can give me an honest answer."

Emma hesitated so long that he was afraid he'd ruined everything. "No," she whispered at last. "It wasn't the first time."

Tyler felt a flash of intuition. "Was it the second?"

Emma remained silent, but he felt her startled movement.

He nodded. "I thought so."

She stiffened, but he tightened his arms around her, turning onto his side and cradling her in front of him, spoon-fashion. She might be more comfortable talking about it if she weren't facing him. He pillowed her head on one arm while he draped the other over her waist.

She relaxed, slowly, finally snuggling close to his warmth. Minutes ticked by in silence, and a log fell into the fire in a shower of sparks.

"How did it happen?" he asked quietly.

"What?" she murmured sleepily.

"How did it happen that this was only the second time?"

There was a moment of silence, then Emma sighed. When she spoke, she no longer sounded sleepy. "There was a boy in college."

"And he seduced you?"

"Not exactly. I fancied myself in love with him. He was a little older than I, and *very* sophisticated." Tyler felt her laugh softly at her own naiveté. "He had a moustache."

"And you made love." His voice was toneless.

"I wouldn't use the word 'love.' Sex, perhaps." She paused, searching for the right words. "It was...not the experience romantic novelists tell one about."

"I see." He knew his voice sounded cold, but that was better than giving in to the anger welling up in him. "So you didn't choose to repeat the experience."

"No."

"I owe you an apology," Tyler said at last, his voice tight with self-recrimination.

She turned to look at him. "What for?"

"For pushing you into something you couldn't have wanted. I'm sorry. It never should have happened."

Emma was still and silent for a moment, then she twisted in his arms so that she could look him fully in the face. "Who do you think you are?"

He blinked. "Huh?"

"Who gave you the right to decide what's best for me?"

"But I just—"

"Nobody!" she snapped. "It's not for you to decide what should or shouldn't have happened. I make my own decisions, Tyler! I'm not a child."

Startled by her vehemence, Tyler studied her face for several seconds while the depth of his mistake became clear to him. "You're right," he said slowly. "I apologize."

Emma searched his face before she nodded. "Very well."

Tyler felt her withdrawal and caught her hand before she could roll away. "Emma, I didn't mean to hurt you. I . . . I know I'm no good at this kind of thing, but . . ." He looked down at his hand, engulfing hers. "I know I'm not the kind of guy you're used to. I—" He hesitated, searching for words. "I don't want to hurt you, Emma. I care about you." He said it in a rush, as if afraid he might not get the words out if he hesitated.

It wasn't a flowery declaration of devotion, but it was more than Emma had dared to expect. Tyler shied away from emotional entanglements, he kept others at bay, yet he had let her past his defenses. An unexpected surge of tenderness washed through her. He wasn't just a loner; he was lonely. And whether he realized it or not, he needed people. He needed her.

When he tugged on her hand, she let him draw her back down and tuck her into place beside him, enclosed in his protective embrace. "Comfortable?" he murmured against her hair.

"Uh-huh. Lovely." She rubbed her cheek against his palm.

"You're tired." He stroked the silky hair off her forehead. "You need to sleep."

"So do you," Emma mumbled.

Tyler chuckled beneath her ear. "Go to sleep, Emma." The last thing she knew was his breathing, slow and regular, ruffling her hair.

Emma didn't want to wake up. She was wonderfully warm, utterly relaxed, and the wakefulness that nagged at her was nothing more than an intrusion on this blissful state of being. When the bed shifted beneath her, she burrowed her head into the pillow and tried to slip back into sleep.

The bed was cooler, though, sleep not so easy to reclaim. The scent of coffee, drifting from the kitchen, finally teased her fully awake. She sniffed, sniffed again and groaned. It was irresistible, and she lifted her head from the pillow, squinting at the bright morning sunshine before she focused on the room and her eyes opened wide in surprise. This wasn't her familiar bedroom in New York, or even her childhood room in Scotland. It was—

Uncle Larry's cottage. Memory came rushing back. She was at Uncle Larry's cottage in the Catskills...in Tyler's room. She collapsed onto the pillow. In Tyler's bed.

And judging from the sounds in the hallway outside, she was about to receive a visitor. Emma stared frantically around the room, but her gown and robe were out of reach on a chair across the room. When the doorknob turned, Emma slithered deeper beneath the covers, pulling them up to her chin.

All Tyler's attention was on the tray he carried. He was dressed, if one could call it that, in his jeans and nothing else, but his hair was wet from a shower and he'd shaved. Emma felt rumpled and groggy by comparison, and very much at a disadvantage without her clothes.

China rattled gently as he brought the tray over and set it on the nightstand. Only then did he shift his attention to Emma.

"Good morning." He smiled, but the expression in his eyes was uncertain, almost shy. He handed her a cup of coffee. "Hope you like strawberry preserves. I couldn't find any of that marmalade you have at home."

"Strawberry is lovely, thank you." She surveyed the toast, jam, coffee and juice he'd brought, and smiled. She could feel him relax when she'd approved the breakfast tray. "This is lovely, but you didn't need to go to all this trouble."

"I wanted to." He bit into a piece of toast. "What do you want to do today?"

She thought about it. "I don't know."

"Do you have any ideas?"

"I hadn't thought about it."

"Okay. Will you trust me to make the plans?"

Emma raised an eyebrow. "Should I?"

"Sure. You'll love it."

"Target shooting?" Emma looked from Tyler to the paper target.

"Sure. I knew this target range was here, and it's good for your competitive instincts."

"But why not tennis or something?"

"Because I thought this would be more equal. Shooting doesn't give an advantage to muscular strength, so it'll be fair for you."

"Oh, I see." Emma lowered her eyes. "That's very thoughtful of you, Tyler," she said, her voice softer than usual.

"Ready?" he asked.

Emma nodded, smiling sweetly.

"Okay. Hold it like this. This is the safety and you release it just before you shoot. Just aim for the target and see how you do. Don't worry about hitting the bull's-eye. Nobody's keeping score."

She nodded. "Okay. I'm ready."

The shooting range provided ear protectors. Emma fitted them over her ears like oversize earmuffs, as did Tyler, then she lifted the pistol he'd brought for her. A .38 Police Special, it fitted her hand well, but it felt odd after the skeet guns she was accustomed to firing. She raised it at arm's length, bracing her right wrist with her left hand, sighted carefully and squeezed the trigger. The gun spat a burst of flame, and Emma lowered it, squinting slightly to see the target.

"Damn!" Tyler muttered.

There was a hole just to the left of the bull's-eye.

"It sights a bit to the left," she said, and lifted the gun again. The second shot entered the bull's-eye. Tyler remained silent, but Emma could see a muscle tense in his jaw. Four more shots and the cylinder was empty.

Without comment Tyler retrieved the paper target and handed it to her, shaking his head. The first shot had been two inches to the left of the bull's-eye while the remaining five were clustered within the red central spot. Emma nodded, then set the target down. "It's not a bad little gun."

Tyler finally spoke. "I know. You're a hustler."

"I beg your pardon?"

Her haughty tone made him smile. "A hustler. You must have seen the movie with Paul Newman and Jackie Gleason."

"Pocket billiards?"

"Pool, actually. The concept is to let the sucker, that's me, believe you're a novice at pool, or in this case, shooting. You get him to make a fat bet and then you clean him out." He nodded toward the gun she was holding with the care of the practiced marksman. "You didn't tell me you could shoot."

"I thought Uncle Larry mentioned it."

"He never said a word."

"Well, I can shoot." Emma smiled, wickedly. "I'd think you'd be pleased that you're going to have some real competition."

"Competition." Tyler smiled back at her, rather like a shark. "Yeah. Tell me, Emma, do you shoot skeet?"

Emma batted her lashes at him. "I have, once or twice."

"Once or twice, huh?" Tyler nodded judiciously. "Well, why don't we go check out the skeet range?"

"I'd be happy to."

Tyler looked up at the clear morning sky and whistled a couple of notes through his teeth. "Care to put a little money on it, say, a dollar a shot?"

Her smiled widened. "I'd say you'd best be prepared to lose a little money."

Chapter 13

That makes—'' Emma added figures on a notepad "—thirty-six dollars.''

"*Thirty-six?* That's impossible.''

"It's right here.'' She showed him the scorecard. "See for yourself.''

He scanned the columns on the pad. It was late afternoon, and they'd returned to the cottage after a day of shooting, with lunch at the shooting range snack bar. The shooting had been challenging and fun. The lunch was best forgotten.

"Hustler was right,'' he said, shaking his head. "How long have you been shooting big game, anyway?''

Emma took a bottle of mineral water from the refrigerator. "Never, actually. Would you prefer soda, mineral water or beer?''

"Beer, thanks. What do you mean never? Don't you hunt in Scotland?''

"I've gone on hunts, but I don't shoot live things. I like target shooting, but the idea of killing a grouse, a rabbit or a deer?" She shook her head. "I couldn't do that."

"What about a man?" Tyler poured his beer into a glass. "What if it was Stefan Alexandru, with a gun pointed at you, and it was you or him?"

Emma hesitated. "I don't know." She studied her mineral water, fizzing gently in the glass. "Does anyone really know how they'd react until they've faced that situation?"

Tyler shook his head. "Not really. You can think about it, but you can't know what it's like until you're there."

"I wouldn't think you could." Emma sipped her water, then looked up at Tyler. "Have you ever... been in that situation?"

His face went still, in the way she was coming to know he used when he wanted to conceal his emotions. Seconds ticked by before he said, "Yes."

She knew he was waiting for her to ask the obvious—who, where, how—but that wasn't what she needed to know. "And was the reality as you had imagined it?" she finally asked.

He looked across at her, his eyes bleak. "No. It was nothing like what I'd imagined."

"I only hope," Emma said after a moment, "that I would have the courage to do the right thing at the right moment."

Tyler reached across to take her hand. "You will."

"You think so?" She squeezed his fingers.

"If I didn't believe you can handle it, I'd pull you out of this thing right now."

"But you can't do that! It's Uncle Larry—"

"Yes, I can. I have veto power over this operation."

"I didn't know that." She pulled her hand away and frowned. "If you can, I'm surprised you haven't already thrown me out."

Tyler was taken aback, but didn't let that show. "I considered it," he drawled. "But since I *didn't* pull you out, don't you think you might owe me something?"

"Such as?" Emma was justifiably wary. Tyler leaned back and folded his arms. It was Emma's bad luck that she couldn't help noticing the way the muscles bunched in his arms and shoulders. "Such as?" she repeated, her voice slightly husky.

"Such as thirty-six bucks?"

Her mouth dropped open, then she threw her napkin at his head. It missed, but she was laughing too hard to care. "Not a chance!" she gasped between giggles. "You made the bet, Tyler Davis, and you'll have to honor it!"

"You're a hard case. Do you know that?"

"The very hardest." She extended her hand, palm up, and wiggled her fingers. "So where's my thirty-six dollars?"

"I'll make a deal with you. It'd cost that much to eat at a restaurant, so how about I make dinner tonight to pay the debt?"

"How about you make dinner tonight and I decide if it's worth the price?"

"Like I said, a tough cookie."

"At the risk of repeating myself, the toughest."

"Not so tough," he said quietly, then pushed back his chair and rose. "Why don't you go sit by the fire while I whip up a gourmet masterpiece?"

"I'll go shower and change," Emma said loftily, "and reserve judgment on the gourmet issue."

"Always a skeptic!" Tyler was already rummaging in the refrigerator as she left the kitchen.

"Well?" he prompted an hour later.

Emma took another bite, ate it slowly, then sipped her wine and tasted her salad again.

"Give me a break here!" Tyler caught her wrist, and a bit of lettuce fell back onto the plate. "Is it gourmet or not?"

"Wel-l-l—"

"Tell me!"

"Yes, then! Yes! It's very good!"

"It took you long enough to decide." He released her hand and took another bite of his own meal.

"I had to be sure. Now I'm sure."

The meal he'd prepared—salad, chicken, rice pilaf and asparagus—was simple enough, but he'd done a bit extra with each item. The chicken had a wine and mushroom sauce, the pilaf was fragrant with herbs, the asparagus dressed with lemon and chopped egg, and the salad had a homemade dressing. It was all delicious.

"I can hardly wait to see what's for dessert."

"It's pretty simple," he warned her.

Though the dessert was simple, it was far from plain. Fruit with kirsch and whipped cream was accompanied by French wafer cookies and dark, dark coffee. They took it into the living room to the sofa in front of the fire.

Emma finished and set her dish aside, then slid down into the cushions, propping her feet on the raised hearth. "That was all absolutely delicious. My compliments to the chef."

"Thanks. Was it worth thirty-six bucks?"

"Undoubtedly." She lay back against the sofa cushions and grinned at Tyler. "I'll forgive the bet, since we both know who's the better target shooter."

"I guess you're going to bring that up every time you can."

"Naturally. I'll take any advantage I can get."

"Not that you need an advantage." Tyler slid lower in the cushions and rested his feet next to hers. "But it's hard to look forward to a future of repeated embarrassment."

"Coward," Emma teased gently. She closed her eyes, wondering about Tyler's choice of words. *A future.* Had he meant that? She wanted him to mean it, with an intensity that surprised her. She wanted a future with Tyler Davis.

She was, she'd come to realize during that day, very close to falling in love with this strong, enigmatic man. The knowledge both thrilled and frightened her. She had no idea what Tyler was feeling. She knew what he thought of her money and her title, and though he knew her better now, she couldn't assume that his fundamental opinions had changed.

Was there really any sort of future for them?

It was odd to think that she'd only met Tyler Davis a few weeks ago. He'd become such a large part of her life that she could scarcely imagine it without him. She hoped he was her friend, she cherished the knowledge that he was her lover, yet what did she really know about him?

She knew almost nothing of his life up to the point when she'd dashed into that airport lounge. She knew he was a man of honor, and a strong yet tender lover. But who was he? She glanced at his face, closed and secretive, hiding his thoughts, then turned away to stare into the fire, wondering why she suddenly felt so alone.

"Emma?" He broke the silence. "You haven't asked about Mina."

"I've been a bit afraid to."

"Afraid of bad news?"

Emma turned to look at him. "A bit afraid. Have you examined the information she gave you?"

"Yeah. That's why we're out here in the woods." He settled back, watching the flames dance.

Emma waited several seconds, then poked him. "Are you going to explain that or not?"

Tyler caught her hand and pulled her over so that she fell across his lap.

"Tyler!" Emma protested. "Let me up!"

"No. You need to relax. Go on, relax." He turned her in his arms so that she lay across his lap, her head resting on his arm and her legs stretched out on the cushions. "There." He ran a hand lightly over her hair. "Comfortable?"

"Yes, thank you. But are you?"

"Oh, yeah." He stretched his legs out again and rested his heels on the hearth. "Now, about Mina."

"Yes, what about Mina?" Emma started to sit up, but he put a hand on her head and pushed her back down. "What about her?"

"If you'll relax for a minute, I'll tell you." He took his hand off her head, but kept it ready. "You going to stay put?"

With an exasperated sigh, Emma folded her arms across her chest and lay still. "Yes, all right. Just tell me about Mina!"

"Okay. We went through all the information she gave us, with the proverbial fine-toothed comb, not to mention cryptographers and microscopes and X rays. As she said, there were microdots with maps on them and information encoded in the text. We ran everything through the State Department, military and intelligence computers and gave it to the experts to verify. It's taken time, but it's been done."

"And?" Emma stiffened in his arms, and Tyler covered her hand with his.

"And it looks really good."

"You verified it all?"

"Everything we could. Some of the information was new to us, and if it's true, it's valuable stuff."

"Do you think it's true?"

He nodded slowly. "Yes, I think it's true, certainly to the extent that Mina's been given accurate information."

"And...do you believe Mina now?"

After a moment of consideration, he nodded. "I believe her, and I'll do everything I can to see that she defects safely."

Emma's eyes widened in the moment before she threw her arms around his neck and reached up to kiss him in relief and gratitude.

His mouth tasted of coffee and kirsch and strawberries, and the passion caught like fire in dry leaves, racing through them both. Emma arched her back, straining toward Tyler as he wrapped her in his arms.

This was dark and deep and dangerous, like summer storms on sultry nights, and Emma fancied she could hear thunder off in the distance. The air in the room was heavy and close with unspent tension as Tyler twisted, lifting his legs onto the sofa to tangle with hers. Lightning seemed to crackle around them, sparking where their bodies touched.

He twisted again, turning her beneath him, pressing her into the soft cushions. The barrier of clothing was still between them, and Emma gripped his shirt in her fists, jerking it free of his waistband to slip her hands beneath and find his skin, hot and smooth and firm.

Muscles flexed beneath her fingers, and he brought one hand between them, seeking her buttons. The first finally came free, and he fumbled for the second. Emma stroked her hands down the length of his spine and dipped her fingertips inside the waistband of his jeans. The thunder rumbled closer, and Tyler jerked at her blouse. He muttered against her mouth as a button popped off and slid across the floor.

He pushed the fabric aside and slipped his hand against her skin, seeking her warmth. Another button popped free, then a third, and he jerked the blouse open and impatiently tugged up the hem of her silk camisole. He pulled it over her head, along with her blouse, and levered himself away long enough to strip off his own shirt, then came back to her, filling his hands with her breasts.

"Do you know how many times today I thought of seeing you like this?" His voice was rough in her ear, his face, with the day's growth of beard, rough against her face. "Do you know how hard it was to look at you and not touch?"

Emma heard the thunder drawing closer, felt the lightning flickering around her. She had looked at him, too, remembering the strong, lean body under the clothing, knowing it was but a matter of time until she was in his arms again.

"I know." Her whisper was ragged with need.

He took her mouth again, sliding his hand over her breasts and ribs to her waistband. The lightning crackled again, electric discharges in the waiting air, sparks of sensation running from her breasts to her center, from his touch to her veins. Suddenly his touch was everywhere—hands, lips, body—driving her on into the dark, swirling center of the storm.

It was all around her, within her, thunder building, wind swirling, carrying her whispered, formless pleas. She thought she'd known passion last night, but this was more. This was desperation as somehow, clumsy in their haste, they stripped off their remaining garments and came together.

The thunder rolled and crashed, the wind howled, and Emma clung desperately to Tyler, dizzy and blind as the tension built and built until she was swept into the heart of the storm.

Aeons later she drifted slowly back to earth, to the cottage in the woods, to the sofa in front of the dying fire. As she floated toward sleep she was dimly aware of Tyler settling her comfortably in his arms and pulling an afghan up to cover them both. Tomorrow would bring questions and planning and the possibility of danger, but for the night, at least, she was safe in Tyler's arms. She needed nothing more but the renewal of sleep.

The last thing she knew was his quiet murmur against her hair, "Good night, my love."

"How will we do it?"

Tyler glanced at her, then turned his attention back to driving, for they were nearing Emma's apartment.

Emma had enjoyed the three-hour drive, but she would have enjoyed anything that allowed her to spend time alone with Tyler. About the time they crossed the Tappan Zee Bridge, Tyler had reached over and taken her hand in his, resting it on his thigh and covering it with his own. Though he'd had to put both hands on the wheel when they got into city traffic, hers still rested lightly on his thigh, moving with the flexing of his muscles when he braked or shifted gears.

"All *you* have to do," he replied, "is arrange for Mina to go to Chicago. Then the professionals will take over."

Emma refrained from comment. She would deal with Tyler's overprotectiveness when the time came. "How am I to get her there? And why Chicago in the first place?"

Tyler glanced at her. Emma knew he was wondering why she'd given in so quickly, but he didn't follow it up. "You have a branch office there. We've decided it might be easier to get her away if she's out of Washington. D.C. is familiar territory for them, and all their people are here. They'll be off their home turf in Chicago, and it'll be easier to identify the undercover people they might send with her."

"How is that?"

"We watch people getting off planes. We watch people watching Mina. We look for anything unusual."

"And once she's in Chicago? What happens then?"

He passed a delivery truck and smoothly slid into the right lane in time to turn. "That still has to be worked out. We have a safe house for her, and people to work on her political asylum, but the details of the actual escape will depend on the reason you give her going to the Midwest."

"Then I'd best think of a good reason."

"Thinking of it soon would be good, too."

"Very well." She subsided into thought, looking out the window at the passing buildings without seeing them.

"Hey." Tyler patted her hand, startling her out of her reverie. "We'll figure it out. I didn't mean for you to go into a blue funk over it."

"Go into a brown study over it," Emma corrected absentmindedly.

"Brown study." Tyler grinned. "That's a good name for it. Either way I wouldn't want you to feel bad."

"You wouldn't?" She softened the question with a teasing grin, and he grinned back.

"Nah. You're pretty impressive for an earl's daughter."

Emma shook her head. "You won't give that up, will you?"

"The life-styles of the rich and aristocratic hold an endless fascination for us ordinary Americans."

"I've come to the conclusion that there's very little that's ordinary about Americans. That's one of the things I like about living and working here."

"It is, huh?"

"Yes. You can't assume someone's status or success by their accent or where they came from. A millionaire can come from poverty and no one sneers at him for his background."

Tyler only grunted, then slowed for a light. It changed and he accelerated through the intersection.

"Tyler, I've talked about myself until you must be bored to tears."

He shook his head with a soft chuckle.

"But," she said with just a hint of shyness, "what about you? I don't know anything about your family or anything."

"Nothing to say." The terse answer was paired with the closed-in expression that concealed his thoughts.

"Where are your family now?"

"I don't have any family."

"No brothers or sisters?"

"No."

"What about your parents?"

"My mother's dead."

His reluctance to answer was obvious, but it increased her curiosity. She cared for him, she was interested in him, and after the intimacy they'd shared over the weekend, she felt entitled to ask. "Well," she asked, "where did you grow up?"

"In a town."

"But what town? Where?"

"What the hell difference does it make!" he snapped. "It was a little town, just like a million other little towns. And what's with this damn inquisition, anyway?"

Emma stiffened. "Asking where you grew up is an inquisition?"

"All these damn questions are!"

"I'm sorry if it seems that way, but, Tyler, I'm interested in you. I don't see any reason to apologize for that."

He scowled blackly at the road ahead. "What difference does it make where I grew up? I'm not some English lord or something, and I know you're probably not used to bums like me. You're probably already regretting what happened. Well, let me tell you, lady, you don't regret it any more than I do!"

He yanked the car into her parking space with a squeal of protest from the tires, jerked to a stop and slammed open his door. "Well?" he demanded, and bent to look in at Emma, sitting in the passenger seat with her mouth open in shock. "Are you coming, or are you just going to sit there."

Before she could answer he was striding into the building, carrying her suitcase.

Chapter 14

Emma followed more slowly as Tyler stalked inside. By the time she reached the lobby, he was already on his way up in the private elevator, leaving her to wait until it came down again. He also left her with a bit of time to think, and her thoughts weren't happy ones.

Regret, he'd said, but she hadn't regretted a thing, not one moment, until Tyler had said those unbelievable things. Now she wasn't so sure.

The bitterness that had come spilling out with his accusations was deep and poisonous. He hadn't told her where the bitterness came from, but it had to have something to do with his past. She'd been disappointed in men before, but the sense of betrayal this time was overwhelming.

She knew what it was like to be desired for her money or her title, what it was like to be pursued by a scalp collector. In America they were one of two types. Men who'd grown up wealthy, but who still felt inferior in some way, pursued her because of her title; they seemed to feel they gained status by trying to seduce her. The other scalp hunters were men who'd grown up poor and wanted to conquer a woman of wealth or title, just to be able to say they had.

Either way they were using her to feed their own shaky egos. The bell pinged, the elevator started back down to her, and Emma shook her head. She could usually spot the scalp hunters straight away, but she'd thought Tyler was different.

He'd been quite blunt about his opinion of her money and title and hadn't tried to get close to her. Then she'd believed that he was coming to know and care for Emma herself. She'd believed that he was different, but had she been wrong?

He'd gotten past her defenses, under her skin...and into her heart.

Emma bit her lip against the tears that stung her eyelids as the elevator doors slid open. She stepped inside, and by the time the doors opened again, her eyes were clear and her chin high. Her entry hall was empty, with her suitcase standing by the door. Emma walked past it into the kitchen and began filling the teakettle.

"I've checked the apartment," Tyler said from the doorway behind her. "It hasn't been disturbed."

Emma nodded and took the tea canister down from the shelf.

"Will you be okay?"

She nodded.

He started to move away, then paused and sighed. "I don't like leaving you."

Emma put the canister down with a bang. "I can't imagine why not." She worked at keeping her voice cool and clipped. "You've made it quite clear that you don't want to stay. Go on, Tyler." She turned her back. "Only the private lift serves this floor, and Mr. Koback looks out for me."

"Ah, yes, the doorman," Tyler said dryly. "He must be at least eighty, Emma. He'd be a swell defense against a gang of well-armed thugs!"

"Right." Emma stalked to the front door and threw it open, revealing the elevator landing with its Oriental rug, small console table and gilt-framed mirror. The elevator car was there, open and waiting.

"See for yourself, Tyler. No thugs. Not even a badly behaved boy with a slingshot and a pocketful of rocks." She stood in the doorway, waiting for him to leave. "Go home, Tyler. I'm tired. I want a cup of tea and a good night's sleep. Go home."

"Home. Right." He brushed past her, stepped into the elevator, then paused and turned back. "Lock up."

"I always do."

Tyler looked at her searchingly for a moment, then nodded and pushed the button. The doors slid together, hiding him from view, and Emma closed her front door. She locked it and leaned her forehead against the cool wood, only pushing herself away when the teakettle began whistling frantically in the kitchen.

Her taste for a cup of tea seemed to have disappeared, so she switched off the flame, then stood uncertainly in the middle of the kitchen. She was too agitated to sleep. Crying might have helped, but her eyes were aching and dry. She drummed her fingers on the tabletop and felt the pressure of emotions bottled up inside her. If she didn't *do* something, she would explode.

With jerky movements she stripped off her jacket and sweater and tossed them onto a chair, then rolled up her sleeves. She turned on the water in the sink, added dishwashing soap and began taking her grandmother's bone china tea service out of the Welsh cupboard against the wall.

The next day dawned gray and chilly, and by late afternoon a cold rain was slanting from heavy clouds, carried on a cutting northeast wind. It spattered against Emma's office window—a perfect match for her gloomy mood.

She glanced at her watch. It was after six, with evening drawing in, and she wanted nothing but a comforting cup of tea and an early bedtime. She couldn't go home just yet, though. Uncle Larry and Tyler were coming to her office at six-thirty to begin planning for Mina's defection. Emma wished she felt alert and ready for them instead of tired and jaded.

"Miss Campbell?" Her secretary looked in the office door. "Will there be anything else?"

"Not tonight. Thank you."

"Good night, then." With a smile the secretary closed the door behind her.

Emma's smile faded and she leaned her elbows on the desk, propping her head in her hands to massage the nagging ache at her temples. She should expect to have a headache after spending half the night washing dishes.

It had been long after midnight when she'd finished her orgy of cleaning and had gone to bed, exhausted. She'd drifted into an uneasy sleep that had left her groggy with the aftermath of nightmares. Despite strong tea, a stinging shower and aspirin, she'd been tired and headachy all day.

Fatigue and a headache were minor annoyances, though, compared to the bottomless aching well of hurt. She'd given Tyler her trust, and he'd thrown it back in her face. The pain was so raw and new that she couldn't yet confront it, but could only use a mask of composure and wait until the hurt eased enough to be faced.

She'd dealt with a day filled with clients and problems and telephone calls, but she didn't think she could cope with Tyler.

Perhaps a cup of tea. She was in the outer office, pouring boiling water into the pot when she heard men's voices in the hallway and sighed. So much for tea and a few minutes of solitude. She set cups and spoons and a packet of tea biscuits on the tray, then went to admit Tyler and Uncle Larry.

With her best deportment-class manner, politely controlled, and very, very cool, she opened the door.

"I still say we do it straight. The less civilian involvement there is, the better." Tyler had his back to her, but Uncle Larry smiled at her over Tyler's shoulder as he replied.

"This isn't a textbook situation, Tyler. Unusual situations call for unusual solutions. Hello, Emma."

Tyler whirled around, eyes narrowed, jaw tight.

"Shall I assume that means I'm an unusual solution?" Emma wondered aloud. Her smile didn't reach her eyes.

"In a word," said Lord Latham. "How are you, my dear?" He walked into the office and gave Emma a hug, then stepped back and held her at arm's length, studying her face and frowning. "Are you well, Emma? You look pale."

"I'm fine." She turned away to pick up the tea tray. "I just have a bit of a headache. Probably the weather." She carried the tray into her office and poured for everyone before she took her chair, barricading herself behind her desk.

The men sat opposite her, and Uncle Larry took out a notepad and fountain pen.

"Well," she asked, looking at them, "where do we start?"

Tyler leaned back in his chair. "At the beginning."

"Which is?" Emma was in no mood to appreciate the sarcasm.

"Mina is the beginning," he explained with exaggerated patience. "How do we get her to Chicago?"

"Is it truly necessary to take her there? It seems that it would be easier for me to go to Washington."

"It would be easy enough if that's all you're interested in," Tyler told her, sarcastically. "But it would be far more difficult to get Mina away safely."

Tyler felt a pang of shame when she stiffened at his words. He was being boorish and rude, but that ice maiden manner of hers got on his nerves.

He could barely recognize the Emma who'd lain in his arms, passionate and loving and generous. This Emma was a cool, disdainful aristocrat with centuries of breeding in her fine-boned face, centuries of wealth and privilege in her clipped, accented voice. This woman wouldn't share raccoons in the moonlight with him, for she'd grown up in a castle with a nanny to take care of her, accustomed to diamonds and French champagne and antique rugs.

She wouldn't even want to know a bum like him, someone who'd grown up in a series of squalid trailers and rented rooms, wearing charity clothes from the Salvation Army store. He'd gone to school on breakfasts of stale beer and potato chips and hadn't owned a brand-new pair of shoes until the navy had issued them to him.

His mother had done the best she could, but she'd been sixteen, pregnant and unwed when her father had thrown her out. The only jobs she could find were waitressing in truck stops and little cafés, and she'd worked hard to care for her son the only way she knew how.

She'd done her best for him, but the hard life they'd lived had robbed him of his childhood.

When she'd died the doctors had talked about heart failure and valves, but he was still convinced that she'd died, quite simply, of overwork. How could Lady Emma understand his childhood? The two of them had nothing, *nothing* in common.

He'd wanted to convince himself that she wasn't like the rich girls he'd grown up with who'd seen him as the boy from the wrong side of the tracks, dangerous and attractive. They'd alternately despised him and come on to him as if he were a sort of sexual trophy.

Being despised was no problem, for he didn't care if they looked down on him, but being used had been harder to deal with. He'd been taken in when one of the golden girls had tried to seduce him, because he'd wanted so badly to believe that she cared. He'd learned the truth later. They'd had

a bet on it. He had never let them know what he'd over-
heard, but after that he'd never allowed anyone within his
defenses again.

Until Emma. He'd wanted nothing to do with a woman
who was not only rich but titled, as well. However, things
had changed, for she hadn't been what he'd expected.

She wasn't a shallow, overprivileged dilettante, but gentle,
compassionate, hardworking and intelligent. She was
beautiful, dressed in silk or in denim, she smelled of summer flowers and her kisses set him afire. Just remembering
those kisses was enough to start a slow flame.

"Tyler?" Lord Latham asked, regarding him quizzically.

He dragged his attention back to the business at hand.
"What did you say?"

"You were miles away."

"Just thinking. What was the question?"

"It's not a question," Emma told him. "I have a way to
get Mina and myself to Chicago."

"How?"

"Tractors."

There was a moment of utter silence. "Tractors?"

"Tractors," Emma repeated.

"That's the most ridiculous thing I've ever heard!" He
turned to Lord Latham, laughing. "Tractors?"

Lord Latham sat back and folded his arms. "I've been
subjected to far too many ridiculous ideas in my lifetime,
Tyler. This isn't one of them. Emma, would you explain it
to him?"

"You have an explanation for tractors?" Tyler knew he
sounded like a bad-tempered adolescent, but he couldn't
seem to stop himself. Emma's lady-of-the-manor composure was bringing out the worst in him. "By all means, go
ahead."

"Part of this loan we've been negotiating is for agricultural equipment—tractors, combines, seed drills and

things—for collective farms." Emma's lips curved into a small smile. "There's a farm equipment show in Chicago in two weeks. She can go for that."

"Won't the secret police be a little suspicious of going all the way to Chicago just for some farm equipment show?"

"It's the biggest farm exhibition in the western hemisphere. Exhibitors come from all over the world, and people attend from all over the hemisphere, even South America."

"For tractors?" He frowned. "Where do they hold this bash?"

"McCormick Place." She kept any hint of smugness out of her voice as she named Chicago's enormous convention center.

Tyler sat back, feeling the sarcastic retorts seeping out of him like air from a leaking balloon. "McCormick Place." His brain was beginning to work now that he'd pushed his emotions out of the way. "It's that big?"

"Very big," she agreed.

"Lots of people wandering around?"

"Mobs."

"Hot dog stands, free souvenirs and radio deejays?"

"That's only the beginning. There will be television coverage, music and dancers, pretty girls driving the tractors, balloons and T-shirts and hats to give away."

"I see." He sat back, tenting his fingers beneath his chin, his expression thoughtful. "Lots of noise and confusion, lots of people milling around and a good reason for her to come." He nodded slowly. "It could work."

Emma was unable to completely suppress a small smile of satisfaction. "I'll plan a busy trip for Mina. Arrange a tour of a tractor factory, maybe some equipment demonstrations.

"I like it," Lord Latham said. "It provides a solid reason for the trip, and with the tours and demonstrations and such, she can plan to stay for several days, thus giving us a larger window of opportunity. However," he said, leaning forward, his smile fading, "that brings us to the more difficult problem of how to get Mina away from her guards."

"Do you have any ideas?" Emma asked.

"I've discussed a few with Tyler, and I'll leave him to tell you. I have a dinner appointment. Tyler, you'll see Emma home?"

Tyler glanced up. "Of course."

"That's not really necessary—" Emma began, but Lord Latham shook his head.

"It's dark, it's raining and I'll feel better knowing you aren't going home alone."

"You needn't baby me, Uncle Larry."

"I'm concerned about you. Let Tyler take you home, won't you?"

"Very well," she said, giving in with a resigned smile.

"Thank you, dear." He turned to Tyler. "I'll see you tomorrow."

"Yes, sir." The men shook hands, then Emma walked Lord Latham to the door. She looked back to make sure Tyler couldn't hear her before she said softly, "Thank you for not laughing at my idea, Uncle Larry."

"There was nothing to laugh at, my dear. It's an excellent idea." He glanced back at Tyler, scribbling notes on a pad. "I noticed that something seems to be bothering Tyler."

Emma shrugged. "We've had a disagreement."

Lord Latham waited, then sighed when she said no more. "Well, don't worry about it, my dear. He'll come round."

"But come round to what?" Emma asked rhetorically. "Never mind. I hope your appointment goes well."

"So do I." He patted her cheek. "Good evening, Emma."

"Goodbye."

She watched him enter the elevator, then returned to her office. She didn't sit down, but gathered papers in to her briefcase. "Could we finish this meeting somewhere else?"

"Why? Is something wrong?"

"Nothing except that they turn the heat down at night and I don't fancy freezing."

"Oh. Well, you want to go to your place?"

She looked at him with honest gratitude. "I'd prefer it. Shall we go?"

"Sure. Just let me make a phone call, okay?"

"Of course."

She went into the other office to give him privacy, and had her coat on when he joined her. The short cab ride was made in silence, each absorbed in their own thoughts. Emma walked into the lobby while Tyler paid the cabbie.

"Miss Campbell, good evening!" Mr. Koback greeted her happily. "This gentleman has a delivery for you."

"A delivery?" Behind the doorman was a young man wearing a baseball cap and holding a large paper bag. "I didn't order anything."

"I did," Tyler said from behind her. "Thanks, pal." He paid the delivery boy, took the bag and caught Emma's elbow to pull her toward the elevator. "Come on, Emma. We've got to eat this before it gets cold."

"Eat what?" Emma asked as he shoved her into the elevator.

"This." He punched the button, then tapped the bag.

"I figured that out, but what *is* it?"

"Dinner," he said smugly.

"But why was the delivery boy already here?"

"I called from the office and told him to meet us here. I'm hungry, and even if you're not, you should be." Upstairs, on her landing, he stepped out and waited while she unlocked the door and swung it wide.

"Where would you like to eat?"

"The kitchen," she replied. "I'll make some tea."

"Sure you don't want to eat in the dining room like you rich girls usually do?"

"The kitchen's fine."

"Okay. I guess you rich girls always get your way."

"I wish you would stop this bloody nonsense!" Emma banged plates onto the table. "Just what is it about *rich girls* that bothers you so much?"

He slapped the container of soup onto the table, spilling a few drops. "You really want to know?"

"Yes, I do! I want to know what it is that makes you behave like a twit!"

"Twit?" Tyler repeated with a sneer. "I suppose that's the best insult someone like you can come up with."

Emma stiffened. "Oh, I haven't even tried to insult you yet. And believe me, when I do, you'll know it!"

"I'm shaking in my boots," he retorted. "And as for why I don't like rich girls, that's easy enough to figure out. I don't like anybody who grew up spoiled, who thinks the world owes them something just because of who and what they are. I don't like girls who think they're better than everyone else, just because they happen to have been born to money. I don't like snobs and I don't like users." He stopped and deliberately lowered his voice to a conversational level. "And I don't like being used."

Emma was silent for a long moment. "Someone must have hurt you very badly," she said at last. She sat down, took a plate and spooned some almond chicken onto it.

"That's old news." He sat down and opened a carton of fried rice. "It's the lesson I learned that matters."

Emma shook her head. "I don't think so. The hurt is still there."

"I'm not a kid anymore, Emma. I survived all those childhood traumas the shrinks talk about and I grew up."

"Inside each of us is the child we once were, with all the hurts and fears of childhood. We never get rid of those. We just learn to deal with them."

"What do you have to deal with?" he scoffed. "You had everything right from the start."

"I suppose that depends on how you define 'everything.' I had a comfortable life and the love of my family. But there is disillusionment waiting for everyone."

"Yeah, right."

"For me," she said, as if he hadn't spoken, "it was discovering that many of the people I meet only see my title or my family's money. Some of them like me for the money or the title, and some of them, out of jealousy or prejudice, dislike me for the same reasons. And if I'm very lucky, there are a few people who have the perception to see me for myself. They become my friends." She looked across the table at him, her eyes weary and a little sad.

"You know, I had begun to think you were different. I thought, or hoped, that you were one of the perceptive ones. I guess I was wrong." She pushed away the plateful of food she'd scarcely touched. "I'm not hungry." She got up and walked out of the room.

Tyler sat there for some time, alone with unpleasant thoughts and the beginnings of doubt. Emma was gone for twenty minutes, and when she returned, Tyler was standing at the sink, washing the few dishes they'd used.

He glanced around at the sound of the door opening and saw that Emma had changed into a pale pink sweat suit with thick socks in place of slippers. Her hair was loose around her shoulders, and she was beautiful. When he realized he was staring, he jerked his gaze back to the dishwater.

"Are you okay?" he asked roughly.

She turned away to take the teakettle from the stove. "Of course. Disillusionment never killed anyone."

That stung, but Tyler was damned if he would let her see that it did. "I suppose not." He put the last plate in the draining rack and dried his hands. "Are you ready to talk about getting Mina away from her guards?"

Emma dropped into a chair at the table. "The sooner we start, the sooner we'll be finished."

And the sooner you can go home.

Tyler understood the unspoken message, and his lips tightened. "All right," he said. "Let's get to it."

Chapter 15

I want to do a switch. Mina has to physically get away from whoever's guarding her for long enough to request asylum."

"How does this 'switch' happen?"

"The best way would be to have a substitute take Mina's place. The longer the substitute can maintain the charade, the more time Mina has to get away to a safe house."

"I see." Emma thought about it. "Then I'll be the substitute."

Tyler jerked his head up. "No, you won't."

"Why not?"

"Because there's no way you're going to be involved in something like that. We'll find a female agent to do it."

"That's completely unnecessary. In case you've forgotten, I'm already involved. And if you look at me, you'll see our faces are the same shape, Mina and I are the same height and the same general build."

"The same build?" He looked her skeptically up and down.

"Yes, Mina's curvier than I am," Emma admitted, "but clothes can disguise that. With a wig and makeup I could pass for her at a short distance."

"It's ridiculous. You're an amateur."

"I'm an amateur who arrived at the airport in disguise a few weeks ago. I've been thrust into a totally unexpected situation, and I've managed to deal with it, Tyler. And might I remind you that this amateur can outshoot you three times out of four?"

For a moment she thought he might actually laugh. He controlled it, though there was a gleam of amusement in his eyes. "That's a low blow, Emma."

"So are most of your opinions about me, if you must know. They're hurtful and unfair." She sighed tiredly. "I don't want to fight with you, Tyler, but I'm going to tell Uncle Larry I want to do this. I think he'll agree."

Tyler shook his head. "He probably will, and I can't figure that out. He loves you, yet he let you get involved in this."

"If I shouldn't be involved, who should? Mina came to me for help, and I *will* help her. I'm all grown up, Tyler, and I'll take responsibility for my choices."

"Yeah, I guess you will. There doesn't seem to be anything I can do about it, but at least you know where I stand."

"Yes, and you know where I stand." She pushed her chair back from the table. "If that's everything we need to talk about I'll contact Mina."

It was a clear dismissal, but Tyler didn't take the hint. He leaned back in his chair, his face thoughtful, considering a question he had to ask. Perhaps the answer would solve the puzzle that was Emma Campbell. "There's something I've been wondering about," he said.

Emma walked to the sink. "What's that?" Though her words were polite, her tone was cool.

"On the way back from the cabin, why did you ask about my family and childhood? What did you want to know?"

"Does the reason really matter? You made it obvious that you took exception to my asking."

Tyler sighed heavily. "I thought I knew what you wanted, but . . . maybe I was wrong."

Emma looked over her shoulder. She let one eloquently raised eyebrow speak for her, and Tyler shifted in his chair.

"Okay," he said. "I was wrong. Why did you ask those questions?"

"Why *not* ask?" she demanded. "After what happened . . . between us . . ." She turned away, blushing.

"After we'd made love."

"Yes," she agreed without looking at him. "We'd shared so much that I wanted to know something about you. Just as a way of being closer to you. I was interested, that's all."

Tyler sat in silence for a long time. "I was born in Virginia," he said abruptly, "in a little town between Culpeper and Charlottesville. That's on the edge of the Blue Ridge Mountains. Pretty country. It was a country town, the kind of place where gossip's a way of life." He paused, gazing at the tabletop while Emma sank quietly into a chair.

"My mother wasn't married. She was sixteen when she 'got in trouble,' as they say, and her father threw her out of the house. I don't know how she managed to survive until I was born. Maybe she went to one of those homes for unwed mothers. My first memories are from when I was four or five. I remember her going off to work. She waited tables."

He glanced at Emma, then looked away again. "With a tenth-grade education that was about the only thing she was qualified for. She worked at truck stops, little greasy spoon cafés and for a while at a grill in a drugstore. Fancy restaurants wouldn't hire her because she was an unmarried woman with an illegitimate kid. It was hard work and she didn't earn much. Truckers and coffee shop patrons aren't big tippers." He smiled to himself with a trace of bitterness.

"She worked the three-to-eleven shift when she could, because dinnertime tips were bigger than breakfast tips. I'd fix her some supper when she got home. It was usually a baloney sandwich or canned spaghetti, but she'd try to eat it, even when she was almost too tired to chew." He looked up at Emma, with something in his face that was almost a challenge. "She took good care of me. She did the best she could."

"I'm sure she did. You obviously love her."

"Loved her. She died when I was seventeen."

"I'm sorry."

"So was I. The doctors told me some mumbo-jumbo about heart failure, but I've always thought it was nothing more than overwork that killed her."

"You said you were only seventeen. What happened to you?"

"I packed everything I wanted in a knapsack, told Goodwill to take the rest and hitchhiked to Newport News. I lied about my age and joined the navy."

Emma could read between the lines of his terse narrative. There was a great deal he hadn't said about his position in a small town. As the illegitimate son of an unwed mother, his life would have been difficult at best.

"It must have been hard for you."

Tyler looked at her sharply, suspiciously, but there was no pity in her face.

"I had a mother who loved me. Lots of kids don't have that much."

"Thank you for telling me." All he'd said, and the things he hadn't said, explained so much. "I know it wasn't easy."

He studied her face for twenty full seconds. "You don't care? You're not disgusted by all that?"

"Of course not! Where you were born and how you grew up make no difference, except that they contributed to making you the man you grew up to be."

He got to his feet and walked across to the window to push the muslin curtain aside and look down at the street. His voice was muffled when he said, "You make me ashamed."

"No." Emma walked over to him and lifted her hand, but stopped short of touching him. "Don't feel that way. I've been trying to tell you ever since we met that it's not who we were born that matters. It's who we've become." She did touch his shoulder then, and he turned to her.

He brushed his fingertips over her cheek, then slid his hand beneath her hair to draw her close, lifting her face to his to kiss her tenderly, almost reverently, with gratitude and a bottomless sweetness.

Almost, Emma thought, with love. She returned the kiss with compassion, understanding and with all the love that was within her, winding her arms around his waist, holding him as tightly as he held her.

When Tyler broke the kiss, he framed Emma's face in his hands, gazing down at her in wonder. "I want you."

"I know." Emma's voice was soft and shaky.

He drew the ball of his thumb across her lips. "I want you, but I'll go if you ask me to."

Emma shook her head, sliding her hands up to wind her arms around his neck. "No," she whispered. "I don't want you to go."

Tyler caught his breath, then bent swiftly to scoop Emma into his arms. She gasped as her feet left the floor, then hung on tight while he strode down the hall to her bedroom, shouldered the door open and carried her in. He lowered her feet to the bedside rug and bent to kiss her again.

The passion rocketed through her, sweeping away everything but the moment, and Tyler. There was no world outside the room—no spies or defectors or international politics. There was only the room, and the bed, and their burning need.

Emma was pulling at his shirt even while their mouths were still locked together, and Tyler was busy stripping off her clothing, until they were both nude and the carpet littered with discarded garments.

He eased her back onto the bed, covering her body with his, pressing her into the mattress as he kissed and caressed her with feverish intensity. Emma was as frantic as he, pressing kisses to his heated skin wherever she could, running her hands over his body, desperate to memorize each muscle and sinew.

She was dizzy and hot, burning with the need that only he could ease. She whispered wordless pleas against his skin, clutched at him with desperate hands and gasped aloud when he joined their bodies.

He took her in a burst of sensation that built and grew in an ever-quickening rhythm until Emma thought she might die from the tension. She raked his back with her fingernails, held him with fevered limbs, going higher and higher until she cried out and the world burst apart into a storm of light and heat and pleasure.

She came slowly back to awareness, reluctant to leave that far plateau of fulfillment. She snuggled against Tyler when he drew the sheet and blanket up to cover them, tucking her head beneath his chin and rubbing her cheek against the crisp hair on his chest as she slid toward sleep.

"Hey." Tyler rubbed a hand over her back.

"Mmm?" Emma stretched luxuriously.

"You asleep?"

She chuckled under her breath. "Just about."

"Yeah." He stroked her back again, and she arched in pleasure. "Do you think you could stay awake for a few minutes?"

"It'll be tough." She turned her head to kiss his shoulder. "What is it?"

He let his head fall back so that he was looking up at the ceiling. "What was it like," he asked softly, "growing up part of the landed aristocracy."

"What?" Emma was much more awake than before.

"This room. It's so different from what I knew. I just wondered. Your family, for instance." He indicated a photo on the nightstand, Emma with her parents and brother, taken when she was in her late teens. "What are they like?"

"Just parents. My father always indulged me a little more than Mama did, but I guess all fathers do that. They were proud of me when I did well in school and they punished me when I misbehaved." He could feel her grin against his shoulder. "I'm afraid I was punished rather frequently."

"You must have been congratulated on your grades, too. Otherwise you wouldn't have done so well in college."

"Mr. Murdock, the dominie, saw to—"

"The what?"

"Dominie. It's a Scottish word for a schoolmaster. Mr. Murdock saw to it that I did well in school. We used to think he had eyes in the back of his head."

"So did Miss Krueger. She was my fourth-grade teacher. Do you suppose they issue those extra eyes at teachers' college?"

"Doubtless they do." She chuckled.

"Okay, I know that you got into scrapes and that you got good grades in spite of yourself. What was your childhood like? What did you do outside of school?"

"Drew and I went exploring. We'd go down to the loch and fish—not that we ever caught anything. Or we'd go over the hills, walking or riding ponies. One time we rode too far and got caught when the mist came down. We spent the night in an abandoned croft, scared to death because we thought it was haunted. He was twelve and I was nine, and we were so terrified that we were actually glad to see Father the next morning, despite the punishment he was planning."

As Emma described her early life, in bits and snatches and little anecdotes, he developed a picture of a happy childhood, spent mostly in Scotland, running through the hills, playing in the sheep pens. She told him about her years at the village school there and about the London boarding school where she'd met Mina. She told him about coming to America for college, the culture shock and the gradual process of coming to love living in the U.S.

Underlying it all was the thread of stability provided by her loving parents, who were careful not to allow their titled children to become spoiled or arrogant, careful to instill in them a sense of responsibility to balance the wealth and position they would someday have to manage.

"That was the most important thing," Emma murmured sleepily. "Knowing my parents loved me. The rest of it—the money and title and everything—was incidental. The most important thing has always been that my parents love me, no matter what."

Tyler nuzzled her hair. "You're right. That's the most important thing."

"Mmm."

She was drifting toward an exhausted sleep, and Tyler shifted her into a more comfortable position against his side. "Go to sleep, Emma."

"Mmm." He listened as her breathing slowed and deepened, lost in thought.

She was right. Love was the most valuable thing a parent could give to a child, far more important than money or things. He might not have had much in a monetary sense, but he had always known that his mother loved him. There must have been "rich kids" in his town who didn't know that kind of sure parental love. He should feel sorry for them, for without that love he would have been utterly lost. He should thank Emma for reminding him.

He shifted position, and Emma murmured his name.

He looked down at her. "Yeah?"

"I love you," she whispered, turning her cheek into his shoulder. And just that quickly she fell asleep.

Tyler lay very still, holding her, wondering why she'd said that. Did she think she was in love with him because they'd made love? Or had she realized that he was in love with her? He'd known he loved her when he'd kissed her on that damn rock and nearly dropped her in the pond, but he'd thought he'd managed to conceal it. For her sake he had to.

She deserved better than him. He couldn't offer her a stable life with a husband who was there when she needed him. He might be called away at any time to some political crisis-in-the-making. He might be gone for hours, or weeks, and there was always the possibility that he might never come back at all. Even if the difference in their relative wealth didn't matter, that was no life to offer her.

He turned his face against her hair and breathed her light floral perfume. For the rest of his life he'd know that scent. His mouth twisted bitterly. Though he was going to walk out of her life as soon as Mina was safe, he knew that whenever he smelled that fragrance, wherever he was, he would remember how it had been to hold Emma, kiss her, love her.

It was nearly dawn when he fell asleep, and he felt as if he'd barely dropped off when the sound of the doorbell woke him. Beside him Emma stirred and mumbled, and the doorbell stopped, to be replaced by the hammering of a fist on the door.

"I don' want— What?" Emma came awake with a start, blinking owlishly at him. "What's that?"

"Somebody at your door." She was irresistible with her hair tousled and her cheeks flushed with sleep. "Are you expecting anyone?"

"No." The pounding continued unabated. "But somebody's obviously here. I'd better go before they wake the whole building."

"No!" Tyler rolled out of bed, grabbing his slacks off the floor and hauling them on. "It's too early for a casual caller. I'll answer it just in case."

"In case of what?" Emma yanked a robe out of the closet and looked around to see him taking a snub-nosed revolver out of a holster inside his suit jacket. He tucked it into the back of his waistband as Emma stuck her arms into the robe's sleeves.

"In case there's somebody at the door you don't want to see."

"Such as whom? A vacuum salesman?" Emma followed him down the hall, holding her robe closed, the silk billowing behind her.

"More like an acquaintance of Mina's. Not the friendly kind."

Emma's eyes widened. "Would they really come here?"

Tyler stepped into the front hall and waved her back. "It's always a possibility," he said sotto voce. "Get out of sight!"

Emma peered around the living room doorframe as Tyler walked to the front door. He undid the locks and swung the door open to reveal a tall red-haired man of about thirty. The initial expression of blank surprise on the man's face gave way to a thunderous glare. He looked Tyler up and down, missing no detail. Unshaven and wearing nothing but his pants, Tyler had all too clearly spent the night.

"Who the *hell* are you?" the redhead demanded. "And where's Emma?"

"Emma's fine," Tyler retorted, not answering the question. "And who the hell are *you*?"

"I'm her brother, damn it!" He shoved Tyler aside and stormed into the apartment. "And I demand to know where my—"

"I'm right here, Drew," Emma interrupted before he could work himself into a full-blown Campbell temper. She stepped into view, tied the sash of her robe, put her hands on her brother's shoulders and reached up to kiss his cheek.

"It's good to see you, Drew. Did Mr. Koback let you up? I'm sure you'd like a cup of coffee as much as I would. Or would you rather have tea?" She was already walking away when he replied.

"Coffee will be fine," he said. "And, yes, your doorman let me up—*after* I showed him my passport and driver's license."

Both men followed her into the kitchen, standing on opposite sides of the room while she measured coffee and water into the machine. She switched it on and turned around to see Drew glowering, and Tyler stonily impassive.

"I'm sorry," she said cheerfully. "I'm forgetting my manners. Tyler, this is my brother, Andrew Campbell, Viscount Corrie. Drew, this is Tyler Davis, with the United States government." They hesitated, then shook hands grimly.

"I'll go get dressed," Tyler said, then nodded curtly at Drew. "Campbell."

"Davis." Drew nodded in return, and Tyler left the room.

As soon as they heard a door close at the end of the hall, Drew caught Emma's elbow and pulled her around to face him. "What the hell is that man doing here, Emma?"

"Drew!" she protested in mock reproof. "I don't ask you about your lady friends, do I?"

"This is different," he insisted. "You're my sister."

Emma raised one eyebrow. "Most of your lady friends are someone's sister. That never seemed to bother you."

Drew's neck reddened, but he saw no humor in the situation. "You're my sister," he repeated stubbornly. "I worry about you."

"And I appreciate the concern, but you needn't worry." She patted his arm comfortingly. "Tyler will keep me safe."

"I'd think you'd need protection from him. And what do you mean, keep you safe? Safe from what?" Drew studied her face. "Emma, what are you involved in?"

"It's a long story."

"I have time. My flight to L.A. doesn't leave until this afternoon." He sat down and waited. "What's going on, Emma?"

"Well, it has to do with the government and it's a little hard to explain."

"Give it a go. You're good at explaining."

"Well...do you remember Mina Grigoras?"

"The girl with the huge, dark eyes? The one you were such good friends with at school?" He frowned, thinking. "Wasn't her father an ambassador from Yugoslavia or somewhere?"

"Romania. Yes, that's her. Well, you know I've been working on an agricultural development loan for the Romanian government. I was to meet with a Romanian representative several weeks ago, and the representative who came was—"

"Mina Grigoras," Drew supplied.

"That's right. And she wasn't there just to talk about soybean seeds and interest rates. Drew, she wants to defect."

"What?"

"That's right." Emma explained all that had transpired since that first meeting with Mina, and how Tyler and Uncle Larry were involved. "So that's what will happen," she concluded. "I'll switch places with her, and she'll be spirited away to a safe house until she's granted asylum."

She sat back, folding her hands on the tabletop. Drew remained silent for several long seconds.

"Are you *insane*?" He slammed a fist on the table, and Emma jumped. "You could be killed!"

"I could be killed crossing Third Avenue any day of the week, Drew. This is something I have to do."

"Why?" he demanded. "Because *he* is forcing you to?"

Emma plunked her hands on her hips. "As a matt—"

"As a matter of fact," Tyler interrupted from the doorway, "I think it's crazy, but she's got some idea that Mina won't trust anyone else. I'd like to think Lord Latham would overrule her on it.''

Drew looked at him for a long, assessing moment, then shook his head. ''She always *was* foolhardy.''

''I'll have you know—'' Emma began, but Drew ignored her.

''And Uncle Larry has always admired what he calls her 'adventurous' streak. He may just let her do it.''

''You would think he'd have better sense.''

Drew shook his head and grinned wryly at Tyler. ''He was liaison with the French Resistance in World War II. He used to sneak across the Channel on fishing boats and hide out in a convent near Utah Beach. What he considers adventurous, I consider suicidal.''

''I see.'' Tyler turned to look at Emma consideringly. ''Then I guess it's up to you and me to change her mind, isn't it?''

Drew nodded thoughtfully. ''You may be right. Certainly the idea has possibilities.''

''I think so.''

Wearing satisfied smiles, they turned to Emma, who had watched their metamorphosis from bristling enemies to allies—against her. She shook her head in disbelief.

''What do you think, Campbell,'' Tyler asked, ''should we lock her in a closet?''

''Perhaps,'' agreed Drew. ''Or tie her to a chair.''

''I'm going to dress,'' Emma said icily. ''When you children are finished with your puerile little plans, you can pour your own coffee!''

Chapter 16

Y ou still mad?'' Tyler asked.

Emma gave them a severe look. Tyler was fighting amusement, while her brother wore a blandly innocent expression.

Emma didn't buy it for a minute. As a child, Drew had been capable of playing the most heinous pranks and then facing an accusing adult with a saintly smile. Emma had long since decided that Drew's appearance of innocence was directly proportional to his degree of guilt.

Tyler, on the other hand, didn't even bother pretending. He'd been teasing her all day, enjoying it, coming up with ever more bizarre ways to keep her from participating in Mina's defection. Locking her in a closet or tying her to a chair had been just the beginning.

Emma canceled her only meeting, and the three of them spent the day together, feeding the pigeons in Gramercy Park and lingering over a long lunch in a small restaurant before calling a cab to take Drew to the airport. And all the while Drew and Tyler concocted ever wilder plans. Drew favored keeping Emma prisoner on a boat anchored in the middle of the East River, while Tyler leaned toward flying her to Connecticut in a hot air balloon. Emma pretended to ignore them, trying not to laugh while she feigned anger.

"Of course I'm still mad," she replied to Tyler's question. "What do you expect? The two of you are ready to incarcerate me on some kind of prison ship and I'm supposed to be grateful?"

"Why not?" Drew wondered. "After all, we're only concerned with what's best for you."

"I wonder what kind of horrors are committed in the name of 'what's best for you.'" Emma glanced out the window. "There's your taxi, Drew."

He checked his watch. "And in plenty of time for my flight. Thank you, Tyler."

"No trouble at all. I'm glad to have met you, Lord Campbell."

"'Lord' isn't necessary," Drew told him.

"What do I call you, then?"

"'Your Eminence' will do nicely," Drew replied loftily.

With a snort Tyler glanced out at the street. "Well, 'Your Eminence,' you're all set."

Drew laughed. "Thank you, my lord." He turned to give Emma a hug. "Emma, be careful. I know how reckless you can be."

"I won't be reckless, Drew. But Mina's my friend. You understand that I have to help her, don't you?"

"I hate to admit it, but I do understand." He hugged her again, quick and hard. "Just be careful. Tyler?"

"Yeah, Drew?"

"Take care of my sister." They looked at each other for a long, level-eyed moment before Tyler nodded.

"I'll take care of her."

They shook hands, then Drew strode outside, pausing to wave before climbing into the taxi. Emma was very quiet as they left the restaurant and began walking slowly down the block.

"What do you—?" she began, then broke off.

"Hmm?" Tyler glanced at her.

She shook her head. "It was nothing."

"I like your brother."

She looked up, startled. "How did you know that's what I was asking?"

"It seemed like the logical question. And I do like him."

"That surprises you, doesn't it?"

"Well-l-l." He shrugged. "It surprises me less than it would have before I met you."

"So your prejudices weren't just against wealthy women?"

"Hey, I was an equal opportunity jerk. I didn't think much of rich men, either, but I like Drew. He's more concerned with what he does than with his father's title." He threw her a devastatingly sexy grin. "And he wants to protect his sister from her insane impulses."

"The insanity of my impulses is a matter of opinion. I know what you think and you know what I think."

"And we're going to agree to disagree, submit both opinions to Lord Latham and let him decide."

"That's what we'll do." Emma stuffed her hands into her pockets and walked on, confident that Uncle Larry would see her side of the issue.

"You're convinced he's going to agree with you, aren't you?"

"Yes, because I'm right."

"Huh!" He snorted. "I have an answer for that, but it'll have to wait till we get back to your place."

"What about your apartment?" Emma asked impulsively.

"My place?" He frowned.

"Yes. I've never seen where you live." She looked down at her hands, a flush tinting her cheeks. "And at the risk of embarrassing myself, I'll be honest and admit that I'm curious.''

"Really?" He seemed nonplussed.

"Yes, really."

"I don't know. It's not much."

"That doesn't matter. Is there someplace nearby that delivers pizza?"

"Yeah."

"There you are, then." Her tone implied it was a fait accompli.

Tyler hesitated for a few seconds, and Emma could see he was trying to figure out how he'd been outmaneuvered. He'd never had a chance, though, for Emma had learned the art of polite strong-arming from one of the best. Countess Campbell was known for her ability to keep the most obstreperous guest or belligerent workman in line with nothing but a few soft words.

"Well, okay," he said after a few minutes. "If that's what you want to do." He stepped to the curb to flag down a cab, then gave the driver an address in the Village.

Emma smiled to herself as the driver made an illegal U-turn and set off, pleased to think she'd inherited a little of her mother's talent. It was too bad she hadn't shown that talent when she first met Tyler. That's when she should have remembered all those warnings about catching flies with honey instead of vinegar. She might have gotten to know the real Tyler Davis much sooner. The Tyler she liked, respected, cared for... loved.

Tyler glanced at her. "You're awfully quiet. Something wrong?"

Emma quickly arranged her face into a smile. "Not at all. I was just thinking of something."

"You can start thinking about what you want on the pizza." The cab rounded a corner and pulled up in front of a building with a pocket park beside it. "Because we're here."

Emma stepped out, smiling as she looked around her. "This is nice," she said. It was also very familiar.

The neighborhood was a mixture of smallish apartment buildings and old manufacturing buildings converted into residential and artists' lofts. The residents were a mixture of students, working artists and elderly shopkeepers who'd lived there for thirty years or more.

Several people greeted Tyler as he paid the cabbie and led Emma inside. The halls and stairwells of his building were rather bare but clean and bright with fresh paint.

"This way," he said, taking her elbow to steer her toward the stairs. "I'm afraid it's a walk-up."

"That's all right. Climbing stairs is wonderful exercise."

"I wonder if you'd say that if you were climbing them for the hundredth time with your arms full of groceries." They reached the second-floor landing, turned and kept climbing.

"That's exactly what I said to myself over and over as I carried my groceries to the fifth floor when I lived here."

Tyler stopped short, halfway up the last flight. "You lived in this neighborhood?"

"Mm-hmm. When I first moved to New York after college. I lived just a few blocks away." She told him the street, and he nodded in wondering comprehension.

"You lived over there, huh?" Shaking his head, he continued up the stairs and along the hall to one of the front apartments. He unlocked the door and swung it wide with a flourish that Emma suspected might cover nervousness.

She stepped in, took a long look around and saw that he had no reason to be nervous. "Tyler, this is lovely!" The living room was large for a New York apartment, with high ceilings, long windows facing the street and a pair of French windows leading to a tiny balcony on the sunny south side, just big enough for a café table and two wrought-iron chairs.

It was furnished in a comfortable men's club style, with an Oriental-patterned rug and overstuffed furniture. There were some good prints on the walls, abstracts, a Monet and a Constable landscape.

"You have England on your wall!" She turned, smiling at him. "You didn't tell me that."

"You have a castle in the family," he said, shrugging. "A print on the wall didn't seem to have much relevance."

"It does if we share an affinity for the moors. The place where I take walks by the loch looks a lot like that—wild and empty and peaceful."

"Yeah. I like the feeling I get from it." He studied the picture for a minute, then stepped back. "You want the grand tour? It won't take long."

"Of course I want the grand tour." Emma tucked her arm in his. "Everything, from the attic to the cellars."

"How about from the kitchen to the bath and back again?"

"Lead on!"

He led her through a small, bright kitchen that didn't look as if he used it much, to an even smaller bathroom, complete with clawfoot tub, a second bedroom he used as an office and a surprisingly large bedroom at the rear of the apartment, furnished with an antique bedroom suite. The bed was covered with a quilt that Emma guessed was also antique.

"This is all lovely. And this suite is beautiful. Did you find it in the city?"

He shook his head and touched the finial on the bedpost lightly. "At an antique barn out in Connecticut. If you're interested, I'll get you the address."

"I'd like that." Emma touched the ornate door handle on the armoire. "I'd like to go there sometime."

She looked over her shoulder at Tyler, standing beside the bed, and caught her breath. His eyes were glowing with a light that told her he wasn't thinking about antique sales.

She felt her cheeks warm, and she curled her fingers around the armoire door handle, as if for support.

"Maybe you can," Tyler said in a voice gone husky and low. "Go there, I mean." He held out his hand.

Emma slowly unclamped her fingers from the handle and reached across the distance that separated them. She laid her hand in his, and he drew her gently to the bedside where he rested his hands lightly on her shoulders.

"How can you be real?"

"I don't understand."

"You're so beautiful, so rare and special. Too special to be real, and yet..." He slid his hands from her shoulders to her throat, tipping her face up for his kiss.

It was almost a vow, a question, a statement and a promise, gentle and sweet. He lifted his lips, his eyes dark with emotion, then wrapped her in his arms and kissed her again with all the hunger that burned inside him.

Emma felt the heat catch within her, sparking flame from the embers that seemed always to smolder when he was near. She clutched his waist, rising onto her toes to meet his kiss. He groaned deep in his throat, tumbled onto the bed with her and let the flames take them.

There seemed to be no separate sensations to Emma, only a swirling whirlpool of need and demand. She let herself go as the familiar storm enveloped her, quick this time, like a sudden summer storm breaking the tension of a sultry afternoon. The thunder rolled, the lightning flashed and they rode the swirling wind to the top and over into infinity.

"I believe this is what they mean by decadent," Emma said with her mouth full.

Tyler reached out with a fingertip and dabbed a spot of pizza sauce off her chin. "I thought decadent was European aristocrats in decline from too much wine and caviar."

"I'm not so sure." Emma sat back, tucked the folds of his shirt, her only garment, around her, and took another piece of pizza. She grinned at him. "This aristocrat feels positively decadent eating pizza in bed at seven o'clock in the evening."

"How about the wine? Isn't that part of the whole decadent experience?" He poured more of the grocery-store Chianti into her heavy tumbler and held it to her lips.

Emma sipped and smiled. "I doubt the Rothschilds have much of this in their cellars."

"Their loss." Tyler drank a deep swallow, then set the glass aside and pulled Emma close for a kiss redolent of red wine and spices.

"Mm-hmm." Emma sat back and popped the last bite into her mouth. "That was delicious."

"Glad you liked it." He closed the box and got up to carry it back to the kitchen, and Emma watched him with a hunger she didn't even try to deny. He'd pulled on a pair of ancient jeans to open the door for the pizza man, and they snugly outlined the muscular lines of his narrow hips and long legs. His back was tanned and smooth, and muscles flexed excitingly beneath the skin as he bent to pick up a fallen napkin.

He winked at her as he left the room, and Emma winked back. Was this love that set her heart racing when she watched him leave a room? Was it love that made her breathing quicken when she heard his voice, or warmed her cheeks with a blush when he looked at her with hunger in his eyes?

If so, it was an aspect of love she hadn't expected, though there was something pleasant about being capable of these giddy feelings at the ripe old age of twenty-eight. It gave the world a new glow, as if she were seeing things for the first time in the warm light of dawn. She snuggled contentedly into the pillows, and she was smiling when Tyler returned to the room.

"You're looking pretty pleased with yourself." He lay down on the bed beside her, drawing her into his arms.

"Mmm. Not pleased with myself, just happy." She tucked her head into his shoulder. "It feels like the world is new."

"The world is new," he repeated. "Yeah. That's a pretty good way to describe it." She felt him press a kiss to her hair, then rest his face against it.

The minutes ticked past as they lay together, listening to music playing softly from the living room, enjoying their closeness, needing nothing more.

"Tyler?" she murmured sleepily.

"Hmm?"

"Is this love? Feeling this way?"

He tensed, then lifted his head. "Love?"

"It must be love that makes me feel like this. Mustn't it?"

"I don't know." He loosened his arms and rolled slightly away onto his back. "I don't think I believe in love."

"Not believe in it?" Emma looked at his averted face. "How could you not believe in love?"

He paused before answering her, then seemed to reconsider. "Emma." He caught her hand and drew her onto her side, facing him. "If you love me, will you do something for me?"

"Of course." She laid her hand against his face and shivered when he kissed her palm. "I'll do anything I can for you. You must know that."

"Then get out of this operation," he said urgently. "Now."

"What?"

"Get out of it. Write to Mina, tell her to go to Chicago, but you get sick on the day of the defection."

"I can't do that!" She pushed herself away, shaking her head in shock and dawning anger.

"You can!" He gripped her chin in his fingers and forced her to look at him. "You can. Say you have the flu and are too sick to go. Let us put a female agent in your place. Mina can see all the tractors and plows and things, and the agent can make the switch, not you.''

"No!'' She sat up. "Tyler, I can't do that!''

"You *can*.'' He sat up, too, his face inches from hers. "If you tell Lord Latham you don't want to do this, you know he won't insist. Just tell him you don't want to do it.''

"But I *do* want to ! I have to!'' She tried to pull her wrist out of his grasp, but he held on. "Can't you understand, Tyler?''

"No.'' He shoved himself up off the bed and stalked across the room, his movements jerky with anger. By the window, he spun around to face her. "No, I can't understand. I have never understood why you'd want to do such a damn fool thing in the first place!''

"Because I promised to help my friend,'' Emma told him. "A friend who is afraid for her life. I won't renege on that promise.''

"Not even for me?'' He looked across the room at her. "You say you love me. I don't know much about love, but I've heard it means doing things for the person you love. I'm asking you, Emma. Don't do this.''

She shook her head slowly. "Try to understand, please. I have to do this. Mina and I, we're more like sisters than friends. If I need help, I know I can always ask her—for anything. If something's wrong, I can see it in her eyes, and she in mine. A stranger can't do that, Tyler. Only I can.''

"Emma, if you love me, don't do it.''

"That's not love, Tyler. It's blackmail. And I won't let Mina down.''

"But you'd put yourself in that kind of danger? Even though I'm asking you not to?'' He slammed his hand against the wall in frustration, and Emma jumped. "That's crazy, Emma, and I won't let you do it.''

"You won't *let* me?'' Emma's voice rose along with her temper. "I decide for myself what I do, Tyler. I've been in the middle of this from the very beginning, and there's no way I'll back out at the critical moment."

"You talk as if you can't be replaced," he scoffed. "You're not James Bond, Emma. You're an amateur. What makes you think you can even pull this off?"

"The fact that I have to." She walked across the room and reached out as if to touch him. When he folded his arms and stepped back, turning his shoulder to her, Emma let her hands drop to her sides. "I don't want to fight with you, Tyler."

"Then don't," he interrupted. "Call your Uncle Larry and tell him you want out."

"No." She had said it as gently as she could, but the word hung heavy in the silence. "Tyler, we can work this out some other way. We just have to talk about it. Don't you see?"

He turned slowly to face her, and Emma shivered when she saw his eyes—cold, and empty of affection. "Will you change your mind?"

Emma half lifted her hands, palms up in a plea for understanding. "I can't."

"Then we don't have anything to talk about."

He brushed past her and strode out of the room, leaving her alone and staring at the empty doorway.

Chapter 17

Damn!'' Tyler jerked his hand back as the cup shattered in the sink, splashing coffee over the countertop. He turned his back on the mess and strode to the living room. The hell with coffee. He would rather have a drink, anyway.

He took out bourbon and a glass, poured himself a good measure, then carried the drink across the room and dropped into a chair by the window. The view of treetops and the evening sky usually soothed him, but not this time.

It had been barely a day since he'd driven Emma back to her apartment in tense silence. When he'd pulled up in front of her building, she hadn't even looked at him. Instead, she'd slid out of the car and walked quickly inside. His last sight of her had been of her back, disappearing through the door as the doorman had held it wide for her. Tyler might have imagined it, but he'd thought Mr. Koback had shot him a disapproving look before he'd pulled the door closed.

Though Tyler liked old Mr. Koback, he could tolerate his disapproval because he knew he was right. But being right didn't do much good when he couldn't talk some sense into

Emma. Who could talk sense to a woman in a mood like that?

She was an intelligent woman, so how could she do something so stupid? She was naively placing herself in danger, as if she thought she were Wonder Woman, perfectly capable of handling anything that might go wrong. Well, Tyler knew what she was up against, and he was terrified that Lady Emma was going to find herself up to her pretty little neck in very hot water.

And there wouldn't be a damn thing he could do about it!

Tyler muttered a disgusted oath under his breath and took a too-large gulp of his drink. He coughed as it went down, then waited, hoping for the liquor to relax him, waiting for the peace of his living room to help him unwind.

He was sitting in his favorite chair, sipping his best bourbon, looking out at the evening sky…and none of it helped.

It was his own fault. He'd known from the start that it was a mistake to let himself care about her. Emma Campbell was a willful woman who didn't listen to advice—especially good advice. So why should he think she would listen to him when he tried to keep her safe?

He raked a hand through his hair and swore under his breath. He'd known all along that involvement with a woman like her would lead nowhere. He'd known from the very beginning that the smart thing to do was to walk away.

Well, he'd walked away, so why didn't he feel better?

He raised the glass to his lips again, then set it aside untasted. He didn't want bourbon; it wasn't the solution to his problem.

He'd made the right decision. He knew that, but why did the right decision feel so wrong?

Emma sat curled on the window seat, looking out at the night. The midnight sky was clear and starry, with a cold wind blowing the last of the autumn leaves off the branches, sending them swirling down the street.

"Yes, Drew," she said into the telephone. "I'll be careful. Uncle Larry wouldn't have me do anything foolish." She listened for a moment. "No, you will not phone Uncle Larry up and have a talk with him! He was spying against the Nazis before you were born, Drew. He knows what he's doing. And Tyler does, too."

She listened again and tried to keep her voice level when she replied. "No, he isn't here right now. Yes, I'll give him the message. No, there's nothing wrong. I've had a bit of a cold and it's made my voice sound odd. Drew, I'll have to go now. You'll be in Scotland next week? Well, enjoy your time in sunny Los Angeles. Give my love to the family. Yes. I'll be careful, I promise! Goodbye, Drew."

She replaced the receiver and sat back, staring blindly outside and biting her lip. It was foolish to want to cry. Crying didn't solve anything. She swiped a hand roughly across her cheek and blinked hard.

She should have known Tyler Davis was trouble, from that very first meeting. She'd known he was the type of overbearing man who would insist on bossing her around and then become unreasonable and furious when she made her own decisions in spite of him.

She should be thanking her lucky stars that she was well rid of him. She should be glad, and she would be . . . if only she hadn't fallen in love with him.

"Are you all right, Emma? You look tired."

"And so would you," Emma replied, "if you'd traveled a thousand miles to spend two very long days looking at tractor engines and combine blades."

She'd flown to Chicago three days ago, checked into a large hotel, touched base with the Strathclyde Bank's Chicago office and then spent two days attending trade shows with Mina.

"What's a combine?" Jim asked with a grin.

"A huge machine to harvest wheat. They need several for the collective farms, but they're shopping carefully since combines cost as much as three hundred thousand dollars each."

Jim whistled, and Emma nodded. "They're terribly technical and complicated, and I'm devoutly grateful that no one expects a banker to understand their inner workings." She chuckled. "The high point of my day was watching Stefan Alexandru and that Petru person try to act as if they knew what they were looking at."

"Did they?" Tyler asked.

Emma looked at him for the first time since she'd walked into this midnight meeting. There were four of them—Tyler, Uncle Larry, Jim and herself—sitting around a tea table in the sitting room of her hotel suite. The lights were low, and they stayed well away from the windows, even though the curtains were tightly drawn against prying eyes.

"Not the first thing," she replied. "Even in another language it's obvious they're completely ignorant of plow angles and corn shellers."

"What's a corn sheller do?"

"Takes the corn kernels off the cob," Emma replied without missing a beat. "This has been a very educational two days. I've learned more than I ever wanted to know about agricultural equipment."

"And Mina? How has she enjoyed it?"

Emma smiled at Uncle Larry. "She's done just as we told her to do. She's looked at absolutely everything the factory representatives had to show her and she's asked questions constantly."

"Is it working?"

She grinned at Lord Latham. "The watchdogs are bored to tears."

"Bored enough to be careless?" Tyler asked.

Emma answered carefully, for this was the most important question. "I think so. When we first started out, they were very wary, very alert. They stayed close to Mina, one on each side of her, close enough to grab her if she tried to run."

"And after two days?"

Emma smiled. "It's difficult to maintain constant vigilance when you're desperately bored. I could see their watchfulness wearing away as Mina asked all those questions. The factory representative who showed us around today was a bonus."

"How so?"

"He has to be the most boring human being I've ever encountered. He never answers a question with one word when ten will do, and he tells you everything at least twice. The poor interpreter you sent along was going crazy."

"So he said," Uncle Larry told her. "According to his report to me, if he has to spend another day in a tractor factory, he's applying for a transfer to somewhere above the Arctic Circle. He says they don't have tractors there."

"Well, he's done translating about tractors," Jim said. "By tomorrow afternoon it should all be over."

"Damn it, Jim! Couldn't you put that another way?"

Jim glanced at Tyler's angry face, then turned to Emma. "Hey, I . . . I didn't mean it that way. It's just that everything will be finished . . . er, done with . . . um . . ."

"That's all right, Jim. I know what you mean." Emma smiled and sipped her cooling tea.

"He could've said it some other way," Tyler grumbled.

"Be that as it may," Lord Latham said, pouring oil on the waters, "tomorrow is the big day. Do we all have the plan well in mind?" There was a general murmur of assent, and he nodded. "Very well, then. Emma, you'll call Mina in the morning and tell her you're not feeling well. You're very sorry, but they'll have to visit the trade show on their own. You hope to see her for dinner tomorrow evening."

Emma nodded. "I'll call at eight-thirty."

"Jim, you and I will be in place inside the convention center before they open."

"Right."

"And, Tyler, you'll bring Emma to the convention center at the same time that the limousine is meeting Mina, so she can be in place before there's any chance of someone seeing her."

"Right," Tyler said, parroting Jim's reply.

"Then I think this meeting's adjourned." Lord Latham stood. "Jim, you'll stay in the room we've taken downstairs."

"Okay." Jim picked up his jacket and walked to the front door. "I'll see you guys tomorrow." He gave them a thumbs-up. "Break a leg, Lady Emma."

She smiled and waved, and he left, closing the door behind him.

"I'll go quite openly back to my own hotel," Lord Latham said, "and hope that they waste their time watching me. If you could call a taxi for me, Emma?"

"Of course." She got up and walked over to the phone.

"I'll go on down with Jim, then—" Tyler began, but Lord Latham interrupted him.

"No. I don't want Emma to be alone tonight. You'll stay here with her, Tyler."

Emma jerked around. "What?" she and Tyler said in unison.

"I don't want you to be alone, Emma. I want Tyler here in the suite as a precaution."

"Uncle Larry, that's really—" She broke off, turning back to the phone. "What? Oh, yes. Room 2814. Ten minutes? That will be fine. Thank you."

She hung up and turned to the men. "Uncle Larry, it really isn't necessary that Tyler stay here."

"That's what I'm counting on." He was pulling on his topcoat, gathering up his gloves. "If I thought they might take any action tonight, I wouldn't let you stay here at all."

"But, Uncle La—"

"I'll see you tomorrow, Emma." He patted her cheek lightly and walked to the door, where he paused and glanced back. "Turn the lights off and make it clear to anyone watching that you're going to bed, won't you?" He smiled. "Good night, dear, and good luck."

Emma stared at the closed door for a moment, then let her breath out in an exasperated hiss and turned back to the man still standing in the hall. "Tyler, I don't really think—"

"You'd better go ahead and turn out the lights," he interrupted. "He's probably right that someone's watching."

Emma's lips tightened, then she turned on her heel and walked over to switch off the lamps. When the room was dark, she lifted the curtain aside a fraction and peered down at the street far below.

"See anything?" Tyler murmured beside her ear, startling her so badly that she jumped and their heads bumped painfully.

"Ouch!" Rubbing her head, she turned around and found herself hemmed in between the window and Tyler, who was rubbing his chin.

The warmth of his body reached out to her, treacherously tempting, but she couldn't get away without pushing past him. "Don't sneak up on me!"

"Don't worry, I won't," he replied with feeling. "Did anybody ever tell you you have a hard head?"

"Frequently." If her voice was sharp, it was because he was too big, too strong, too male...too close. "Especially when they're opposite me in negotiations. Will you please move?"

"Move?"

At first she thought he hadn't understood. "Move, please. You're blocking my way." She looked up into his eyes and realized he'd understood perfectly.

"Yeah, I am." He didn't move, but somehow he seemed to loom closer. He wanted her. She could see it in his eyes and could feel the answering desire rising in her. She fought it, tensing her muscles, narrowing her eyes.

"Tyler!" She didn't realize she'd fallen into the upper-class drawl of her London classmates. "Let me go." He wasn't touching her, in any way, but neither commented on her choice of words. He was holding her there, as truly as if he gripped her wrists or held her in his arms.

"I can't hold you." His voice was low, rough. "It's all wrong...."

He'd held his hands stiffly at his sides, but now he touched her arms lightly, brushing his fingertips over her elbows, his warmth reaching through her silk blouse as he slid his hands up to her shoulders, to her throat, caressing the delicate skin there.

Emma caught her breath as he sought her pulse. It hammered against his fingertips. "It's wrong," he whispered, "and that doesn't seem to matter a damn!"

So suddenly that she gasped, he dragged her against him and captured her mouth in a kiss of savage intensity.

Emma fought the need, and lost, reaching up, locking her arms around his neck, kissing him with all her passion and power. Time flowed past as they clung together, linked in a desperate web of need and passion denied.

She was still clinging when he took her wrists and pulled her hands down, setting a distance between them before he released her and backed away.

"Go to bed, Emma."

"Tyler?" She hated the tremor in her voice that she couldn't control.

He turned away, raking a hand through his hair. "Just go to bed, please. For your sake and mine."

She stood uncertainly for several seconds, then nodded, though he still had his back to her. She remained silent, but turned to go. She was nearly at the doorway when Tyler said softly, "Good night, Emma."

"Good night," she replied, and walked away.

"Are you okay?"

Emma glanced at Tyler, surprised by the question. "Why?"

"Because you look pale." He pulled the car into a space in the parking area reserved for convention center officials and glanced at her as he killed the engine. "And frightened."

"I'm not frightened." He made a noise of dissent, and she shrugged. "Edgy, maybe. I wouldn't be ready for this if I was completely relaxed, would I?"

After a moment Tyler nodded once. "No. If you were too relaxed, flat-footed, you wouldn't be ready. Just don't look so frightened."

"I'm not frightened!" Emma got out when he did and glared at him across the car. "I'm just not very relaxed."

"No kidding." He reached into the car and pulled out a canvas tote bag. "You look like you're about to jump out of your skin."

"What are you trying to do?" She hurried after him when he strode toward the staff entrance. "Make me lose my temper?"

"Yeah." He turned a key in the door.

"Why?"

"To take your mind off your nerves. It's working, isn't it?"

Emma stared at him as he walked calmly inside, and finally moved when the door started to swing closed. She had to smile as she followed him into a bare, utilitarian corridor. He was right; it *had* worked. She was still alert, ready for action, but she was no longer a bundle of tightly strung nerves.

When they emerged into the cavernous exhibit area, it was quiet, peopled only by the singers, models and salesmen who would be showing the exhibitors' products, along with hot dog and pizza vendors, and a few custodians setting out trash cans and ashtrays, moving among the looming cultivators and combines like ants prowling around enormous metallic dinosaurs.

Emma and Tyler threaded their way between the steel monsters, coming at last to a ladies' room tucked around a corner, away from the main exhibit area. It was a fairly large room with several cubicles and sinks, a diaper-changing area and a sitting area at one end. Unlike most of the other ladies' rooms in the building, this one boasted a window, a window that was part of their plan.

Tyler stopped outside the door. "Here you are. Do you have your gun?"

Emma indicated the tote bag. "It's in there."

"Good." He glanced at the door and frowned. "Are you going to be okay?"

Emma shrugged. "Certainly. It's simple, really. I just wait in the ladies' loo until Mina comes."

"But you could be in there for hours. What if somebody asks why you're staying in there so long?"

"Nobody will ask. That would be nosy. And rude."

"But what if they *do* ask? What'll you say?"

"That I'm feeling ill, or perhaps tired."

"What if they don't believe that? What if somebody's really persistent?"

"I'll play my trump card." She smiled.

"Which is?"

"I'll say I came in to escape an obnoxious man. No woman would argue with that."

"Oh." His surprise showed. He shook his head and turned to look around the vast space of the exhibition hall. It was due to open in ten minutes.

A janitor walked past, emptied an ashtray into the waste bin on his rolling cart and moved on. A few yards away an attractive young woman in red-sequined overalls climbed on top of a huge yellow tractor and settled in the seat, ready to demonstrate all its new and improved features. The smell of hot dogs drifted from a steam cart not far away, competing incongruously with doughnuts and coffee from another stand. In the distance music began to play, a pop tune from the sixties, with lyrics rewritten to extoll the latest in cultivators.

"So you have it all covered?" he asked, turning back to her.

She tapped the tote bag he held. "I have a book to read, along with the other things I'll need."

"The signal?"

"It's in there." She smiled. "It's a bit unorthodox, but I suppose it'll serve the purpose."

"It'll do fine." He looked around again at the increasing bustle. "They're about to open."

"Then I'd better go into hiding." Emma reached out for the tote bag, mustered a smile and stepped back. "Wish me luck."

"Wait." He caught her arm.

"Tyler, I have to go in before anyone comes and sees me."

His grip tightened on her wrist. "I can't—"

"What's the matter?" She watched his face change, his expression go grim. "What is it?"

"I don't want you to do this." His voice was low, but the words seemed to burst out of him, impelled by something he couldn't control. "You can't do it. It's too dangerous!"

"It's too late!" The doors had opened, and she could hear the rising noise of an incoming crowd. "Tyler, I have to go!"

"After this—" He hauled her into his arms and kissed her, then lifted his mouth and gazed down into her eyes. Then he twisted a hand into her hair, tipped her head back

and kissed her again, long and hard and deep. When he finally released her, she was breathless, her lips bruised. He
let his arm slide from her waist, keeping one hand at the
nape of her neck. "Be careful," he said. "For God's sake,
be careful." He kissed her again, quick and hard, and gave
her a little shove toward the ladies' room.

As Emma went through the swinging door, she glanced
around in time to see Tyler rounding the corner into the exhibition area. She watched for a moment after he disappeared, then walked calmly into the loo.

Emma nodded politely at two women near the mirror,
walked into a cubicle and fastened the door. She stood there,
listening as they finished their conversation and left. When
the door had squeaked closed behind them, leaving silence
in its wake, she left the cubicle and surveyed the room that
was going to be her domain for the next several hours.

As public rest rooms went, it wasn't bad. Certainly it was
clean, with a lingering atmosphere of disinfectant. The
vinyl-upholstered daybed at one side of the room wasn't the
most comfortable piece of furniture she'd ever encountered, but it was as clean as everything else and infinitely
preferable to spending most of the day in a toilet cubicle.
Emma settled herself comfortably, using her tote bag as a
pillow, and opened the paperback novel she'd brought.

That kept her from being bored for all of half an hour.
Then she sat up, swung her legs off the couch and marched
impatiently to the room's single window, high in the end
wall. It opened easily enough, swinging out to be propped
open by a folding brace. She fastened the brace and stood
on tiptoe to look out at a concrete-paved service yard, then
closed the window again. She counted the sinks—six—and
the cubicles—eight—and was actually eyeing a band of dark
gray tiles that set off the lighter gray walls when she caught

herself. If she was counting the wall tiles after half an hour, how was she going to survive until midafternoon?

She had to be patient, Emma reminded herself, patient yet ready for action. She returned to the daybed and opened her book with all the patience she could muster.

Chapter 18

I'm fine, thank you. I was just taking a break."

"From looking at tractors?" The plump woman who'd asked after Emma's health shook her head. "I don't blame you. I've looked at so many different pieces of equipment that my head's spinning, and my Bill isn't done yet!"

Emma made a little sound of sympathy and agreement.

"I don't know what the fascination is." The plump woman tucked her lipstick back in her purse and patted her hair. "I'd have bought the first tractor we saw when we came in the door, and that would be the end of it, but Bill's determined to look at every single machine they have. Do you know how many machines are in this place?"

"No, I'm afraid I don't."

"Well, there must be thousands of them!" She tucked her comb away and gave Emma a solicitous smile. "Enjoy your rest, dear."

Emma murmured thanks and waved goodbye, then sank back on the daybed, smothering her laughter.

The plump lady's complaint was a common refrain among the women attending the show with their husbands, fathers, uncles, brothers and boyfriends. It appeared that very few women shared their men's fascination with agricultural machinery, for the only enthusiasm had been shown by a pretty young woman who was engaged to be married. She came in with a friend, talking about two things—her engagement ring and the tractor her fiancé had selected. She didn't know much about it, but she was deeply impressed with her young man's knowledge of machinery.

Emma opened her book, then closed it again. It was past three o'clock, and she'd managed to plow through nearly half of it, but it was slow going. The combination of boredom and tension left her too distracted to get involved in the story, but she'd plodded doggedly on, turning the pages in between looking at her watch, peering out the window and occasionally pacing. Around noon she'd nibbled a small packet of wholemeal biscuits and drunk some of the tea she'd brought in a thermos. As the high point of her day so far, that wasn't much.

She got up and walked to the window once again. When she stood on tiptoe to look out, she could see Jim down below in a service yard, wearing a maintenance worker's uniform. He'd spent his day acting the part of a maintenance worker, emptying the occasional trash barrel, then taking a "break," sitting in the sun to smoke a cigarette. Emma wondered if he was as bored and edgy as she.

Waiting was driving her crazy. She wanted things to start happening, wanted to do the job she was there for. Jim glanced up when she opened the window, but he didn't wave, for that might draw attention to the ladies' room window. He let his gaze slide past the window to the sky as he adjusted his cap. Then he drank from the can of soda he held and sat down again.

Emma understood his message. He was on duty and alert, he knew she was there and there was nothing they could do until Mina appeared. Emma closed the window, returned to the daybed and uncapped her thermos. After drinking the last of her tepid tea, she picked up her book and applied herself unenthusiastically to the next chapter.

"...look at another plow, I'll scream!"

Emma glanced up as the door swung open and two women in their thirties walked in.

"Be patient, Jan. You wouldn't want him to spend seventy-five thousand on just any old tractor, would you?"

Laughing together, they disappeared around the corner, and Emma went back to her book. While water was running in one of the sinks, the entry door squeaked again. She looked up...and dropped the book.

She was on her feet before it thumped to the floor, started for the door and was ready to fling her arms around Mina when she remembered there were strangers in the room.

She glanced at them, standing by the mirror, combing hair and applying lipstick, then gave Mina a smile that was only a little strained. "Mina, what a surprise to see you! Are you here looking at tractors?"

"Combines, actually." Mina spoke carefully, aware they weren't alone, trying to minimize her accent. "It's been a very interesting day."

"I'm sure it has." Emma led her toward the sitting area. "Do you have a minute to sit down and tell me how you've been?"

"Of course."

As Mina replied, Emma turned to look deliberately at the strangers, who'd been following the exchange with interest. "Hello."

Caught eavesdropping, they flushed, mumbled hello and left. Emma peeked out the door as it closed, then pulled it shut and locked it.

She turned to Mina, and then they were in each other's arms, hugging as if they would never let go. "Oh, Mina," Emma said when she stepped back, "this is it."

"Yes," Mina said, her voice trembling slightly. "What do we do first?"

"First, I put out the signal." Emma rummaged in the tote bag and pulled out a white towel, which she took to the window. She opened the window, hung the towel outside, then closed the window again, trapping the towel securely. Down below she could see Jim glance up. He stiffened, then settled his cap with a flourish and disappeared inside. "Jim's seen it."

"That is good. And now we change into each other?"

"More or less." Emma grinned. "I change into you and you change into a total stranger. Here's your wig." She pulled it out of the tote bag. "I'm wearing the rest."

"Wearing it?" Mina eyed Emma's black stretch pants and matching tunic. "That is an . . . unusual outfit, Emma."

"Do you like it?"

"It looks like winter underwear!"

"It's the latest thing." Emma pulled the tunic over her head and handed it to Mina. "You'll be the essence of style."

"I'm trembling with anticipation." Mina dropped her coat on the daybed and began unbuttoning her dress.

"How are things going outside?" Emma handed over the stretch pants and sneakers and took Mina's dress in exchange.

"I have bored them beyond endurance," Mina told her with pride. "When I expressed a desire to answer nature's call, they were so relieved they almost cried. They've gone to get hot dogs, and I am to meet them near the seed drills."

"I know where those are. They're near one of the exits, aren't they?"

"I believe so. At the northwest end."

"Okay." Emma finished buttoning the dress and looked down at it. The blue silk was a snug fit on her, but it had been generous on Mina. "You've lost weight, Mina."

"A little. I have been . . . distracted lately."

Emma glanced at her. "I know." She buckled the belt around her waist. "Where are your shoes?"

"Here."

Mina passed the dark blue pumps across, and Emma slipped them on, then stood up, hands on hips, and looked down at herself. "How do I look?"

"Like me, with red hair. Do you have a wig?"

"Of course." Emma produced a second wig from the tote bag, along with a comb, some hairpins and a cosmetic bag. "Come on, Mina, let's make ourselves beautiful."

"Just a moment." Mina was sitting on the daybed, bending over her foot. "These are very complicated shoes."

"They're quite easy, actually." Emma knelt and took the laces from her hands. "You tie the laces, like this, then fasten this Velcro strap, and this one, and voilà, you're ready!"

"Is that all? That is not so difficult." Mina flexed her toes experimentally, then stood up and bounced a little. "They are very comfortable shoes, are they not?"

"Very. Now let's finish up before someone reports the loo out of order."

In front of the mirror they pinned up their hair, Emma's copper waves and Mina's black silk, then carefully donned the wigs. Their reflections looked back at them, not quite right.

"Makeup!" Emma picked some items out of the cosmetic bag for Mina. "With that blond hair you need a slightly darker complexion. Use these and put on extra eye makeup. They'll never know you."

While Mina darkened her porcelain-fair complexion and emphasized her eyes, Emma covered the dusting of freckles on her cheekbones and carefully darkened and elongated her eyebrows, mimicking Mina's elegant facial structure. The finishing touch was black mascara for Emma, blue for Mina, then they turned to face each other.

"What do you think?" Emma asked.

Mina shook her head. "I would not have believed you could look so much like me. Even your eyebrows! And how do I look?"

"Thanks to the wonder of cosmetics, you look like a Chicago college student."

"Is that good?"

"It's about the farthest thing I can think of from a Romanian diplomat."

"Good." Mina nodded once, her small chin set at a determined angle. "They will not know who I am, and from a distance they will believe that you are me."

Emma looked at her reflection in the mirror. "If they get close to me, they'll be able to tell, but I only have to stay away from them for ten minutes or so, long enough for you to get away."

They looked at each other, suddenly sobering beneath their disguises. This was no child's game they were playing. It was deadly serious and deadly dangerous.

"Are we ready?" Emma asked.

"Yes," Mina said quietly. "We are ready."

"Okay," Emma said briskly without emotion. "You go out first. Turn right, away from the hot dog stand they went to, and walk directly toward the exit. You know where it is. Hurry as much as you can without attracting attention. You need to get outside quickly. Jim will meet you."

Mina nodded. "I will do that."

"You'll need about eight minutes, maybe a little more. If I can make them think you're still here for that long, you'll be away, free and clear."

"Free," Mina breathed. "How wonderful that sounds."

"Everything will be all right, Mina. This will work." Emma reached out for a hug, and for a moment Mina hugged her tightly.

"Good luck," Emma whispered as she unlocked the door. "I'll see you soon."

"I can never repay you for this, Emma." Mina's voice threatened to break. "Keep safe. Please keep safe." She looked at Emma, her dark eyes wide and frightened, then she pushed open the door and walked out, turning to the right and walking quickly away without looking back.

Emma forced herself to count slowly to ten, then she took a deep breath, pulled the door open and walked out into the exhibit. She tried to be calm, but her heart was hammering in her chest and her knees felt distinctly shaky. She walked straight ahead, past the hot dog stand and toward the display of seed drills. It was probably only her imagination, but she felt a prickling between her shoulder blades, as if someone were watching her.

As soon as she reached the first pieces of equipment, Emma stepped out of the aisle and began weaving her way between the machines and the people, using them as camouflage. She paused for a moment behind a lime-green combine, took a chance and looked back the way she'd come.

She could see no dark overcoats and fedoras in the crowd, but that didn't mean her pursuers weren't there, looking for Mina—looking for her. Cravenly she wanted to stay out of sight, but eventually she had to let them catch a glimpse of her, to distract them from looking elsewhere.

She walked on more slowly. She avoided meeting anyone's eyes, though she searched the crowd for Tyler or Uncle Larry. They were both there, trying to stay out of sight, since the secret police had seen both men with her.

When she finally reached the seed drills, she positioned herself on the far side of the display to watch for Stefan or his thin, gloomy partner, Petru. She picked up a brochure and studied it with every evidence of interest, glancing from it to the seed drill as if comparing the description in the leaflet with what she could see on the machine. She had actually begun to relax a bit when she looked up and saw them, and the fear came rushing back.

They were forging their way through the crowded exhibit, looking neither to the right nor the left, grim-faced and intent on their goal. Emma watched them for a moment, then stepped behind a tractor's huge tire just as Petru, the taller man, moved his head as if to look toward her. When she glanced out again, he was scanning the area on the other side of the aisle.

Emma stepped away from the tractor and watched the two men move around the display. She kept moving, keeping track of their whereabouts with quick glances. The seed drills weren't really tall enough to hide behind, but some were displayed with tractors, and while she was screened from view by one of those, Emma risked a look at her watch.

Four minutes. It had been four minutes since Mina had left the ladies' room. Eight minutes for Mina to get away, a minute or two more for Tyler to join Emma. She had to keep up the pretense that long. She swallowed hard, moved away from the tractor and found herself scarcely four yards from Stefan and Petru.

She saw them in profile as they looked from side to side, walking slowly between the machines. They were looking away at the instant she saw them, but they were going to look back, and she had to be out of sight before they did....

She dodged back toward the head-high tractor tire she'd been sheltering behind and crashed into someone. Gasping, she staggered, off balance from the impact.

"Hey, there, little lady, are you okay?"

A very large hand caught her arm to steady her, a very large voice boomed out the question, and Emma found herself face-to-face with the very large man to whom the voice and the hand belonged. Sixty or so, tall and bulky, he was wearing a shiny corduroy sport coat, a string tie and a baseball cap advertising a seed company. His face was weathered and kind, and he kept a solicitous grip on her elbow.

"Are you all right, little lady?"

His voice boomed above the noise of the crowd, and Emma winced. No one in the vicinity could help but hear him.

"I'm fine, thank you." She tried to pull free, knowing she had to get away, and quickly.

"Well, I want to apologize for bein' so clumsy. My wife is always telling me to look where I'm going."

"It's quite all right," Emma assured him desperately. "Really it is. It's as much my fault as yours. I wasn't looking where I was going."

"It's nice of you to say that, little lady, but I'm still real sorry."

"Think nothing of it, please." Emma pulled again, but he kept his grip on her elbow. "I must go now."

"You sure you're okay?"

"Perfectly. And I really do need to go. I have to meet—"

"Me," said a deep, heavily accented voice. Stefan's voice. "She is to meet me."

"That right?" the farmer asked.

Emma nodded, keeping her face averted. She couldn't let them see her face. For as long as they didn't, they might still believe she was Mina.

"Well, I guess that's okay then. You have a nice day, little lady."

"Thank you," Emma murmured, trying to pitch her voice higher, like Mina's. "You're very kind." She moved away as soon as he released her, but immediately another hand gripped her arm, far less gently.

"Come this way," Stefan said as he pulled her almost roughly down the aisle. She could hear Petru behind her.

Oh, God, it's too soon! she thought. Why couldn't she have had just a little more time? Why had she been so clumsy, so inept? All she'd needed was a few more minutes, but she'd bungled things, and now Mina was in terrible danger.

She kept walking, quickly, trying to stay half a step ahead of Stefan, easing open Mina's purse, which now held the small automatic Tyler had given her that morning.

They'd walked perhaps ten yards when he spoke, a rumble of incomprehensible Romanian that ended on a questioning note. Emma shook her head and kept walking, fear a brassy taste in her throat. She spoke French, Spanish and a smattering of Japanese, but after years of friendship with Mina, she understood only a word or two of Romanian. Now that it was too late, she cursed her lack of knowledge.

He repeated the question, whatever it was, his voice slightly louder, more emphatic, demanding. Emma tensed and shook her head again, lengthening her stride. He jerked her to a halt, and in the instant before he swung her around, he barked out another incomprehensible question.

Then he looked into her face. His eyes widened in surprise, then narrowed again in icy rage. He barked something at Petru, and though Emma didn't understand the words, she could recognize swearing. He spoke to her, still in Romanian, and swore again when Emma shook her head in blank incomprehension.

Stefan had frightened Mina, and he frightened Emma, as well. He was only an inch or so taller than she, but stocky and muscular, barrel-chested beneath his dark overcoat. His face was heavy-featured, his hair dark, his mouth set in a grim line, but it was his eyes that frightened her. They were eerily empty, devoid of any spark of feeling or humanity.

"Where is she?" he demanded, low and furious. "Tell me, right now. Where she is!"

"She's gone." Emma didn't even try to keep the note of triumph out of her voice. "She's already gone." She slipped her hand inside the purse, touching the cool, hard metal of the gun barrel.

"Where?" His grip on her arm, already painful, tightened even more.

"I don't know." She pushed her hand farther into the shoulder bag. She just had to grip the gun and flick off the safety.

"Don't lie to me!" Standing close so that no one could see, he twisted her arm painfully. Petru, taller and thinner, but with the same dark hair and empty eyes, stood close at her other side, blocking escape.

"Tell me where she is."

"I don't know!" Emma's voice rose, and he gave her twisted arm a vicious jerk. She felt the gun slip away from her fingers and bit her lip in frustration.

"Be quiet! Do not draw attention."

"You won't do anything to me! I have a gun—"

He laughed. "So do I." His hand was in his coat pocket, and something round and hard pressed into her ribs. "And I will shoot you, and Petru and I will carry you out of here."

"No, you won't!" She tried to scoff, but it didn't come off very well. "People would hear a gunshot."

"It is silenced."

She tried again. "A dead body would be pretty obvious."

"It is easy. We carry you. We say you are ill, or drunk, or on drugs, and we are taking you to a doctor. Easy."

He smiled, and an icy finger slid down Emma's spine. He could kill her with no hesitation and no regret, feeling nothing more than satisfaction for a job well done.

She finally wrapped her fingers around the gun butt and felt for the trigger. "I'll fire this thing and every cop in the place will come."

"If you fire a gun in here, you risk killing some innocent farmer," he sneered. "You will not do that."

He was right. She couldn't risk injuring anyone but her captors. "If you kill me, you have no chance of finding her."

"If I kill you, I will feel a very great satisfaction. And I will find her, whether you are alive or dead." There was no hint of doubt in his voice. He said something unintelligible to Petru, who caught her free arm in a painful grip.

"Now, Petru will take your hand from that bag and hold it where I can see it, and you will give the bag to him."

Emma resisted, and Petru dug his fingertips into the inside of her arm. Pain shot along the nerves, her fingers went numb, and suddenly she couldn't make her muscles obey her commands. When he pulled her hand out of the bag, she could do nothing to resist. He took the bag, looked inside and muttered something to Stefan, who nodded shortly. "So your threat was not an idle one. You have tried my patience already and I am not a patient man. You will come with us now, quietly."

He turned toward the exit, giving her no choice but to go along. She dragged her feet, trying to hang back, but she was exquisitely aware of the gun barrel pressed into her side. As they walked, he spoke to Petru in Romanian. Petru's English was somewhere between rudimentary and nonexistent, but Emma knew it would be useless to appeal to him for help. His loyalty was unquestionably to Stefan.

Stefan turned to Emma. "We will leave," he murmured, "and you make no sound."

"You can't take me out of here!" Emma whispered harshly. "I'm a foreign national, and... and I have diplomatic immunity!"

"Do you?" Stefan smiled like a shark. "So do I. Come." The gun barrel nudged her ribs again, and she did as she was told.

Stefan set a quick pace, moving Emma along with the punishing grip on her arm and the gun barrel at her side. She stared around her as they moved, frantically searching for a sight of Tyler, Uncle Larry or anyone she knew. She scanned the sea of faces in the crowd, moving and shifting like a restless tide, all of them strangers.

They were at the exit and Petru was pushing the door open when the sea parted for just an instant and she saw Tyler's face in the gap.

Painfully aware of the gun against her side, she didn't scream or try to run but mouthed "Help!" at him in the instant before the crowd surged together again, blotting him from view.

Chapter 19

My God!'' Tyler had only a glimpse of Emma before she was hidden by the crowd, but that instant was long enough to make his blood run cold. He'd recognized Stefan Alexandru holding Emma's arm, and from his posture he knew the man had a gun on her.

They'd all known that the disguise would only hold up from a distance, so disaster was already a fact. They knew Mina was gone, and that Emma had played a part in it.

He had a gun on her, and from the looks of it he'd found the one she'd been carrying. As Tyler shoved his way through the crowd, that knowledge was a cold sickness in the pit of his stomach. They'd hoped she could bluff her way out of trouble if she were discovered, but that hadn't worked. They'd hoped she could defend herself as a last resort, but apparently that had failed, as well.

His way toward her blocked, Tyler stepped up on a cultivator and looked over the sea of heads. Alexandru's hat was beside Emma's dark wig, with Petru in front, opening the door. He swore viciously. They were kidnapping her!

He jumped off the cultivator and pushed his way through the crowd, heedless of the people he shoved aside.

"Hey, pal! Watch where you're going!" A burly young man in jeans and a denim jacket grabbed Tyler's arm. It stopped his progress through the crowd briefly.

He turned to face his accuser. The burly young farmer was a few inches taller than Tyler and powerfully built and angry, but when he saw Tyler's face the aggression melted out of him like spring snow in a warm sun. There was a cold, implacable danger in Tyler that made a mockery of the young man's clumsy anger.

"What do you want?"

"N-nothing." The young man released Tyler's arm as if it were red-hot. "I don't want nothing."

"Good." Tyler didn't spare him another glance as he forged on through the crowd. He'd reached the edge of the exhibit area when he saw her again.

She was outside, with Alexandru and Petru close beside her. She looked back as Petru opened the rear door of a dark sedan and Stefan forced her into the car, but Tyler knew she couldn't see him.

He broke into a run on the fringe of the crowd, running along inside the windows, helpless to do anything to prevent Petru from climbing into the driver's seat and starting the engine. Tyler dashed out onto the sidewalk as the dark car pulled away, then whirled around and ran to a nearby taxi stand.

A cab was parked there, the driver slouched in his seat, reading the paper. Tyler hammered on the hood, startling the driver out of his *Sun-Times*.

"What the hell? What you doing?" He was obviously a recent immigrant, his English an odd amalgam of the old country and the unmistakable accent of Chicago.

"You see that car?" Tyler pointed down the street. "The black sedan?"

"The big one. Yeah, I see it."

Tyler yanked open the door and flung himself into the back seat. "Follow it!"

"Like in the movies?" The driver grinned happily. "Follow that car?"

"Don't sit here blabbing about it!" Tyler snapped. "Follow the damn car!"

The cab lurched away from the curb, then screeched to a halt as a well-dressed silver-haired man jumped into the street in front of it.

"What the hell?" The driver flung open his door and leaned out. "Get out of the road, crazy old man!"

Lord Latham ignored him. He grabbed the back seat door when Tyler flung it open and swung himself into the cab. "Did you see the car?"

"Yeah." Tyler nodded.

"The black one," the driver agreed.

"Well, follow it, then!" Lord Latham commanded.

Engine screaming and tires squealing in protest, they took off in pursuit.

"You will stay here."

Stefan gave her a hard shove, and Emma stumbled across the carpet of the suite's smaller bedroom. By the time she'd turned back to the door, he'd already closed and locked it behind her.

"Damn, damn, *damn*!"

She stood in the middle of the pretty hotel room, fists clenched in rage. She had failed, and she was furious with herself. So now she was locked in a hotel bedroom inside a suite on the thirty-seventh floor, and unless she could figure out how to climb down the sheer side of the building, she was stuck there. And it was her own stupid fault.

She paced the length and width of the narrow room like a caged tiger, practically snarling with anger, stopping at the window to lift the heavy drapes. It was early evening outside, with a cold gray sky above, and far, far below her, rush-hour traffic creeping past.

No one would hear if she screamed or banged on the window. No one but Stefan, and he would probably shoot her to silence her.

For a moment her anger ebbed, fear rushing in to take its place. Stefan would enjoy killing her. She was only alive because she was useful as bait. Emma was expendable once he had Mina back, or if he found that he couldn't use her for that purpose.

Once he realized that the governments and agencies involved were not going to give Mina back, Stefan would have no further use for Emma.

Her hands were shaking. She clenched them to stop the trembling, fighting the fear. Fear would paralyze her, rob her of her ability to think and act.

"Think!" she commanded herself sotto voce. "Think!"

"Who are you talking to?" Stefan's question came from just outside, and Emma whirled around to face the door, shaking with tension. "Who are you talking to?" he asked again, louder this time.

"Myself!" she yelled back, making her voice irritable. "Who else do I have to talk to in here? And how long am I going to be in here, anyway? It's boring!"

"You will be there as long as I say you will. If you are bored, watch the television!" His voice was heavy with irritated disgust. Emma tiptoed to the door and pressed her ear to it, listening as his footsteps moved away. After a moment she heard him in the suite's living room, talking to Petru. She stood with her ear pressed to the door for a full minute, but they didn't leave.

Emma nodded and tiptoed over to switch on the television. She set the volume at a comfortable level, loud enough to cover small sounds from her room, but not so loud as to attract attention. She felt suddenly stronger, braver, ready to act. Without knowing it, Stefan had given her a gift, or—

dering her to turn on the TV, providing her with background noise to cover the sounds of her activities.

Surely Tyler would have tried to follow her, since he'd seen her leaving with Stefan and Petru. If he'd managed that, he would at least know the hotel she was in. And if he knew that, all she had to do was let him know which room.

She snapped her fingers. What could be simpler? She tiptoed over to the door again and stood with her ear pressed to it for several moments. She could hear voices from the living room and the clink of glasses as they made use of the courtesy bar.

Very well. They were safely occupied, at least for the moment. Emma changed channels to a game show with nonstop sound effects and laughter. While it played merrily on the television, she slipped into the bath and grabbed the largest towel she could find.

She ran lightly over to the window, opened the drapes as far as they would go, then fingered the window frame, looking for a latch. As she'd suspected, it was there. The window had been rigged so that it would slide open far enough for ventilation, but not so far that someone could jump out. She opened the latch and pushed the sliding glass sideways about five inches. Cold air rushed into the room, but a window screen still blocked the opening.

Muttering to herself, Emma pushed and pulled all around the aluminum frame. There was one spot, halfway up the side, that wiggled when she pushed on it. She pushed harder, pressing it out an eighth of an inch, a quarter— The frame snapped back, pinching her fingertip.

"Ah!" She jumped back, holding the injured digit in her hand, biting back the exclamation of pain, holding her breath, praying fervently that the television's canned laughter had covered any noise she'd made.

It appeared that it had. When a full minute had ticked past and no one had come to investigate, Emma let herself relax, just a little.

She could do it. All she needed was some sort of tool to pry the screen out of its frame. The ashtray? She picked it up, turning the heavy glass over in her hands, looking for an edge small enough to slip under the screen. It wouldn't work, but she'd remembered something that would. She set the ashtray back on the table with a clunk and hurried into the bath.

She returned to the window in seconds, triumphantly carrying a toothbrush, still in its cellophane wrapper. The room was getting chilly, but Emma didn't notice. She ripped the cellophane off the toothbrush and wedged the green plastic handle against the screen's frame. She pushed hard against the aluminum frame, wedging the toothbrush into the opening, forcing the gap wider and wider.

The frame bowed, then bent with a piercing squeak. Emma froze, her heart thundering in her ears, straining to hear above the sounds from the TV. Fifteen seconds passed, then twenty, and no one shouted, no one burst through the door to discover what she was doing.

Quickly, her heart in her throat, Emma shoved the screen out to create a two-inch gap. She snatched the towel off the floor and mashed the thick fabric through bit by bit, muttering impatiently under her breath. Finally, after what seemed an age, the bulk of the towel was outside.

The wind caught it unexpectedly, almost tearing it from her hands. Emma gripped the one corner she still held with her fingernails and pulled a few inches back inside before she jammed the screen back into place. She'd kinked it so that it wouldn't go all the way back, but it closed tightly enough to hold the towel. She peered out, watching in satisfaction as the white terry cloth flapped against the bricks.

If they'd located the hotel, they couldn't miss this. How many thirty-seventh-floor windows had bath sheets flapping out of them? She was pushing the window closed when she heard the door lock rattle.

Frantically staring at the door, she shoved the window closed and dragged on the drapery cord. The drapes were heavy and they moved slowly. They weren't quite closed when she saw the doorknob start to turn. Emma left the drapes open several inches and leaped toward the little sitting area.

By the time the door opened to reveal Stefan Alexandru, she was sitting in the armchair, staring at the television, painfully aware that the draperies behind her were still swaying slightly, as if in a gentle breeze.

Stefan stood in the doorway, as if he expected Emma to try to run past him. She sat back comfortably in the armchair and very deliberately crossed her legs. He looked quickly around the room, then back at her.

"Are you comfortable?"

Emma didn't for a moment believe that the man had any interest in her comfort. He was just checking to make sure she wasn't up to anything.

"I'm bored." She gestured at the television. "I've never developed a taste for American game shows."

He didn't consider that worth addressing. "It is cold in here," he announced.

"I know. Perhaps you could turn up the heat." Emma's words were quick and a little loud to draw his attention back to her before he noticed the swaying draperies and the unlatched window. "I'm hungry, too," she told him, petulant and demanding.

"You are not fool enough to think we will go out to get food for you."

"There's always room service. I'm told this hotel has an excellent kitchen."

"Perhaps." Stefan backed out the door. "It is good that you are being sensible. It would go badly for you if you crossed me."

Emma didn't respond, and after a moment he closed the door. She listened to the lock turning, then tiptoed over and waited until she could hear Stefan in the living room again, talking to Petru. The voices were clear enough, but the words were Romanian and meaningless to her.

They talked for several minutes, then Stefan's voice moved farther away. She thought he was speaking English but couldn't understand the words. After several fruitless minutes, she gave up listening. She checked that her towel flag was still flapping bravely out the window, then returned to the armchair, where she sat, idly watching the flickering television screen, waiting.

"Is that the car?"

Tyler squinted at the license plate as the cabbie obligingly cruised slowly past the valet parking area. "Same license number. That's the car."

"Any sign of Emma?"

Tyler shook his head, his expression grim. "They must have taken her inside."

"Do we follow that car?" The cabbie was eager for action.

Tyler just looked at him. "It's parked."

"Could they have walked through the hotel and caught a cab on the other side?" Lord Latham wondered.

"Don't know." Tyler turned to the cabbie. "Drive around the block. Not too fast."

"You got it!" Grinning, he complied. Tyler scanned the crowded sidewalks as they drove, trying to see the faces beneath hats and scarves. On the far side of the block, opposite another entrance to the hotel, Lord Latham suddenly grabbed the cabbie's shoulder.

"Stop! Stop right there!" The cab jerked to a halt.

"What is it?" Tyler demanded.

"Look! Up there!" While Tyler searched the sidewalks, Lord Latham had been looking up at the hotel tower itself.

Both Tyler and the cabbie craned their necks, following Lord Latham's pointing finger, and there it was. He had to fight the urge to laugh through his terror, for far above them, halfway to the sky, a white banner flapped raggedly in the cold wind.

He met Lord Latham's eyes and nodded. "She's here."

"Let's be off, then." Lord Latham was already out of the cab. Tyler followed him, pulling bills out of his pocket without looking at the denominations.

"What is that?" the cabbie asked, still looking up at Emma's signal.

"It's a message from a lady." Tyler tossed the bills through the window and strode quickly away.

The cabbie muttered under his breath, then looked at the money. "Thank you, sirs!" he called after them. "Thank you very much!"

"How do we get to her?" Tyler muttered to Lord Latham as they crossed the lobby. "Kick the door in?"

The older man snorted. "Subtlety, my boy. Subtlety." He strode toward the desk. "We find the manager."

Five minutes later the manager was escorting them to the hotel kitchen.

"How'd you do that?" Tyler whispered. "He was ready to kiss your ring."

"A bow is perfectly adequate," Latham replied in his best upper-crust accent. "Americans love aristocracy. And they love to help."

"The diplomatic passport didn't hurt, either."

"Whatever it takes." Lord Latham lifted his chin and followed the manager into the hot, noisy kitchen, where it appeared that the British lord's wish was the manager's command.

He listened to Lord Latham's request and nodded. Yes, he could do that, he told them, and summoned the room service supervisor to explain the situation to him.

"You're in luck!" The supervisor returned from checking a large bulletin board near the stoves. "They just called down to order some sandwiches."

Tyler grinned at Lord Latham. "We won't even have to pretend to have the wrong room."

"It's an excellent plan, my boy." Lord Latham turned to the supervisor. "How soon will the food be ready?" he asked, and the supervisor passed the question to the chef, who shrugged.

"Fifteen minutes, maybe twenty."

"That's too long," Tyler said flatly. "Give us somebody else's order!"

"Sir, I couldn't possibly—"

"A woman's life is at stake! Are you going to tell me somebody's eggs Benedict are more important than that?" There was a barely leashed violence in Tyler that had the supervisor warily stepping back.

"Oh, no, sir. Of course not, sir. Philip!" He gestured to a waiter. "Get these gentlemen a cart and a tray of food, please."

"But the order for 3720 isn't ready yet."

"Just get them a tray." He dropped his voice to a conspirator's mutter. "It's a matter of life and death."

The waiter's eyes widened. He looked from the supervisor to Tyler and Lord Latham, waiting grim-faced, and nodded quickly. "I'll get that tray." He hurried away, returning almost immediately with a large tray bearing three meals.

"You take it up on a cart, right?" Tyler asked.

"Yes, sir. Like this, with a cloth covering it."

There was a white linen cloth covering the stainless-steel cart. He placed the tray on top, then covered the whole thing with another linen cloth. The two layers of linen fell nearly to the floor, brushing the cart's wheels, while in the space within the cart, concealed by the linen, there was a plastic bin for used dishes and utensils and room for coffee urns, punch bowls and the like.

Tyler lifted the two cloths, studied the space and nodded. "It'll work." He pulled the plastic bin out and set it aside, then dropped the cloths back into place. "Are we ready?" he asked, directing the question to both Lord Latham and Philip. They nodded, and with a small, grim smile he said, "Let's go, then."

"How many do you think there are?" Tyler asked as they rode up.

Lord Latham shrugged. "Possibly only the two who took her from the exhibit hall. Possibly others."

"Let's hope there's only two."

"Hope for the best," Lord Latham agreed, "but be prepared for the worst."

At the thirty-seventh floor the elevator stopped, its doors opening onto a small service lobby. Philip pushed the cart off the elevator but waited inside the door to the hallway used by guests.

"You got your gun, Larry?"

"Right here." Lord Latham patted his side, where the shoulder holster hung. "And you?"

"Right here." Tyler drew his revolver from the holster at the small of his back. He turned to the waiter. "You roll this thing into the room and then get the hell out, okay?"

"But you're—"

"Just get out. There might be shooting, and I don't want innocent bystanders involved. Get out and get help. Got it?"

He waited until Philip nodded, then lifted the cloths away from the side of the cart and gave Lord Latham a little bow. "After you."

"Right."

The waiter watched in disbelief as Lord Latham folded his length into the smallish space inside the cart. Tyler followed, grunting as he hunched his shoulders and ducked his head to fit inside the cart.

"Can you move over any more?"

"My boy, this is the best I can do." Lord Latham muttered an oath as he banged his head against one of the steel struts. "I'm getting too old for these shenanigans."

Tyler gave a snort of disbelief and pulled the cloths down again. From within the linen tent he said, "Okay, Philip, let's move it."

Heavily laden with its unusual burden, the cart rumbled slowly down the hall. They lurched to a halt, and Tyler tensed as Philip rapped on the door. "Room service!"

Emma heard the knock and the distant sound of the room service waiter's voice. She darted across to press her ear against the door, clutching the heavy glass ashtray in her hands. She'd spent the time since she'd hung the towel out the window making a plan. It wasn't a particularly good plan—in fact, it was ludicrously simple—but even if the odds of succeeding were miniscule, the knowledge that she was *doing* something was a lifeline to cling to.

Waiting passively was sure to drive her insane. If she had a plan, she could stay calm, stay sane. Without that she was afraid she would simply start screaming.

Standing behind the door, listening to voices and the rattle of a serving cart, she lifted the ashtray, tightening her grip on it. She'd figured it out. In a moment or two someone would open the door to bring in her food. Whoever it was, while he was at a disadvantage with a plate in one hand and the other on the doorknob, she would bash him over the head with the ashtray and run.

She just might be able to get past the man who would still be in the suite's living room. If he didn't shoot her. And she might, just might, be able to get out into the hall and run away...if he didn't shoot her.

She'd heard that bystanders hesitated to come to the rescue if they heard someone shouting "Help!" but other women living in the city had told her that shouting "Fire!" would bring people out of their apartments or hotel rooms. Emma would sprint down the hall, yelling "Fire!" at the top of her lungs. If he didn't shoot her.

The murmuring voices became clearer. "Shall I put it over there, sir? By the window?"

Stefan's voice was a rumble of impatient agreement.

Dishes rattled, then she heard a shout. "Where is she!"

Emma's mouth dropped open. That sounded like—Stefan shouted. There was a crash of dishes as he shouted again, furiously, then two gunshots and another shout.

It was him.

"Oh, God!" Frantically Emma shook the doorknob, desperate to get out. "Oh, God, let him be all right! Please let him be all right. Please let—"

The door crashed inward from a violent kick, knocking Emma backward, the shattered lock flying off the frame. Emma staggered back, swinging the ashtray up as a man burst through the door. He had a gun in his hand. She was on the downswing when she saw his face.

"Tyler!" The ashtray slipped from her suddenly lax fingers and thudded to the floor. The room began to blur, the floor to sway beneath her feet, and she was reaching for Tyler when the world went black.

Chapter 20

I still can't believe it.'' Emma chuckled weakly. "Uncle Larry hiding in a serving cart?"

"As he put it, he's 'too old for these shenanigans.'" The elevator stopped, and Tyler ushered her across the landing to her front door. "I got the feeling that he enjoyed it, though. I think it reminded him of his days as a spy."

"It probably did. I believe he was quite a good agent."

"He impressed me today. He had that hotel manager eating out of his hand in about thirty seconds, and he didn't hesitate to ride a serving cart into that room and then come out with a gun drawn." He chuckled. "I wish you could have seen the look on Stefan's face when we suddenly appeared out of that cart."

"I heard shots," Emma said, preceding him into the apartment.

"The other guy, Petru, got one shot off, but when Larry and I pulled our guns and fired a warning shot, Petru decided the odds weren't in his favor. Stefan tried to make a break for the door, but Philip, the waiter who brought the cart up, tackled him." He shook his head. "I told him to get the hell out, especially if there was any trouble, but he ignored me. I guess he used to play football in high school or something. Stefan never knew what hit him." He helped Emma out of her coat. "And then I came in to get you."

"I had a plan, you know." She stood before him, pale with exhaustion. In the hours since Tyler had burst into the hotel room they had given statements to the authorities, signed them and flown back to New York on a chartered plane. It was now nearly four in the morning.

"I'm sure you did." Tyler steered her into the kitchen and pushed her into a chair. She slumped there, elbows on the table.

"I did! I was standing behind the door with that big glass ashtray. Whoever brought my food, I was going to hit him over the head with the ashtray and run."

"I know you were. For a minute there I was afraid you were going to clonk me."

"I wouldn't hit you." Her voice was slurred with tiredness, and she rested her chin on her hands. "Not that I haven't wanted to now and again."

"You have, huh?" Tyler was opening cupboard doors, looking for something. "Where's your liquor cabinet?"

"I don't have one." She lifted a hand. "Look at that. My hand won't stop shaking."

"If you don't have a liquor cabinet, where do you keep that lethal, straight-off-the-moors Scotch of yours, then? You need a bracer."

"It's in that cupboard." She pointed.

Tyler opened the doors, and from behind some cooking sherry and an unopened bottle of schnapps, retrieved the plain, unlabeled bottle of golden liquid. He uncapped it and sniffed warily. "Do you want ice in yours or water?"

"I'll have it as it comes. Anything else is sacrilege."

Tyler shook his head, poured and handed her a glass. "Drink up. It'll make you feel better."

"You sound like Nanny. She has a 'wee drop' to build up her blood."

"To your health, then. Cheers."

"To your health." She clinked her glass against his, tipped it up and took a good mouthful. Tyler watched her swallow, then close her eyes tightly as the first shudder ran through her. She released her breath in a gusty sigh before she opened her eyes. "Perfect."

Tyler sipped his, enjoying the mellow, smoky tang. It was still strong enough to make him blink. "It's good. I'll be spoiled for the ordinary stuff after this."

"All the better. That's rotten stuff, anyway. Look." She lifted her hand from the tabletop. "It's not shaking anymore."

"Good," he said. "Are you okay now?"

"Yes. Nothing happened to me, after all."

Nothing much, Tyler thought in bitter guilt, except that she'd been threatened and kidnapped and frightened half to death, and it was his fault. He remained silent, but took a jolting swallow of his drink.

"Mina's all right, isn't she?" Emma asked.

"I must have told you ninety-seven times already that she's fine. She found Jim and got out of the building with no problem and she's at a safe house now. Her letter requesting asylum has already gone in."

"And Mina herself? Is she feeling okay?"

"Yes," Tyler sighed, "she is. They tell me she's a little frightened, a little shaky, but she hasn't changed her mind. She still feels she's done the only thing she could."

"Good." Emma sighed and sipped her whisky. "When will I be able to see her?"

"Not for a month at least, maybe longer. They know who you are, and we don't want you to lead them to Mina until she's officially received asylum and Stefan and Petru have been deported."

"I see. You'll tell me as soon as I can see her, won't you?"

Tyler hesitated a fraction. "Somebody will let you know."

"Oh." Emma set her glass on the table, her hands cradling it. "I see." And she did.

She understood a great deal. She had refused to do as Tyler asked and get out of the actual defection plan, and he wasn't going to forgive her. He'd asked her, if she loved him, to keep herself safe and let someone else help Mina. She'd refused, and it appeared he wasn't going to forgive her for that.

She rose and walked to the window, where she stood looking out at the night, still dark, with dawn three hours away. "I'd do it again, you know," she said, and sipped her whisky.

"What?"

"Help Mina. Take her place so that she could get away. I'd do it again because I think I was right to do it."

"Oh, sure!" He rose from his chair but stayed on the other side of the room. "You took her place and look what happened!"

"Mina got away!" Emma turned to face him across the width of the kitchen. "She trusted me and she knew that I was there just for her, not for some obscure government purpose. That was important."

"And it wasn't important that you were kidnapped?" he demanded. "Damn it, Emma, he could have killed you! Don't you think that matters just a little?"

She smiled wryly. "It certainly mattered to me when Stefan was poking me in the ribs with that bloody great cannon of his!"

"It's not funny!" He slammed his glass down on the table and was across the room in two long strides, catching her shoulders and shaking her. "My God, Emma, this isn't a joke! I saw you there with him at the exhibition and I could tell he had a gun on you. I know his type and I know what they're capable of." He swallowed convulsively, and his fingers tightened on her shoulders. "And all I could do," he whispered hoarsely, "was watch as they took you away."

"Tyler." Emma reached up to touch his face, tense with guilt and anger. "It wasn't your fault."

"Then whose was it?"

"Mine, because I bungled it. I didn't keep a close enough watch on Stefan and Petru when I saw them and then I bumped into a gentleman who gave my position away. I didn't even get my gun out in time. It was my own clumsiness that put me in that position."

"I was there to protect you. I didn't." His self-condemnation was total.

"You asked me not to go." A flicker of a smile touched her lips. "And then you told me not to go."

"But I didn't convince you."

"You couldn't have."

"I could have done something. I knew Lord Latham would agree with you, but I could have gone over his head. I could have forced the issue."

"How?"

"Through the British ambassador if nothing else. But, no!" He jerked away from her touch on his face and spun around, his back to her. "No, I didn't work hard enough to convince you because I told myself I could protect you. I would be there, watching, and I'd handle anything that came up." He jerked around, his face tight with anguished guilt. "I really handled it, didn't I? I stood there like a damn idiot and watched them kidnap you!"

"Tyler, it wasn't your fault!" When she reached out, he jerked back, so she dropped her hands and clasped them tightly. "It wasn't your fault." The words were inadequate, but they were all she had.

"It was," he said flatly, thoroughly convinced.

"No," she said quietly, then louder, "no! Will you listen to me? It was *not* your fault! If anything, it was mine because I was sloppy and careless. I'm sorry I was careless, Tyler. And I'm sorry I put you through so much worry—''

"Worry?" he demanded. "*Worry?* That was hell!" He slammed a fist against the wall, making Emma jump and dishes rattle. "Hell! Knowing the danger you were in, knowing I should have prevented it and knowing I hadn't! I was so afraid I'd be too late, that the...worst...might happen and I'd never have told you—" He broke off, spinning suddenly away, turning his back to her.

Emma caught her breath, her heart hammering in her throat. She had to swallow before she whispered, "Tell me what, Tyler?"

"Never mind." He shook his head once, sharply. "It doesn't matter."

"I think it does." Emma touched his shoulder. Though he flinched, she didn't take her hand away. "I think it matters."

"Not anymore."

His muscles were tense, rigid under her hand. "Can I tell you something, Tyler?"

He shrugged acquiescence, if not agreement.

"All right." Emma lowered her hand but didn't move away. "I'm sorry I put you through that. You must know I never would have meant something like that to happen."

"Good intentions don't generally count for much."

"I suppose not, but they're better than bad intentions. And I told you before that I would do it again—for Mina."

"I know." He gave a snort of humorless laughter. "You'd do whatever you had to for Mina."

"That doesn't mean I think less of you."

"Doesn't it?" He turned to face her, his face bitter. "Listen to me! I sound like some jealous teenager! Forget it, Emma. This is pointless." He strode out of the kitchen and grabbed his coat off the table in the hall. "It's almost morning. I'm going home so that you can get some sleep."

"Tyler, I love you."

He stopped with his hand on the doorknob. "So you said."

"Yes!" Emma followed him into the hall. "So I said, and I meant it, too!"

"It didn't make much difference to the situation, did it?"

"If you mean I wouldn't let you blackmail me in the name of love, then, no, it didn't make a difference. It wasn't fair of you to ask that."

"Not fair?" He turned around, tense, angry. "All's fair in love and war. Isn't that how the line goes? Fair didn't matter, Emma. I wanted you safe!"

"I know you did. And if you'd been the one in danger, I'd have jumped in front of the bullet. I know how you feel, but I also love Mina and I had to help her. I wish you could understand that."

There was a long moment of silence, then he sighed heavily. "I do. The hell of it is that I do. If you were anyone else, I'd even admire you for it."

"But I'm not anyone else?"

"No. And I couldn't just calmly watch my heart and my life walk into danger."

Emma stared at him, her mouth round in shock.

"I love you, Emma." He walked slowly toward her. "I love you in spite of everything. I didn't want to fall in love with you. Why do you think I treated you so badly at first? I fought it like hell because I know a guy like me doesn't have anything to offer you, but damn it, Emma, I love you! How was I supposed to feel, watching you go off to do a job I knew was too dangerous for you?"

"You tried to stop me."

"And failed. And I tried to protect you and I failed. What can I offer you if I can't even keep you safe?" He finished with a shout that seemed to echo around the hall.

"Your love," Emma whispered into the angry echoes. "That's all I ever wanted. Just your love."

"Oh, yeah! That's a big help when someone's got a gun against your back."

"It is. It was." She reached out for his hand, and he didn't pull away. "When I was with them, and so frightened, all I could think of was you and how sorry I was that I'd been clumsy and gotten myself into trouble. I knew you'd be angry with me, and I wanted the chance to tell you I was sorry."

"Do you think that matters?" he asked, the anger leaving his voice, the tension in his body easing. "Whether I was mad at you?"

"You have every right to be."

"I was never mad at you, except for being so pigheaded. I guess I should expect a redhead to be stubborn, though." He lifted their clasped hands and stroked her fingers. "I wasn't angry at you, Emma, only at myself. Angry and guilty because I'd failed." He looked from their hands to her eyes. "And because if I'd lost you, I would have lost everything."

They looked into each other's eyes for an electric instant, then they were in each other's arms, kissing and clinging with the desperation of those who have come too close to losing it all.

Tyler lifted Emma into his arms and carried her into the living room. He sat on the sofa while she lay across his lap, secure in his arms, and smiled up at him.

"You love me," she murmured in wonder. "You really do."

"Of course I do! Why do you think I yelled at you?"

"Oh, I see." She smiled, teasing him. "You yelled at me because you love me, so you must be kissing me because you can't stand me."

"I'm kissing you because you're the most beautiful, most desirable woman in the world, and because I want you so badly it's killing me, and because I love you desperately."

Emma met his descending lips, kissing him with a fierce hunger to match his. When he lifted his head, she clung, with a little whimper of protest. He resisted, and she opened her eyes to see him frowning.

"Tyler, what's wrong?"

"This." He indicated the room. "Us."

Something cold settled in the pit of her stomach. "What do you mean?"

"I mean, we're both saying 'I love you,' but it's still no good."

"What—?"

"You're Lady Emma Campbell, and I'm just some jerk from a hick town who never knew his father."

"I thought we'd gotten past all that!" She sat up, kneeling on the cushions so that she could look levelly into his eyes. "And you're *not* 'just some jerk.' You could never be! You're a man who's strong and honorable and gentle and brave and—"

"And poor," he put in.

Emma glared. "So what?"

"So you're Lady Emma. You can figure it out."

"And you're a fool if you can't!" she snapped, finally losing her redhead's temper. "Damn it, Tyler, haven't you heard *anything* I've said? I love you! Not your name, or your job...*you*! I love you as a government agent, and I'd love you as a lord or a carpenter! That doesn't matter. *You* are what matters, and your love."

"You think so now." He sighed. "But what happens when you introduce me to your old school buddies?"

"Do you mean the crofters' kids in Scotland or the people in my classes at college?"

He tightened his lips in irritation. "Your parents, then, the earl and the countess. What do you say to them?"

"I say, 'be happy for me, Mummy and Dad, because I've found a strong, brave, honorable man who loves me for me and not for my money.'" She took his shoulders and shook him in frustration. "Tyler, when are you going to stop punishing me for this? Most men would be happy to marry someone with a little money!"

"I won't be kept." He set his chin at an obstinate angle.

Emma's jaw dropped. "Who's asking you to be?" she shouted. "If it makes you happy, I'll see that you pay your part of the rent *and* the groceries!" she shouted. "And you can take the trash out to the dustbin, too!"

"Fine!" he snapped. "Terrific! I'll wash the car and you'll do laundry!"

"Fine!" She glared at him, then her frown turned to puzzlement. "Tyler, what are we talking about?"

"Who's going to take out the trash."

"When? When will we have this trash?"

"When we—" He stopped, his eyes widening.

"When we...get married?" she suggested. Her eyes were wide, too, wide and soft with wonder.

A hint of a smile touched his lips. "Yeah. What else?"

"Oh. Very well." She subsided into his arms again. "Will you check the oil in my car when you wash it? I always forget."

He pretended to consider that. "Yeah, I guess so. I want starch in my shirt collars, though."

"All right. How about starch in your underwear?"

She asked the question so demurely that three seconds ticked by before he gave a shout of laughter. "You starch my shorts and I'll—"

"What?" She grinned wickedly. "What'll you do?"

"This!" Pulling her close, he tickled her ribs.

"Tyler!" She giggled wildly. "Stop that! Stop it!"

He silenced her with a kiss, and they rolled off the sofa onto the thick, soft carpet—kissing, clinging, laughing. When they came to rest, Tyler propped himself on one elbow and looked down into her flushed face. He was still breathless with laughter, but his eyes were dark with love.

"I love you, Emma. Just you, only you, forever."

He kissed her again, a promise and a vow, and as Emma closed her eyes and gave herself up to the delight of it, she could see the future spread out before them, bright and glowing with the love and the life they would share.

*   *   *   *   *

Silhouette Intimate Moments ™

COMING
NEXT MONTH

#333 CORRUPTED—Beverly Sommers

Police officer Sandy McGee is on special assignment to protect Johnny Random, a crooked cop. In a world of false identities and misplaced trust, in which even the double-crossers are double-crossed, Sandy, torn between her ethics and her growing passion for Johnny, must choose: honor or love? Or can she have both?

#334 SOMEONE TO TURN TO—
Marilyn Cunningham

Ramsey Delacroix returns to her grandfather's ranch after a shattering divorce. Instead of the safety and reassurance she craves, she finds murder. Compelled to defend her family, yet helpless against her deepening feelings for the bitter Brad Chillicott, Ramsey is forced to choose between loyalty to her family and a dangerous love for a stranger.

#335 LOVING LIES—Ann Williams

To catch a killer, Lauren Downing finds herself recruited as bait. Working alongside the town's ''bad boy,'' Jesse Tyler, in a race against time, she discovers a deepening passion that goes against all the rules. Despite the odds, they must reveal the killer's identity—will it be in time to save their growing love?

#336 DREAM CHASERS—
Mary Anne Wilson

TV host Jillian Segar, on assignment in volatile South America with her enigmatic former lover Carson Davies, finds herself enmeshed in a web of political intrigue. Irresistibly drawn to Carson, and finding herself falling in love, Jillian must put her life in his hands. Can he be trusted to save her, or will love elude them once again?

AVAILABLE THIS MONTH:

#329 BETRAYED
Beverly Sommers

#330 NEVER SAY GOODBYE
Suzanne Carey

#331 EMMA'S WAR
Lucy Hamilton

#332 DANGER IN PARADISE
Barbara Faith

Just when you thought all the good men had gotten away, along comes ...

SILHOUETTE®

Desire™

MAN OF THE MONTH 1990

Twelve magnificent stories by twelve of your favorite authors.

In January, FIRE AND RAIN by Elizabeth Lowell
In February, A LOVING SPIRIT by Annette Broadrick
In March, RULE BREAKER by Barbara Boswell
In April, SCANDAL'S CHILD by Ann Major
In May, KISS ME KATE by Helen R. Myers
In June, SHOWDOWN by Nancy Martin
In July, HOTSHOT by Kathleen Korbel
In August, TWICE IN A BLUE MOON by Dixie Browning
In September, THE LONER by Lass Small
In October, SLOW DANCE by Jennifer Greene
In November, HUNTER by Diana Palmer
In December, HANDSOME DEVIL by Joan Hohl

Every man is someone you'll want to get to know ... and love. So get out there and find your man!

BIG BROTHERS/BIG SISTERS AND HARLEQUIN

Harlequin is proud to announce its official sponsorship of Big Brothers/Big Sisters of America. Look for this poster in your local Big Brothers/Big Sisters agency or call them to get one in your favorite bookstore. Love is all about sharing.

Silhouette Romances

DIAMOND JUBILEE
CELEBRATION!

It's Silhouette Books' tenth anniversary, and what better way to celebrate than to toast *you*, our readers, for making it all possible. Each month in 1990, we'll present you with a DIAMOND JUBILEE Silhouette Romance written by an all-time favorite author!

Welcome the new year with *Ethan*—a LONG, TALL TEXANS book by Diana Palmer. February brings Brittany Young's *The Ambassador's Daughter*. Look for *Never on Sundae* by Rita Rainville in March, and in April you'll find *Harvey's Missing* by Peggy Webb. Victoria Glenn, Lucy Gordon, Annette Broadrick, Dixie Browning and many more have special gifts of love waiting for you with their DIAMOND JUBILEE Romances.

Be sure to look for the distinctive DIAMOND JUBILEE emblem, and share in Silhouette's celebration. Saying thanks has never been so romantic....

SCANDAL'S CHILD

ANN MAJOR

When passion and fate intertwine...

Garret Cagan and Noelle Martin had grown up together in the mysterious bayous of Louisiana. Fate had wrenched them apart, but now Noelle had returned. Garret was determined to resist her sensual allure, but he hadn't reckoned on his desire for the beautiful scandal's child.

Don't miss SCANDAL'S CHILD by Ann Major, Book Five in the Children of Destiny Series, available now at your favorite retail outlet.